Whimsical Dreams, Book Four

Whimsical Diva

Tiffany E. Taylor

Whimsical Diva

Published by Painted Hearts Publishing

Whimsical Diva

Copyright © 2023 Tiffany E. Taylor

ISBN: 9798390697474

Publication Date: February 2, 2023

Author: Tiffany E. Taylor

Editor: Kira Plotts

Painted Hearts

PUBLISHING

Publisher's Content Guidance:

This work of fiction contains scenes of disciplinary spanking, and other instances of light BDSM. In addition, this story depicts / makes mention of domestic violence / domestic abuse.

Some readers may find this content triggering.

Acknowledgments

To the blessed survivors—who preferred to remain anonymous—who were my resource and navigators through the ugly world of domestic violence. I remain in awe of your strength and determination. And to my wonderful beta team: Sam DeFiglio, Kim Gosselin, Maria Lau, Juliet Pishinsky, Tricia Potter, Ashley Ribeiro, Mysty Ross, and Hazel Tan. Whimsy wouldn't be the same without you.

ARMSTRONG PROTECTION SERVICES (APS)

The APS Management Team

The Armstrong Twins

Bryn Armstrong

General Management
Book 1 – *Whimsical Haven*
Femme Counterpart – Rowan Holland

Riley Armstrong

General Management
Book 2 – *Whimsical Princess*
Femme Counterpart – Kelly Holland

The Seven and the APS Teams

Casey Christensen

MMA/Krav Maga Team (Hades)

- Jess Evanston *(Casey's Second)*
- Campbell Mallet
- Trish Robles
- Nicki Shepard
- Sawyer Stark

Jaime Quintero

Physical Security Team

- Desi Phillips *(Jaime's Second)*
- Chris Chandler
- TJ Cooper
- Morgan Dodson
- Angel McDaniel

Trillian (Trill) Dacanay

Data Analysis/Tech Team (Recon Room)
Book 4 – *Whimsical Diva*
Femme Counterpart – Nova MacLeod

- Darcy Leveque *(Trill's Second)*
- Val Chan
- Peyton Mycroft
- Kendall Quaide
- Melanie Reed

Blake Siebert

Gaming Simulator Team (Utopia)

- Blair Mariano *(Blake's Second)*
- Quinn Abbott
- Kat Krause
- Parker Lyons
- Tracey Nichols

Drew Hollister

Counterintelligence Team (Purgatory)

- Dara Cochran *(Drew's Second)*
- Liz Acevedo
- Toni Bauer
- Ari Mendoza
- Devon Sanders

Kennedy (Kenn) Weston

Armory team (the Cage)

- Dakota Vargas *(Kenn's Second)*
- Jen Fortunato
- Leighton Greer
- Jordan Serrano
- Lee Walsch

Teagan Malloy

Communications Team
Book 3 – *Whimsical Angel*
Femme Counterpart – Delaney Sedgwick

- Remy Baumann *(Teagan's Second)*
- Jo Farnsworth
- Shelby Gregoire
- Harper O'Neill
- Amari Wilson

MAP OF WHIMSY

MAP OF WHIMSY

1 Sweet Expectations
2 Dream Creamery/Whimsy Art Center
3 Haines Investigations
4 Gulf Breeze Inn
5 KitchenWorks
6 Pier House Grill
7 Seashells
8 APS Apartments
9 APS Headquarters Complex
10 Feel the Burn

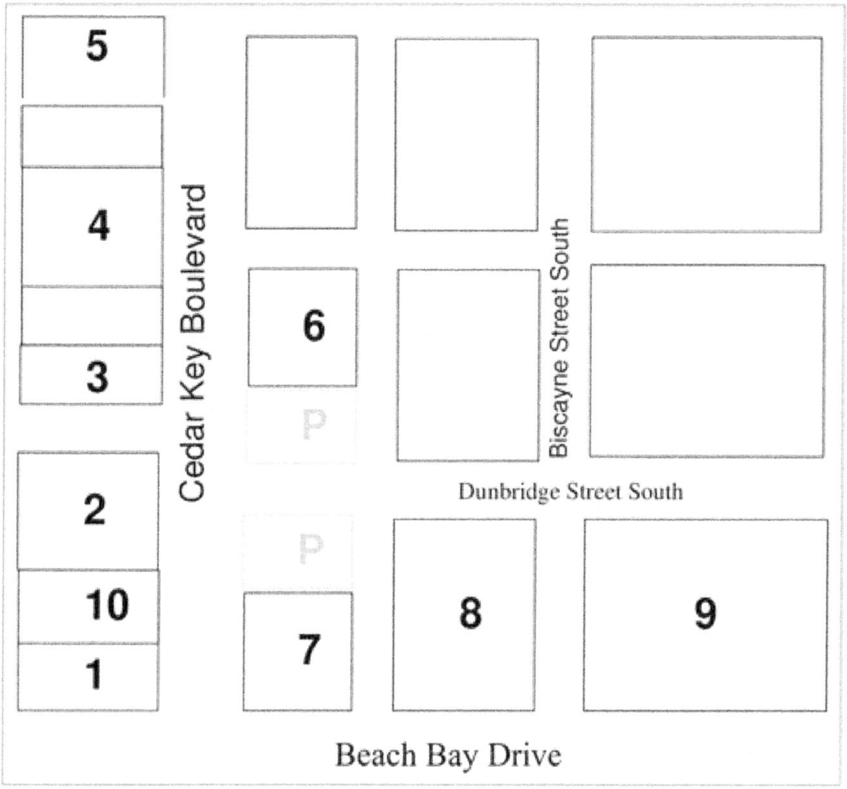

Author's Note

When I wrote Whimsical Diva, I very pointedly made Isadora Nightingale, our fictional domestic violence survivor, a woman who seemingly had it all on the outside: white, straight, wealthy, talented, and loved by millions. It was important to me to make it clear that domestic violence isn't something only restricted to individuals who are poor or marginalized or part of an ethnic or other minority. It's a malevolent cancer that affects females *everywhere*, regardless of their race, color, affluence, or gender identity. Needless to say, it brought me great joy to bring Isadora's abuser to a very satisfying end.

As a licensed hairdresser, my salon and I have been involved for many years with an organization called *CUT IT OUT – The Beauty Community Against Domestic Abuse*. Hairdressers are in a unique position to help abused women: We see evidence of scarring and bruising that most others will never see, a salon is one of the rare places an abused woman is allowed to go to by herself, and survivors often feel safe confiding in their hairdressers when they don't even trust their therapists or their spiritual advisors. Salon professionals who are involved with *CUT IT OUT* have small cards with resource information that they can give to a client, cards that are small enough for the client to hide in her shoe. Ask the salon manager where you go or your hairdresser if they are part of this very important program.

If you or someone you know is in an abusive relationship, you are not alone.

National Domestic Violence Hotline
1.800.799.SAFE (7233) | TheHotline.org

https://www.probeauty.org/pba-charities/cio/charities---cut-it-out-2020

For every domestic abuse victim out there who is lonely, isolated, and filled with fear: You are believed and you are loved.

Prologue

"You've got everything?" Nova looked at the small pile of luggage by the front door then at her older sister, Gillian. "I'll be sending you the rest of your stuff when you're settled, so I guess there's really not much to worry about, is there?"

"No. There's not." Gillian threw her arms excitedly around Nova. "I will never in a million years ever *be able to repay you for everything you've done for me, Nov." Her dark hazel eyes shone with tears.*

"I'll text you and Mom when we stop for the night. It's a long fucking drive to Albuquerque, but Kip has everything under control, he says."

Nova shook her head. "What you see in a dude who has a name that sounds like a small, stinky fish, I don't have the first fucking clue." She grinned as Gillian rolled her eyes.

"Seriously, Kip is a really, really good guy, Gill. You deserve him after everything you went through with that fucktard, Charles." Just then, there came a knock at the door.

Gillian opened it to a man with clear blue eyes and a perpetually sunny smile. "Hey, gorgeous. You ready?" he asked as he stepped inside the apartment and kissed Gillian. Next, he turned to Nova and pulled her into his arms for a huge hug.

"I swear to you…I will protect your sister with my life," Kip vowed solemnly, squeezing the tiny brunette. "I love her, Nova, and it will be over my fucking dead body that anyone ever puts their hands on her again. Not while I still breathe."

Nova hugged him back just as hard. "I know that, and I trust you, Kip. You're a terrific man, you're both so *good for each other, and I kind of envy you…this massive adventure you're going on.*

"I hear Albuquerque is wonderful and the Goddess knows, nurses like you two—you, a critical care cardiac nurse and Gillian a kickass labor and delivery nurse—will have jobs the minute you land in Albuquerque.

"Now go, before you make me cry and ruin my bad ass reputation." Both Gillian and Kip hugged her fiercely one more time then picked up Gillian's luggage and disappeared through the front door.

Nova listened to the silence in the apartment for a moment then sighed and went into the kitchen to get herself a beer out of the refrigerator. She typically didn't drink much—since she had to stay alert at all times—but a beer or a cocktail once in a while was okay.

Christ knew she needed one after the day she'd had today.

She slid back the sliding glass door that led out onto the tiny balcony and closed it behind her after she'd gone out into the balmy night. Seating herself in one of the outdoor chairs, she curled her small bare feet under herself then settled down to think about this shit show of a day.

APS. Now. Knew.

Fuck my life*, she thought with trepidation as she took a healthy swallow of her beer. She stared out unseeing toward the park across the street from her apartment complex.*

"The bad asses"—as she and Clementine Martin had nicknamed the butches of APS—had discovered tonight that there was quite a bit more to Nova MacLeod than they'd ever known.

That she was far more than just a tiny, snarky Whimsy femme and former professional food stylist, who was now a legendary ice cream artisan and worked with Delaney Malloy and Rowan Holland at the Whimsy Arts Center.

During the course of Delaney's rescue, APS had abruptly realized Nova had skills and a certain kind of knowledge no food stylist or ice cream artisan should ever *have. And while they didn't have any details, they'd made it perfectly clear in the aftermath of the whole entire clusterfuck that they would be going after answers from her.*

Nova leaned her head back on the chair's headrest and groaned, the icy beer bottle clutched between her nerveless fingers.

It's not like I'd had a fucking choice, though, *came the acerbic thought. She loved Delaney—Delaney was one of her soul sisters and had been for a long time—and it was going to be over Nova's dead body that Frank Bellwood would touch even one hair on Delaney's head.*

Everything had gone down so goddamn fast—Tina Schaffner's murder, Delaney's hostage situation…but Nova was an absolute master *at rapid rescues, where there was often little time, if any, to think and plan. She had the process down to a science.*

Nova firmly believed that APS was, hands down, the best protection and security company for women in existence. She had anonymously sent more than her fair share of battered women to them for their help over the years, knowing they'd be safe and protected under the APS umbrella.

However, there was a much, much smaller segment of abused women out there who didn't trust anyone. *Their lives were so severely in peril, a woman who even* smelled *like a flight risk could be dead at the hands of her abuser the next day. These were the women that Nova had helped to rescue for years, under the radar and unbeknownst to anyone, even her close-knit family.*

Except Gillian. Gillian knew…because Gillian had once been one of those women.

Her beautiful, happy-go-lucky older sister, who had been spirited and playful in high school and college—and who had actually dated Teagan Malloy for a very short while in high school before they'd both decided they were much better off as friends—had turned into a wraith practically overnight after she'd met Charles Galloway.

Nova's lip curled in hate.

Charles was handsome and personable, an immensely popular graduate student who had charmed everyone around him. He'd lured a starry-eyed Gillian to his side with presents and flowers and all the right words.

Things had seemed perfect between the two of them at first, and Gillian had seemed happy.

Until Nova had noticed her outgoing older sister was becoming more silent, more introverted, and had even started dressing differently—frumpier, drabber, with long sleeves and long skirts even during the hottest days of the Florida summer.

She had repeatedly assured Nova that nothing was wrong and that she was just fine. But Gillian's retreat into herself and her withdrawal from the lives of everyone around her had continued unabated.

It was Nova's first lesson in domestic abuse. When she had unexpectedly strode into Gillian's room one day while Gillian was getting dressed, and Nova had seen the hundreds *of cuts, welts, and deep bruises that had littered her sister's body, she had violently thrown up—and then had demanded to know exactly what in the* fuck *was going on.*

Gillian had tried to excuse it away and lie about it, her fear palpable, but Nova wasn't having it. She'd forced her older sister to tell her about the abuse she'd been suffering at Charles Galloway's hands—and when Gillian had started to scream hysterically that Charles had promised he would kill her if anyone found out, Nova had felt herself going ice cold.

Gillian had been her first rescue.

Nova wrenched her thoughts back to the present. Since that horrible day eight years ago, Nova had become an expert at rescuing women who didn't have anywhere else to turn because they didn't trust anyone—not even an organization as noble and protective and upstanding as APS. They were too afraid and in too much danger to even think *about taking the risk to contact them.*

Enter Nova. Nova gave these women money, set up contacts and safe resources in other cities for them, often arranged train tickets in a circuitous route to hide their tracks, then helped them to simply disappear one day.

In a few cases—like that of that fucking waste of life, Charles Galloway—Nova had been instrumental in making sure they'd ended up languishing in a Florida prison for domestic assault and even attempted murder, afraid to pick up the soap in the shower.

It was a testament to Nova's cunning—and the determination of the women she'd rescued to finally be free of the terror they'd lived with for so long—that not a single one of them had ever been found by their former abusers after they had disappeared.

Nova had managed to keep her secret life secret *for eight years...but now it was all coming to an end because of what she'd done tonight. She knew the Armstrong twins and the Seven weren't going to stop until they'd pried every single detail out of her...and they were going to be* furious *when they found out about the hazardous hidden life Nova had kept from them for so long.*

Delaney had explained Sin One and Sin Two to her during a conversation they'd had not long after Delaney had been punished by Teagan for her Sin Two violation. Nova was uncomfortably aware that she had not only violated Sin Two, according to the principles of APS, but she had smashed the motherfucker into a billion infinitesimal pieces.

She groaned again, a trickle of apprehension whispering its way down her spine.

Trillian Dacanay was going to fucking explode *when she found out exactly what Nova had been up to over the years. Nova lifted her beer bottle to her lips, trying to ignore the slight trembling of her fingers.*

Nova had had a crush on Trill for as long as she could remember. That dark blonde hair, those light brown eyes…and the deep dimples that Nova had always felt she could literally fall into. Trill, one of the APS Seven, ran their Geek Crew, and had a formidable reputation as the smartest one of the APS bad asses—which was saying something, given their collective talents.

If I'm being honest, *she admitted to herself with another swallow of her beer,* I've always been somewhat intimidated by Trill's brilliance.

But Trill was also sensual and predatory, just like the rest of the APS management team. A woman who found herself in Trillian Dacanay's bed would find herself captured and claimed, if only for one night, until her very soul was devoured and her body had surrendered in a submission she would be unable to prevent.

Despite Trill's slightly introverted, techie exterior, Nova knew deep down inside that Trill was anything but *on the inside. Any femme who got mixed up with the handsome team lead would be hard-pressed to stay one step ahead of her, even as she succumbed to Trill's deadly, carnal lure.*

And Trill was coming for her.

Nova shuddered and picked up her empty beer bottle, pausing before she went in to scan the street below. She knew there was no way she could afford to get distracted by this situation, not with what she had on her plate at the moment.

Nova's lips firmed and she narrowed her eyes stubbornly. As much as she wanted Trill—as much as she craved just one single night in her arms and in her bed—she knew better than to fall prey to Trill's lethal charm and handsome, sexy body.

Moth, meet flame. *Nova shuddered again. She was a big girl, she told herself resolutely, steeling herself against Trill's hypnotic appeal. She had no reason to believe she couldn't handle it* or *Trill...and it would be over her dead body that she would let either her raging hormones or the dangerous butch from Armstrong Protection Services take priority over the desperate women who needed her.*

But as Nova pulled open the sliding glass door to walk back inside her apartment, she turned around and let her anxious eyes scan over the street one more time, looking for the gleam of dark blonde hair and a sexy, predatory smile in the moonlight.

Because Trillian Dacanay was coming for her.

Chapter 1

"Are you sure you have everything, Maria?"

Nova MacLeod stood in the waiting room of Tampa Union Station on a bright June morning with a large manila envelope in her hands. The fragile, jittery female standing next to her, clutching a toddler in her arms, nodded.

"I think so."

"Good. Your baggage is checked in and is on the train, except for this small overnight bag for you and the little one." She smiled gently at the tiny girl peering shyly at her from her mother's arms as she slid the strap from her shoulder.

"This is Amtrak's Silver Star train, and it will take you the whole way to New York City. It's a 25-hour trip, so I booked you a roomette in the sleeping car. It's extremely small, but at least you and Valentina will be more comfortable. I can't even imagine a two-year-old sitting still in a train seat for that long." Nova rolled her eyes and Maria laughed, becoming a bit more relaxed.

"Your *mami* and your *abuelo* will meet you at Penn Station. This," she waved the envelope she was holding at Maria before tucking it into the side pocket of the overnight bag, "is everything you'll need to get settled into your new life once you get to New York City, plus a bit of cash."

She smiled into Maria's eyes with warmth and put one arm around her in a hug. "Have a safe trip and text me when you get there so I know you arrived safely."

"Nova." Streams of tears started to flood down Maria's face and she choked, unable to continue for a minute. "There's no way I can *ever* repay you for what you've done for us," she stammered when she finally got herself under control. "You will be in my prayers for the rest of my life. May God go with you always, because surely you are doing His work."

"I've already told you the story of my sister, Maria. It wasn't that long ago that she found herself in a similar situation as you, although she's free and safe now. This is just my way of helping other women who find themselves in a dangerous domestic violence relationship and need to get out." The two women hugged once again, and Nova watched Maria and Valentina as they exited outside to the boarding platform. She crossed her arms and leaned against a large marble pillar, intending to wait until the train pulled out before she headed back to Whimsy, and settled down to think about Maria's story while she waited.

24-year-old Maria Camila Narvaez Estrada and her family had emigrated from Puerto Rico to New York City when Maria was just a child. Five years ago, when Maria was nineteen, she had met 27-year-old Emilio Ramos Morales while working in her parents' bodega and had been swept off her feet. After Maria and Emilio had dated for about six months, Emilio had persuaded Maria to move to Florida with him. *I have a friend who owns a construction company down there*, he'd told her, *and because the weather is so warm all year round and construction never stops, I can make a lot more money there than I can here in New York.*

He'd held Maria tightly and caressed her face. *I want to marry you,* negrita, *and I can't do that until I can save some money for us.* "Negrita" was a Puerto Rican term of endearment, and Maria had been warmed by his affection. Excited, she had agreed to relocate to Florida with Emilio and when they'd arrived in Tampa, she'd looked forward to settling down and starting her new life with him in the Sunshine State.

But no sooner had they stepped foot into their new apartment, the false mask Emilio wore dropped away and he showed his true colors as the cruel, abusive tyrant he truly was. Maria had been shocked and frightened, especially after the first time he'd savagely beaten her then had threatened her life if she told anyone. For several years, Maria had suffered her abuse in silence: broken bones, burns where Emilio had pressed her fingers against the hot stove when he was angry, chunks of hair torn from her scalp. Then, when Maria was twenty-two, she'd been terrified to find out she was pregnant.

Nova felt the rage in her soul when she remembered that Maria's family hadn't even *known* about Valentina's birth when Nova had called them. They'd been shocked beyond measure to find out their Maria had had a child without their knowledge.

Maria didn't have a cell phone or a home phone, wasn't allowed to go anywhere without Emilio, and had been accompanied by him to all her prenatal visits during her pregnancy. Her weekly Sunday calls to her family were made in his presence, where she'd pretended to be healthy and happy for both her sake and theirs, but he had forbidden her to mention her pregnancy to her family—afraid they would want to come down to see the new baby when it was born.

What should have been one of the happiest times in her life was shrouded in secrecy and terror. Emilio had ceased physically beating her while she was pregnant, knowing he couldn't hide the marks of his abuse on her body during visits to her obstetrician, but his campaign of terror had still continued.

Nova's rage simmered even more as her eyes narrowed and she thought about that incredible piece of shit. Maria's account of everything he had put her through still made the hair on the back of her neck stand up on end.

After Valentina was born, the beatings had resumed, and life became even harder because of the presence of Maria's baby daughter. Although she had a new infant to care for, Emilio still expected the house to be cleaned, his laundry to be washed, and his dinner to be cooked, just as it had been before Valentina's birth. Her insides were torn up, unable to heal, because Emilio had ignored the six-week postpartum period needed for vaginal healing and forced her to have painful, degrading sex with him. He had also refused to take Maria to any of her postpartum checkups, saying that she'd had the baby, so there was no need for her to have any special treatment anymore.

Both Maria's days and nights were agony, and even the joy of having her beautiful little girl couldn't keep her from falling into a deep depression.

One day, when Valentina was about to turn two, Emilio had returned home from work to find Maria passed out on the floor, unconscious and in shock from her exhaustion and poor physical health. Emilio had slapped her awake, hollering at her to get her lazy ass up and fix his dinner. Valentina was screaming in her playpen and, as Maria had staggered to her feet, Emilio had smacked the toddler across the face and told Maria she'd better shut the brat up if she knew what was good for her.

That was the day Maria Camila Narvaez Estrada completely broke. Watching Emilio abuse her daughter, just as he had always abused her, lit a fire in her soul and gave her an ironclad determination to escape his evil as her fierce mothering instinct rose with a vengeance.

Although Maria was isolated and wasn't permitted to talk to anyone, she remembered a conversation she'd overheard in the waiting room of her obstetrician's office when she was about seven months pregnant with Valentina.

"Her name is Nova MacLeod and she lives in Whimsy," she remembered hearing the woman say to her friend. "Desirée says she saved her life, I swear. This Nova woman got Desirée away from that piece of shit before he killed her. I guess that's what she does for women, when they're in danger and they don't have anywhere else to turn. She's rescued a ton of battered women, from what I understand."

Maria had flipped through the magazine on her lap, pretending not to hear the conversation, but her mind had raced. She had filed Nova's name away in the back of her mind, knowing that someday—if she was ever brave enough and could find a way to contact this woman—that she would be calling Nova MacLeod herself…before she ended up dead.

After Emilio had slapped Valentina—and Maria had vowed to herself that she would get herself and her daughter away from him once and for all—it had dawned on Maria that Emilio had ceased being as vigilant as he had once been when it came to watching Maria. He had evidently assumed that since she didn't have her own cell phone or a home phone, on top of having a toddler to look after now, she was far less of a flight risk then she used to be.

Emilio had taken to dropping Maria off at the grocery store with the baby, then waiting for her outside in the car while she struggled with the groceries and her daughter all by herself. After Emilio's abuse of Valentina, Maria had decided she would use that opportunity to try and contact Nova MacLeod.

"Excuse me," she'd said politely to another shopper in the back of the store, her heart thundering in her chest, during one of her shopping trips. "I'm such an idiot, but I forgot my phone at home, and I promised I'd pick up a few things for my sister. Would you mind very much if I borrow yours to make a quick local call?"

The older woman had smiled then had handed Maria her phone. “No problem at all, sweetie,” she had assured Maria. “I’m going to step over there and pick out my Sunday roast while you’re chatting with your sister, okay? Just bring it over when you’re done with it.”

Maria had quickly looked up Nova’s phone number and placed the call, looking around nervously and praying Emilio didn’t pick today to come into the store. “Are y-you Nova?” she’d asked, her voice shaking, when the confident, self-assured female voice had answered.

“Are you safe where you are?” the voice had immediately asked her.

“No. No, I’m not.” Maria had felt her eyes fill with tears at this woman’s quick understanding of her precarious situation. “But I want to be. I only have a few seconds, but I heard you help women like me. My name is Maria, and all I want to do is find a way to get back to my family in New York City without my boyfriend finding out. I also have a two-year-old, and I’m scared for her because he slapped her the other night. Please, *please* help us.”

Nova shifted against the pillar as her memories carried her through every event that had brought her and Maria to this point, when Maria was finally safely on her way home to her family with her daughter.

That phone call had been the very beginning of Maria and Nova’s communication. On a subsequent trip to the grocery store, Maria had found another shopper and had fallen back on the “forgotten” phone excuse so she could call Nova. Right away, Nova had let Maria know exactly where she could find the tiny prepaid cell phone that had been hidden for her in one of the aisles.

"The volume is off on the phone and locked, but you should also know I will never, *ever* call you at this number unless it is an absolute emergency. This phone is for *you* to call *me* when you can, and for when we have pre-arranged a time to talk," Nova had told Maria when Maria had called her for the first time from her new phone. "Don't try to hide this in your purse because that's the first place fuckwits like Emilio will search if they suspect something. Bury it in your bra for now until you get home.

"When you get home, even before you've unloaded the groceries, say you really have to pee and run to the bathroom. Then hide the phone in your tampon box. Dudes are *totally* freaked out by stuff like that so he'll never look there."

Maria had managed to hide the phone without incident when she and Emilio had returned from the grocery store that day. Then, she had continued with her life as usual while Nova had put Maria's escape plan together as quickly as she could.

When the day for Maria's escape came, Maria took Valentina into the grocery store just as she normally did, but they had continued through the store to the back and slipped out the freight receiving door, where Nova was waiting for them in her car by the receiving dock. After quickly buckling Valentina into the car seat Nova kept for these purposes, they had taken off and headed for Tampa Union Station, where Nova had put Maria and Valentina on the train under an assumed name, heading to safety with Maria's family in New York City.

Maria's parents and grandparents had been grieved and angered when Nova had called them right before Maria's escape and had told them about everything Maria had been suffering with Emilio while in Florida. They were also shocked beyond words when they'd found out about Valentina's existence…but, after their initial astonishment, Maria's *mami* and *abuela* were clearly eager to start spoiling her right away, grateful and thankful for Nova's assistance in rescuing Maria and her child. It took Nova a little more effort, however, to calm Maria's menfolk down.

"Maria doesn't need your vengeance. She needs your love and your protection," she told Maria's *papi* and *abuelo* frankly, knowing how hot-blooded the Puerto Rican culture could be from her acquaintance with Jaime Quintero and the Armstrong twins of APS.

"I will be doing everything in my power to make sure Emilio Ramos Morales *never* abuses another woman again. In the meantime, the very best thing you can do for Maria is love her, protect her, and make sure she knows she's not to blame for *any* of this. She's going to need medical care and a good therapist for a while, so she can heal and purge herself of everything she's been carrying around for the last five years.

"Maria has been through one hell of an ordeal, and you should all be very proud of her strength. I suspect that because she was also raised in a family as strong and as close as yours is, she was able to survive as she did all these years." After talking to Maria's family,

Nova was confident that Maria would eventually be okay and would ultimately be able to heal the physical and mental scars left on her from Emilio.

Her mouth curled as she watched the train finally pull out then turned to walk back to her car. She wished she could send APS after Emilio, to throw him a beating just as severe as the ones he'd given to Maria all the years they were together. They'd fuck his ass up for sure.

But…although APS had discovered her secret life a couple of days ago, after the whole clusterfuck with Tina Schaffner and Frank Bellwood had gone down, she was still reluctant to involve anyone else in her rescues. These women felt safe with her and her alone—which is why they hadn't gone to APS in the first place, as noble and honorable as they were.

Nova wasn't about to jeopardize any feelings of safety and security she could give to them, no matter how small. The abused women who found her were so severely at risk, it was anyone's guess if they would still be alive tomorrow. They were too frightened at the thought of going to anyone for help—except for Nova.

Nova then rolled her eyes as she thought about the icing on this week's shit cake.

She knew there was a *huge* reckoning with the APS management team in her future. Nova had been avoiding Trillian Dacanay for two days now as a result—because Trill had already proved she was determined to yank every secret Nova had right out of her. Trill would be coming after her for every single detail about her hidden life. Based on their brief interaction the night Delaney had been rescued from her hostage situation, it was not going to be a pleasant conversation either.

Nova sighed as she strode toward the entrance, tired and ready to head back across the Howard Frankland Bridge to Whimsy. She had a new gelato flavor she wanted to test when she got back to the Dream Creamery—plus, her mother had called her about a possible food-styling contract for a local movie that would be starting to film next month. As Nova moved toward the front doors, however, her eyes suddenly widened and she stopped dead in her tracks, surprise and not a small amount of trepidation sending a shiver down her spine.

Trillian Dacanay was standing inside the doorway, her hands on her hips, and her eyes focused with a laser-like intensity on Nova's pale face.

Chapter 2

Trill studied the diminutive brunette who had stopped dead in her tracks with wide eyes when she'd caught sight of Trill. She then saw Nova firm her jaw resolutely as she resumed her stride toward her.

"Dacanay? What the fuck?" Nova didn't hesitate as she marched right up to the APS team lead and narrowed her honey-brown eyes. "Are you stalking me now? Because I'm busy and I've got shit to do."

"Mmm hmmm. You've also been avoiding me for two days, little diva." Trill arched her brow as Nova blushed unexpectedly. "There's an outstanding conversation we need to have, which you well know. So…here's what we're going to do. I'm taking you out for an early lunch. There's a great little pizza place within walking distance and their bianca pizza with spinach and grilled chicken is to die for."

Nova's eyes narrowed even further as she snarked, "I thought bad asses didn't eat anything but rabbit food and protein. Doesn't the thought of eating carbs make your head explode?"

"We break the rules on special occasions. Of course, not as often as *you* break the rules, I'm sure," Trill's eyes bored into Nova's as she crossed her muscled arms and moved out of the doorway, "but we'll get to that part of the conversation later. We're going to eat and have a nice lunch…and then you're going to start talking, Nova MacLeod. You're going to tell me every goddamned secret you've kept from us—from *me*—over the past I-don't-know-how-many years, and why.

"Starting with why the fuck you're at Tampa Union Station watching an Amtrack train depart at ten-thirty on a Wednesday morning."

ৈωৈωৈωৈ

Nova felt her heart sink. The stern look on Trill's handsome face told her the APS team lead was completely serious and wasn't about to let Nova evade her and her questions any longer. And yet…

"No," she replied calmly, keeping her facial expression uncompromising despite her nervousness. The look of astonishment that hit Trill's face would have been comical if Nova hadn't felt like she was going to throw up. Nova swallowed hard but continued with steely determination. "Just like I explained to you the other night, Trill, I am neither an APS wife nor an APS girlfriend. I'm also not an APS employee. The secrets I keep are not always mine to tell either, so I'll be *goddamned* if I'll break a confidence just to satisfy your curiosity."

"Curiosity?" The barest hint of anger edged Trill's usually even tone. "The other night, you sailed right into the middle of a dangerous hostage situation, sight unseen, expertly guided Delaney Malloy through what she needed to do to take down her captor—as cool as a fucking cucumber, from what I understand—and you think we're *curious*? We've known you for fucking *years*, Nova—since the fifth grade, as a matter of fact—so you'll excuse me if we were all just a wee bit taken aback by your transformation from a food stylist and ice cream expert to a fucking special forces operator." With her arms crossed the way they were, Trill looked like she was coiled like a rattlesnake.

Nova snorted and rolled her eyes. "Exaggerate much?" She folded her arms across her own chest in turn and glared at the handsome butch in spite of her trepidation. "Why does APS feel like they need to know so badly? It's obviously something I've been doing for a while now and you haven't been any the wiser. I wasn't fucking *joking* when I said some of the secrets I keep are not mine to tell, Trill! You can't tell me that APS doesn't totally respect the confidentiality of their clients, because I know that you do…so you need to respect that when I say I can't tell you, *I can't fucking tell you.*"

Nova huffed and rolled her eyes again. "Honestly, why the hell do you even care, Dacanay? What difference does it make to anyone at APS what I do or don't do?"

Uncharacteristically, Trill lost her temper. "Because we *care* about you, Nova!" She pulled the tiny brunette into her arms. "*I* care about you!" Nova froze in astonishment when Trill anchored her firmly against her hard body. "You gave me a goddamned *heart attack* the other night when I found out you were involved up to your earlobes with bringing that fuckwit Bellwood down. You remember, the man that had *both a hostage and a gun*? Jesus *Christ*!

"And then, I find out you have all this knowledge about how to manipulate dangerous situations where someone might be at risk, and how to climb into an opponent's head. Why the *fuck* do you know how to do these things, Nova?!"

Trill's light brown eyes darkened and flamed. "You know how much we at APS respect client confidentiality, so I'm not going to ask you for any names. None of us would ever in a million years expect you to break your own confidences. But we're going to lunch and you sure as fuck are going to let me know what's going on with you, so I can figure out why I don't feel like you're safe. And then…I'm goddamn going to make sure you *are* safe."
Unexpectedly, Trill slid one strong hand around the back of Nova's head and kissed her.

Through her shock, Nova felt as though she was drowning even as her body welcomed Trill's touch. She'd never before seen cool, logical Trillian Dacanay display so much emotion, aggravation, or downright anger.

According to Rowan, Kelly, and Delaney, Trill was an absolute machine at work and in the community. She was kind and personable with the public but also somewhat introverted and detached—except for when she was with the Armstrong twins and the rest of the Seven—and was fully occupied by her responsibilities as the head of the data and technical security crew, whom everyone at APS called the Geek Crew.

She was systematic, analytical, and so fucking intelligent, rumor had it there was no one in the seven-county area APS monitored who could outthink her. To see her display so much open emotion like this sent Nova's senses reeling. Before she thought about it too much, however, she stood on her tiptoes and wrapped her arms around Trill's neck to return her kiss, sinking into Trill's dominance and giving herself over to this moment in time.

Although Trill was the shortest one of the APS management team at 5'7", she was still a full six inches taller than Nova's slight 5'1". Nova felt completely claimed, even owned by the handsome butch as they continued to kiss each other.

When Trill finally raised her head, she smiled faintly at Nova's flushed cheeks and wrapped her arms more firmly around Nova's trembling body. "Come to lunch with me, little diva," she whispered, running her mouth over the shell of Nova's ear. "I will not ask you to break a single confidence, I promise you. Nor will I insist you tell me anything you don't feel is relevant to this particular issue."

Nova quivered as Trill's voice grew predatory. "But I will continue to stalk you, Nova MacLeod—and I promise you that you will *not* escape from me—until I find out just what the fuck is going on."

"Now," Trill sat back and downed the last of her iced tea when they were done eating lunch, "where should we begin, Nova? I have a lot of questions. How about we start with why I found you at Tampa Union Station on a weekday morning, watching an Amtrak train depart?"

Nova sighed, fidgeting a bit, and steeled herself for the upcoming conversation. She and Trill were seated at a rear corner table in a little NY-style pizza joint about a ten-minute walk from Tampa Union Station. To her surprise, Trill had captured her hand as they'd started to walk to the pizzeria and had refused to let it go until they were seated.

To Nova's further amazement, she'd discovered that she had *loved* eating lunch with Trill. She was stunned to find out that the normally reserved, taciturn butch was funny and relaxed in a casual setting, when she was able to set aside her massive APS responsibilities for a time. Trill had asked her intelligent questions about the food-styling business during lunch and had been fascinated by Nova's depth of knowledge and years of experience in the field.

When Nova had explained to her that sometimes motor oil was used to mimic pancake syrup in food styling, then smirked as she told Trill about the time some fool key grip on a movie set had arrogantly swiped his finger through the set's pancake dish and licked his finger, Trill had thrown her head back and howled with laughter—the free and easy sound a complete shock to Nova's system. The sight of Trill's gorgeous deep dimples on full display from her laughter had also caused Nova's heart to flutter.

She actually thought she might have fallen right then and there—just a little—from both Trill's sexy-sounding laughter and those devastating dimples. But all too soon, lunch was over, and Trill was back to being her serious, analytical self.

"Just talk, little diva." Nova was surprised at Trill's kind and easy tone, even with her gravity. "I don't want you to become overwhelmed while we're talking, so we'll take things one at a time. Why don't you start by telling me why you were at Tampa Union Station this morning?"

Nova stared down into the dregs of her iced tea for a long minute, resigned to the fact that there was no way to get out of this now.

"I need to start at the very beginning, Trill, or else you won't understand," she finally said slowly as she took a deep breath then looked directly into Trill's eyes. "Eight years ago, I burst into my sister Gillian's room unexpectedly one day while she was getting dressed. You remember Gill, right?"

Trill nodded. "I do. I also remember when she dated Teag for a short while when we were in high school. She was good people, Nov."

"Yeah, well…that day, when I busted into her room, I saw her without clothes on, for the first time in a long time. And she…she was bruised and cut and beaten to the point that I hurled all over her floor from the sight of the violence that had been done to her. It was *bad*, Trill. I can't even describe to you how bad it was." Nova's eyes welled in remembered grief.

A deadly silence fell over their table.

"Turns out, she was being severely abused by her former boyfriend, but she had refused to tell anyone…because he'd told her he would kill her if she did. Long story short, I got her away from him then managed to have that asshole motherfucker put behind bars for a very, very long time. She," Nova hesitated for a moment before plunging on, "she was my first rescue." The dark silence grew.

"I have secretly referred more women than you could ever begin to imagine to APS over the years. But," she paused again, "locally, there is a tiny segment of abused and critically at-risk women out there who don't trust *anyone*, Trill. Not even APS, as awesome and upstanding and noble as you all are. But they'll trust *me*. I am the one exception to the general rule, because I have…I have a reputation out there as someone who can get these women out, safely and completely anonymously. So, I do, Trill. I've been rescuing severely at-risk women for eight years now and no one's ever found out." Nova gave a short, ironic laugh. "That is, until two days ago anyway."

She fiddled with her napkin. "I was at Tampa Union Station this morning because I'd put one of those women on a train and sent her back to her family in New York City with her two-year-old daughter. Her family had emigrated here from Puerto Rico when she was just a child. She moved here to Florida with her abuser five years ago, when she was nineteen and he was still pretending to be Mr. Nice

Guy." She snorted and blew her bangs out of her eyes. "That fucking asshole is still probably trying to find his dick after his pea brain finally registered that she never came out of the grocery store this morning."

Chapter 3

"The boyfriend from Puerto Rico also? What's his name?" Trill's voice was crisp.

Nova nodded. "He is…and I guess it won't do any harm to let you know *his* name. It's Emilio Ramos Morales, may the Goddess cause his dick to rot and fall off. He's still here in Tampa, although he originally lived in New York City as well. I hope that fucker gets exactly what he deserves some day."

Trill held up one finger then rapidly sent a fairly lengthy text before focusing her laser attention back on Nova. "What is it exactly that you do for these women, Nova?" Trill's voice was calm although the dark look remained in her eyes.

"I…um…well, I quit full-time food styling so I could devote more time to them and be more available. When someone contacts me, I'll find out their story. Then I'll formulate an escape plan for them. Give them money and arrange whatever type of transportation they might need. In short, I do whatever I need to do to get them out and away from their abuser."

Nova pleated a discarded straw paper between her fingers, still too nervous to sit still. "I'm lucky I have some pretty hefty savings, but I still take an occasional food-styling contract to stay flush. My sister just moved to Albuquerque with her new boyfriend a couple of days ago—Kip is wonderful, by the way—and I'll have to find a new apartment when the lease is up on our current apartment at the end of next month. It's way too big and expensive for me alone, and I don't need to be wasting my money on something like that when it's just me now. When Gill and Kip are settled, I'll ship their stuff out to them and make other arrangements."

Nova wondered where her unusually hesitant mood was coming from. "I've always been so incredibly busy—first with my food-styling career since I was a teenager, then with doing domestic abuse rescue—that I've never accumulated a lot of stuff on my own…which is actually a good thing. The vast majority of the furnishings in the apartment are Gill's. I have very few of my own possessions. I think I might just stay with my mom and dad for a while until I figure it all out." She subsided, wondering what Trill was thinking and what the dark, uncompromising look on her face meant.

She soon found out.

"Nova." Trill's voice was emotionless. She looked at the ceiling, clearly considering her next words before she continued. "So…what you've been telling me is that, for the past eight years, you've run this one-woman SWAT team show and rescued severely abused women from very dangerous situations. Not only situations that were dangerous to *them*, but also situations that were dangerous to *you*." The first hint of emotion crossed Trill's face.

"Why in the *motherfuck* have you never come to APS for help of any kind, Nova? Do you have *any* idea what could have happened to you, out there all alone like you've been?" A wicked gleam appeared in Trill's eyes. "No one doubts that you are a supremely capable woman, but who the fuck did you expect to keep *you* safe while you were dealing with some of these fuckers? Jesus *Christ*!"

Nova bristled and placed her hands on the table before she leaned forward. "Dude…none of these women give a good *goddamn* who APS is or about your bad ass reputation. What part of, *they weren't about to trust anyone but me*, are you not fucking getting?" she hissed, her hands clenched into fists. "They come to me for help because they *trust* me. They know I'll get them to safety—no matter what it takes—and that I can be trusted to keep my word and my vow of silence. They're too fucking scared to even take a chance on APS. *Why can't you understand that*?"

"Did it ever occur to you," Trill spoke through gritted teeth, "that we could have sat down and figured all of this out if you would have just *come to us*? Why would any of them have ever needed to know that you had silent backup in the shadows?"

"Oh. So you mean fucking *LIE* to these women and let them believe I'm the only one involved when I'm not." Nova was *so* done. She stood up with a grimace of disgust, but before she stalked off, she braced herself on the table with her hands and leaned forward one more time. "I don't *need* your help, Trillian Dacanay. I don't *want* your help."

She wished she understood why her heart felt so heavy under her anger. "I've been doing this for *eight motherfucking years*, all by myself, *without* your permission, and without your fucking lofty superior attitude! I won't lie to these women. *Ever*," Nova spat. She glowered at Trill, who had also risen to her feet. "They're coming from situations where all anyone has ever done is *lie* to them…unless, of course, they're dealing with some moronic dickhead who's beating the shit out of them!

"I'm *through*, Trill. I did what you wanted, I explained to you why I know what I know, and now *you* need to realize I don't owe you one fucking thing more." Her look was scornful. "If I even owed you anything in the first fucking place…which is *highly* doubtful at this point."

"*Goddamn* it, Nova!" Nova had never seen Trill so angry. "*No one* is suggesting we lie to them! I'm offering to provide *you* with APS protection while you do what needs to be done for *them*. We wouldn't get directly involved with your rescue strategies or with any of these women. Their secrets would still be their own."

"No thanks." Nova whirled around and started walking away. "If you can't understand that even *that* would be perceived by them as putting their lives in more danger," she threw over her shoulder defiantly, "we definitely have nothing further to say to each other. Thanks for lunch." Moving quickly, Nova flew out of the door of the pizza place and ran back to the parking lot of Tampa Union Station to get her car, ignoring the two tears that had escaped from the corners of her eyes.

ɞωɞωɞωɞ

Trill didn't think she'd been this fucking angry in *years*. *That little brat.* Trill's eyes narrowed as she walked rapidly to her SUV. Nova MacLeod was asking for her gorgeous ass to be blistered until she couldn't sit down for a week.

When Trill had cupped Nova's cheek during one of the APS self-defense lessons in Hades, not long before Frank Bellwood had taken Delaney Malloy hostage, Trill had made it clear that she would always make time for Nova if she wanted help with her self-defense practice. *Which means*, Trill seethed as she reached her SUV and swung into the front seat, *Nova has been doing dangerous rescue shit BY HERSELF—without ANY type of protection or training or help—for EIGHT GODDAMN FUCKING YEARS. Jesus CHRIST!*

When Trill finally got hold of Nova, in the privacy of Trill's own apartment, she was going to fling the tiny brunette over her knee and give her a punishment spanking she wouldn't soon forget. Nova. Was. *Hers*. It would be over Trill's fucking dead body that Nova would continue putting herself at risk the way she'd been doing over the past eight years.

She understood Nova's concern, she acknowledged, as she navigated south on I-275 toward the Howard Frankland Bridge, calming slightly. The women Nova worked with were probably incapable of trusting *anyone*…except for Nova herself. The sheer size of APS alone had likely been enough to send them into a tailspin and keep them hidden in the shadows, despite the APS reputation. Nova, a single female who worked alone and who had wholeheartedly devoted herself to the safety of these women for years, represented a trusted safe space to them—given the incredible danger they were facing—whereas an organization as large as APS did not, even as ethical and trustworthy as they were.

However…

It just might be acceptable for Nova to take on one lone partner without upsetting the entire apple cart. A partner who didn't interact directly with any of the women who needed Nova's help, but someone behind the scenes who helped Nova procure supplies and resources and money and transportation for them. Someone like Trillian Dacanay.

Trill would make it clear to Nova that they wouldn't lie. Nova could tell these women that she'd taken on a single trusted partner. She could assure them her partner didn't know anything about the women she worked with—not their identities, not their stories—but was someone who could easily smooth their way financially so they could start their new lives without worry until they could get on their feet.

If anyone did ask who Trill was, Nova would be welcome to tell them it was one of the owners of APS—someone who had taken an interest in Nova and her rescue efforts but was providing personal assistance separately from APS. Nova could assure them Trill respected the fact that these women weren't in a position to go to APS themselves or get involved with them in any way. It was a win-win the whole way around.

Trill continued south until she reached the exit that would put her on the road that led to Whimsy. She laughed slightly to herself as she recognized that her predictable, logical, neatly ordered life had been turned on its ear and sent into erratic gyrations after only a few days in Nova MacLeod's orbit. *Nova,* Trill thought with heat, *is beautiful and passionate and has always been everything I have ever wanted.* That long, thick, wavy brown hair, coupled with Nova's amazing honey-brown eyes—along with the nine tiny freckles that dotted her adorable nose—had mesmerized Trill for as long as she could remember.

Those freckles? Trill had been counting them since the fifth grade, when Nova and her family had first moved to Whimsy.

Like the rest of the APS management team, Trill had always expected to be alone throughout her life. Of course, it's not like there hadn't been women. Many women. Trill's cool logical exterior hid the same predatory, highly sensual nature the rest of the APS management team had, and frequent sex was an integral part of their lives. Just as with her best friends, however, Trill hadn't thought it would ever be possible to find a femme who could call to her soul, who would overlook her brilliant, analytical, bad ass exterior to see the true person Trill really was deep down inside.

The "machine" who was also a closet romantic.

But Bryn finding Rowan, Riley finding Kelly, and Teagan finally staking a claim on Delaney, had proved to the entire APS management team that none of them *had to* remain alone as they'd once believed. That maybe it was possible for each of them to eventually find their soulmate, their perfect femme counterpart.

Wanting Nova had always been an impossible dream, Trill had thought. When they had all graduated from high school—since Nova was the same age as the Seven and the Armstrong twins—Trill and her tribe had enlisted in the Marine Corps, while Nova had started to forge a brilliant career as a food stylist. Trill was away for a long time, first with her Marine Corps service, then with college, before she had returned home to start APS with her best friends. When she'd finally gotten back to Whimsy, Trill had been stunned to find that Nova MacLeod had morphed from a pretty, funny high school senior into a fierce beauty who had taken the world of food styling by storm.

Trill had been surprised, then pissed, when Teagan had told her recently that Nova felt intimidated by Trill's considerable education and numerous degrees. She was self-conscious about the fact that she'd never gone to college…feeling a bit inferior, Teag had informed her. Which—oh, *fuck* no. Trill wasn't ever going to stand for Nova putting herself down, especially with her more-than-considerable intelligence level. Her eyebrow quirked as she turned into the APS complex so she could park her SUV before heading across the street to her apartment. Clearly, Trill needed to sit down with Nova and establish some ground rules.

Nova was going to learn right damn quick that she belonged to Trill, she was going to move into Trill's apartment with her, she was going to take the help and money Trill was going to give to her for her domestic violence work—without any goddamned argument—and she was going to keep herself out of harm's way before Trill tied her to the bed to keep her safe. And if she had to resort to that, then Trill planned on fucking her little diva until she was screaming for Trill's mercy and had submitted to her—body, mind, and soul.

She smiled faintly as she unlocked the front door to her apartment complex and moved down the hallway to her apartment. She just might do that anyway.

Chapter 4

"So, then…it's okay if I come home for a little bit after my lease is up? Until I figure out what I'm going to do for sure?" Nova swung her legs from her perch on her mother's kitchen counter.

"Nova." Caprice MacLeod stuck her hand on her hip and rolled her eyes, her face a perfect mirror of her daughter's. She shook her head as she turned back to the stove. "Of course you can come home, baby, for as long as you need to. You're going to miss your sister like crazy for a while, just like we are, and it's probably not a bad idea to be around family right now."

"What's this, pipsqueak?" Max MacLeod entered the kitchen and kissed his wife then leaned over to peck Nova's cheek before tossing his briefcase onto the table. "I thought when parents got rid of their kids, they were supposed to *stay* gone."

"Ha ha ha. Funny, Dad." Nova adored her father, who had been the one to bless Nova with her quirky, snarky sense of humor. She swung her legs faster as she watched her dad go to the fridge and pull out a beer. "Mom, you also said you needed to talk to me about a food-styling contract?"

"I sure do." Nova's mother said as she tossed the contents in her sizzling pan. "Filming is starting next month on a new movie that's being shot on the Gulf beaches. They're shooting on location for two months before going back to the studio to film the rest." Caprice rolled her eyes again as she lowered the heat under her stir-fry. "I don't know what brainiac decided the beginning of hurricane season was the best time to film on a Florida beach, but they didn't ask my opinion, so screw it."

"And isn't *that* just going to fuck up traffic along the beaches for the locals, too," Max observed cynically, taking a sip of his beer. Nova snickered.

"Right? Anyhow, Nova...*guess* who's staring?" Nova shook her head and arched a brow quizzically. "*Isadora freaking Nightingale*. Directed by her husband, Chad Lancaster." Nova's mouth fell open and she stared at her mother in astonishment.

"Mom. Are you serious? Holy shit!" Nova had done more than her share of food styling on movie sets, but she didn't think she'd *ever* worked with a star as big as Isadora Nightingale before.

"Dead serious. And get this: I guess Ms. Nightingale will be playing a *chef* in this role, so the food styling has to totally be on point. Which is why the executive producer wanted one of us for this film and didn't bat an eye when I quoted them the high end of our contract prices. I can't do it because the filming schedule will run right into the beginning of Christmas season for print, and I have that huge spread for *Fine Dining* magazine on my calendar already. So...you're it, kiddo." Caprice pushed her skillet off the burner and turned off the heat. "The contract's right next to you in that manilla folder."

Nova rifled through the contract to look at the terms and felt her jaw go *kerplunk* for a second time. "Are you serious?" she repeated, looking at Caprice with huge eyes.

"I know, right? I suppose they won't spare any expense for one of the biggest box office draws in America. But you're worth every dime they'll be paying you, so I hope they realize *they're* the ones who are lucky, not you." Nova looked at her mother with soft eyes as she jumped down off the kitchen counter.

"Stay for dinner, baby? There's plenty."

"I wish I could, Mom, but I have to get back to the Dream Creamery. I'm trying out a new ice cream for the first time and the mix should be cold enough to churn. It's a honey lavender to herald the start of summer, and I'm excited to see how it turns out."

"Ooh, yum…that sounds *quite* summery. Make sure you save us some. I'll call you tomorrow, okay?"

When Nova got back to the Whimsy Arts Center and the Dream Creamery, she found Rowan Holland standing on the sidewalk, talking to a woman Nova had never seen before. A moving van was pulled up in front of the empty storefront where the Whimsy Taphouse had been located, and a couple of guys were busy unloading what looked like office furniture and bringing it into the storefront.

Rowan's sweet voice reached her. "Nova! Come here a second, will you? There's someone I want you to meet." Nova walked over to the two women and smiled at the stranger as Rowan said, "Meet Piper Haines. She's taking over Juliet and Dana's old taphouse storefront and opening a private investigations office. Piper, this is Nova MacLeod. *Legendary* ice cream artisan, food stylist extraordinaire, and the Whimsy undisputed Queen of Snark."

"My bitch has jokes." Nova leaned over and kissed a grinning Rowan on the cheek then held out her hand. "Welcome to Whimsy, Piper. We're happy to have you. Are you new to this whole area or just to Whimsy itself?"

"Just Whimsy itself." Piper shook Nova's hand with a friendly smile. "I was actually born and raised in Shore Acres and I still live there. I worked for a small investigations firm in St. Pete for a good many years. The owner retired, so I decided to strike out on my own. I've always loved Whimsy and I was *thrilled* to find this storefront." Piper was a pretty woman who stood a couple of inches taller than Nova's own 5'1", with straight ash-blonde hair cut to her jawline in a classic bob, light turquoise eyes, and a friendly, easy demeanor. Nova sensed, however, that Piper wasn't someone you would ever want to fuck around with.

"Can I ask what kind of investigations?" Then Nova snorted. "Ro had a bit of trouble here for a while with a dickhead PI from Virginia, so we know for sure not all PIs are created equal."

"She was telling me." Piper's turquoise eyes darkened. "Bah. Assholes like him give private investigators a bad name. I've investigated suspicions of infidelity and do some legwork for acrimonious divorce proceedings. But I think because I'm on my own now, I'm going to scale back on that a bit. The bulk of my work has always been domestic abuse and human trafficking investigations. I'd like to keep more of my focus on that." Nova's ears perked up.

"I have a close friend who specializes in investigating elder abuse situations," Piper continued, "so we're going to work in tandem when we can and be a resource for each other. Also, my ex-girlfriend works for the Department of Children and Families on their Economic Justice Initiative. We're still friendly, so we'll have a resource there as well."

"Wow, Piper. That's so incredible," Rowan said in her sweet way. "I don't know if there's anything we can do to help you, but let us know if there is, okay?" She smiled and waved as she looked across the street. "Oh, look…there's Trill and Kennedy." Rowan raised the volume of her voice. "Hey, you two. What's up?" She turned back to Piper. "I don't know if you've ever had the opportunity to work with APS before, but they're located right here in Whimsy, just a couple of blocks over. My fiancé, Bryn Armstrong, is one of the owners, and that's Trillian Dacanay and Kennedy Weston of the Seven walking over now. Do you know them?"

"My former firm worked with APS a lot, but it was mainly the owner and the senior investigator who had any contact with them. I've never had the pleasure." Piper's eyes seemed glued to Kennedy.

"I don't know that I'd call it a pleasure," Nova snarked with an eye roll. "I love them all to pieces, but they are the biggest pain in my ass ever. If you look up the word 'bossy' in the dictionary, there's a full color picture of the Armstrong twins and the Seven, smack dab in the middle of the page."

"And just why are we bossy, little diva?" Trill kissed Rowan on the cheek when the pair reached them then turned back to Nova. She regarded the tiny femme consideringly. "Maybe it's because the women of our acquaintance are a bit too cavalier for our liking when it comes to their own safety?" Trill arched an eyebrow as Nova snorted.

Rowan, ever the peacemaker, introduced the two APS team leads to Piper. "Trill, Kenn, this is Piper Haines. She just rented the old Whimsy Taphouse storefront and is going to open a private investigations office there. Piper, Trill runs what's known as the Geek Crew for APS and Kenn is their Armory Master. I'm sure you'll be seeing them around a lot."

After kissing Rowan on the cheek, Kenn put out her hand, looking at Piper with a laser focus. "Pleased to meet you, Piper. Welcome to Whimsy. If there's ever anything APS can do for you, just let us know." Although Kenn dwarfed the far more petite Piper, she shook Piper's hand gently and held it for a long minute before letting go. Nova and Rowan looked at each other with barely quirked eyebrows before Nova decided she'd had enough of the electricity swirling around the group.

"I have to get into the Dream Creamery to work on my ice cream, but I've got some crazy news I need to tell you before I go. I'm starting a contract to do some food styling for a movie that will be shot on the Gulf beaches, and you'll *never* guess who the lead actress is?" Everyone shook their heads and waited.

"*Isadora Nightingale*, if you please. How crazy is that?" Nova laughed as Piper and Rowan squealed in excitement. "Maybe I can even get her to come and hang at Seashells with us one night. Wouldn't that be cool?"

"Oh, my gosh, that would be awesome!" Rowan gushed. "I absolutely loved her in *Master Plan*!"

"*Loved* that movie. Now, I really have to go before my ice cream is ruined, so I'll catch you later." Nova waved at the group as she started to walk to the WAC. "Welcome again, Piper. Ro can text me your number and we'll go hang one night."

After she'd gone about five feet, Nova sighed as she realized Trill was following her back to the Dream Creamery. "What, Dacanay? I've got shit to do, and I don't have time to listen to you yammer on about your bullshit feelings over how I conduct my life."

"Little diva." Trill caught up with her and took possession of her hand. "No matter what the fuck you say, we still have a discussion to finish. I know Clem is off today and Rowan is going to help Piper for a little bit, so we'll have the Dream Creamery and the WAC to ourselves so we can talk."

Nova felt like she was about to explode. "What the *fuck* do you think needs to be said that wasn't already said this morning, Trill?" She snatched her hand from Trill and yanked open the door to the WAC. "You said your piece, I'm not going to change my mind, so anything further would be absolutely pointless. I don't understand why you can't just fucking *let it be*." Nova stomped behind the counter of the Dream Creamery and pulled the ice cream mix from the refrigerator. She nodded to herself when she tested the temperature and found it was ready to begin churning.

"Because I did a lot of thinking on the way home from Tampa this morning, and I think I've come up with the perfect solution, something I think we can both live with." When Nova arched her eyebrow cynically at Trill, the handsome team lead explained her idea.

"This wouldn't be anything APS-sanctioned, Nova. But frankly, none of us gives a fuck what any of the others do with their own money and their own spare time. The only thing the Armstrongs and the rest of the Seven will want to know is if we want or need any help from them. So…I, Trillian Dacanay—who just *happens* to be one of the owners of APS—will be the lone, faceless partner who will provide you with the financial resources you need to get your women safe. But I won't be involved with any of those women nor will I know any of the details about their identities or their situations.

"You will tell them up front that you've taken on a partner so you can give them a lot more by way of money and resources to start their new lives. No one except you, however, will know anything about them, so their secrets will still be safe with you. If they ask who I am, we'll simply tell them. We won't hide anything from these women. But we'll also make sure they understand I'm not doing this on behalf of APS. I'm doing it myself to help *you*.

"And this way, *I* feel better about you doing such dangerous work, because you'll have me at your back in case things start to go sideways. I talked to Kenn and told her I want you to learn to shoot just like Delaney did…in addition to continuing your Krav Maga lessons with Casey and Jess. Nov," Trill's voice softened, "I'm not looking to take your power away from you, little diva. But that also means you need to learn every single way you can protect yourself when you're in the middle of one of these situations."

Nova stopped and considered what Trill had said.

It wasn't the worst idea, Nova thought. If she told the women she helped that she'd taken a single partner so she could provide them with more resources, but her partner knew absolutely nothing about them, they'd probably be okay with that. It would be a whole fuck of a lot less scary for them if they thought Nova was dealing herself with one silent partner for financial and resource support—who knew nothing about the women she helped—instead of having an organization with the strength and size of APS involved.

She drew in a deep breath. "What you say makes sense, and it's quite a bit different than what you said to me this morning. This, I think they could deal with. The other…there was no fucking way. You haven't explained to me where the money for this grand plan is supposed to come from though, Trill. I've already told you I have a pretty decent-sized nest egg, and this movie contract I just took will really add to my coffers.

"But I'm not sure you understand just how expensive something like this can be, despite your experience with APS." She flipped on the ice cream machine and it started to churn. “We’re talking about train tickets. Clothing. Toiletries and some luggage. Food. Water. Some cash so they have a little bit of money to start out with. Sometimes there are kids involved, so I need to make sure the children have what they need.

“More often than not, these women don’t have *anything* but the clothes on their backs when they run. They need to get to where they’re going knowing that they have access to some food and water, so they aren’t going to starve.” Nova bit her lip, willing the tears away. “They need to know they have time to take a wee little breath, before they have to start worrying about jobs and apartments and things like that.”

“Baby.” Trill paused for just a moment before she continued, looking keenly into Nova’s eyes. “We make an absolute *fuckton* of money at APS, even with all our charitable giving. All my living expenses are paid for: my apartment, my utilities, my concierge service, my vehicle maintenance and insurance…in short, just about everything you can think of. The only money I really ever need is for when I go out. I’ve pretty much done nothing but bank my paychecks for the last ten years, Nova.”

Nova’s eyes widened.

“I have more money than I’ll ever be able to spend in this lifetime, baby. I can’t think of a better way to use it than to help some of these women of yours create the life they should have always had. Okay? Can you accept that from me?” There was a long moment of silence. Holding on to her emotions by the skin of her teeth, Nova finally took a deep breath and nodded.

"Good." Trill leaned back against the counter and crossed her arms. "One more thing, because I have to be honest with you, little diva. You did give me that fuckwit's name at lunch today, the abuser of the woman you put on the train at Tampa Union Station this morning. I passed it on to Bryn, Riley, and Jaime…and I let them know what that fucker had done to your friend.

"They were fucking *not happy*, Nov. Bryn and Riley are half Puerto Rican because of their mother, and Jaime is what they call *boricua*—someone who was born on the island of Puerto Rico. It's a proud, passionate culture, and the fact that Mr. Morales had so thoroughly disgraced their heritage means that he landed in the crosshairs of three very pissed-off APS bad asses today. They paid Mr. Morales a visit this afternoon."

Nova's eyes grew huge.

The corner of Trill's mouth quirked up. "I think I can safely say that asshole will never put his hands on another woman ever again. Whether or not you tell her or her family is completely up to you, but your friend was avenged today, Nova."

Chapter 5

Nova felt as though her whole world was spinning. A brief silence reigned over the Dream Creamery, the only sound coming from the ice cream maker, until Trill finally spoke.

"This isn't something that I'll ever do without your knowledge, but today seemed to be a special occasion that warranted it. However…I'd suggest you not tell me any details going forward, as we've already agreed. We deal with some nasty-ass motherfuckers on a regular basis at APS. Because we are a protection and security company, dedicated to keeping women safe in general, we've unfortunately run into more than our fair share of situations over the years.

"I'm just like the rest of APS in that there's *nothing* that enrages me more than someone who will put their hands on a woman. I don't usually get too up close and personal with the details because I'm more focused on the data and technical security end of the business."

Trill leaned over the counter and took Nova's small hands in her own. "But…had I not started APS with the twins and the rest of the Seven, I most likely would have stayed in the Marines and gone the sniper route. I am an expert shot, Nova, and I've been shooting since I was five years old. I don't think any of these motherfuckers need to put themselves in my crosshairs, do you?"

ઋωઋωઋωઋ

Trill squeezed Nova's hands gently then reached over to stroke Nova's pale cheek. She was *done* with this bullshit. She was going to take Nova out to dinner, then she was going to take Nova to her own apartment so she could pack a bag. And then, they were going to Trill's apartment—which was now Trill *and* Nova's apartment. Because Trillian Dacanay fucking refused to spend another night apart from her woman.

"Nova." Trill's voice was gentle but stern—with an edge of dominance that made Nova's heart flutter. "Come here, baby."

Slowly, Nova moved around the counter. When she reached Trill, the blonde APS team lead wrapped her arms around Nova and secured Nova's petite body against her. She slanted her mouth against Nova's and kissed her deeply.

ઋωઋωઋωઋ

Nova whimpered and she knew her panties were soaked. She was still trying to wrap her head around the fact that, for as many years as she'd wished for one night in Trillian Dacanay's bed, it looked like Trill had felt the same exact way about her. Just as Nova felt she was on the verge of passing out, Trill finally raised her head. She ran her hands up and down Nova's back. "How long before you're done here, baby?" she murmured.

After a minute, Nova was able to come back to herself and focus. "Umm. Maybe about forty minutes, tops. Why?"

"Because when you're done, we're going to go out to dinner so we can talk a bit more, little diva. Then I'm taking you to your apartment so you can pack a bag, and you're coming home with me."

Nova made a sound of disbelief in the back of her throat.

"I'm *done* being without you, Nova MacLeod. In case it hasn't occurred to you yet, you've been mine since the fifth grade." Trill bent slightly and rested her forehead against Nova's. "You've wanted me and I've wanted you…but the biggest reason we've been kept apart in recent years is because of your dedication to the battered women you help. You weren't about to expose them to anyone for any reason, even if it meant denying your own wants and needs to do it."

Trill kept running her hands over Nova's petite frame as her gaze bored into Nova's honey-brown eyes. "I love you for that, you know. You found a small but still very critical gap in the realm of protection for women that none of us knew about, and you filled it. Do you have any idea how many lives you've probably saved over the years, Nova MacLeod?"

Nova couldn't help it. The tears started to flood down her face.

"Be that as it may, Nova." Trill's voice became stern again. "I am still *furious* that you put yourself into such danger for so long. Over the years, you've clearly taught yourself a fuckton about the psychological aspects of battered woman syndrome. I doubt there's anyone out there who knows more about how to get an abused woman away from her abuser than you do.

"But making sure you had adequate physical protection for yourself while you were getting these women out? Working to make sure you had enough self-defense knowledge in case one of these motherfuckers tried to hurt *you*? *Big. Fucking. Fail*, baby." An edge appeared in Trill's tone again. Nova shuddered instinctively.

"Do you have any idea how easily you could have been beaten or killed during a rescue? You were all alone out there, Nova, without the *first* fucking clue how to defend yourself if you found yourself facing a threat."

Nova gulped when she saw the look in Trill's eyes. However, to her shock, she felt even more moisture slide out of her, responding unbidden to Trill's dominant nature.

She was confused by her almost submissive reaction to Trill. Nova was fierce and snarky, she didn't take shit from *anybody*, and she would have told anyone else to go pound fucking salt if they'd tried to lecture her like Trill was. But Trillian Dacanay was a dominant alpha butch who only had to *look* at Nova to make her want to obey her. Within the safe shelter of Trill's arms, Nova felt herself succumbing, unable to help herself.

Trill grew even more stern. "Do you know what Sin One and Sin Two are, Nova?"

"Del-…Delaney explained them to me one day when she told me about the punishment spanking Teagan had given to her," Nova whispered, relaxing from the soothing strokes on her back, even though she knew she was in a world of trouble.

"Good. So…you'll understand when I tell you that I think you've managed to smash even Kelly Armstrong's record for the severity of a Sin Two violation, little one."

Nova winced.

"Eight years, Nova. *Eight fucking years* you've put yourself at daily risk—without backup, without adequate resources, out there all alone *and* unprotected—and I'm here to tell you it will be a cold goddamn day in hell before my woman *ever* puts herself at risk like that again." Trill ran a strong hand over the back of Nova's head again before she lowered her mouth and once more took possession of Nova.

In a blinding flash of clarity, Nova realized that, for all her snarking, for all her blustering, for all her attitude and defensiveness and caustic sarcasm, one thing was certain—she'd fallen so far under Trillian Dacanay's spell of dominance and possession that she knew she would belong to Trill without question for the rest of her life. That she had *always* belonged to Trill, even during their years apart. There were complex, hidden layers to Trill that weren't readily apparent on the surface—facets of her personality that were easy to overlook behind her slightly introverted, brilliant, techie exterior.

Nova knew the handsome team lead would keep her safe and support her in her work without question…although she would fully expect Nova to defer to her when it came to matters of her own safety from now on. Nova had never thought of herself as a woman who would easily submit to anyone else. To put herself in a position where she would obey someone else without question, without being certain her own wants and needs would be honored? That was some epic bullshit right there.

However, Nova was as sure as she could be that Trill had no intention of taking any of her freedom away from her. All she wanted was for Nova to be safe—and Trill would always expect Nova to listen to her when it came to her safety—but, beyond that, Trill would be her partner and her sounding board and her safe harbor in the midst of her often chaotic life.

For the first time in her life—and especially for the first time in the last eight years—Nova MacLeod didn't feel alone.

"Little one." Trill nuzzled her ear after she released her mouth once more. She banded her strong arms tightly around Nova's body. "You understand you've earned yourself one hell of a punishment spanking for putting yourself at risk the way you have for so long, right?"

Nova stiffened.

"Alpha butches discipline and spank, little diva. When our femmes don't take care of themselves the way they should, when they knowingly walk into unsafe situations—or, like in the case of a Sin One violation, they put themselves down and bring about psychological harm to their mental state of mind—these are all spanking offenses, Nova."

A humorless chuckle came from Trill's chest. "It sounds ironic as hell, talking about domestic violence in one breath and punishment spankings in the next. But we both know they are night and day situations…because punishment spankings exist to keep you safe, not to subvert your will or control you."

Nova nodded her agreement against Trill's shoulder.

"We will, on occasion, give a pass for a transgression, but that's not something we do often. The long and the short of it is…I am an alpha butch, you are *my* femme, and you've behaved in a way that is completely unacceptable to me as far as you remaining safe, happy, and healthy. Do you understand?"

Nova drew in a long, shuddering breath.

"I don't know if I can do this, Trill," Nova whispered, burying her face in Trill's chest. "To submit to you for a punishment spanking? I know what I did wasn't permissible by APS standards, but I…I'm not sure I can. I didn't even *know* about the rules until now, so it doesn't seem fair to me that I should be punished for something I didn't even know existed."

"Little one. You've always known, deep down inside, that you belong to me. You've also known, whether you admit to it or not, that I would be way less than happy about what you've been doing over the last eight years. Well…not so much *what* you've been doing, but *how* you've been going about doing it." Trill kissed her temple.

It was true. Nova fidgeted, discomfited. She really had no excuse.

"I think when we're done here, little diva, we're going to grab a few things from your apartment and then go directly home. You're nervous and I see no reason to drag this out. We'll take care of what we need to do, then you can take a shower while I fix us something light to eat."

"You cook?" Nova was surprised, forgetting her dilemma for a moment.

"Basic stuff. I can broil a steak, scramble some eggs, throw together a stir-fry…things like that. My mom knew when I left for college that I would be gone for a long time, so she tried to make sure I at least knew the basics. Because of your background, however, I'm sure you far outclass me in the culinary realm."

"I've spent a lot of years doing food styling so, yeah…most of us cook. Food stylists throw some epic dinner parties, actually. Gill and I used to have people over all the time. Of course, I have to admit sometimes it's hard to get excited about making a juicy steak for people when you've spent time painting realistic grill marks on one with eyeliner."

Trill chuckled and nuzzled Nova's temple again. "It's going to be okay, little diva. I promise you. Believe it or not, I'm going to hate this *far* more than you will. You will shockingly have a sense of release you've never felt before, despite the discomfort. And when it's over…we'll be exactly where we need to be. Together, with nothing between us, for the rest of our lives."

Chapter 6

Discomfort??? Nova screamed as Trill's hand came down firmly on her bare bottom again.

When Trill and Nova had finally arrived at Trill's apartment, Nova had stood at the end of the entranceway and looked around. She'd been inside Delaney and Teagan's apartment a couple of times, and she saw that the layout of Trill's apartment was identical. But while the Malloy abode was filled with soft blues, greens, and the symbolism of Teag's Irish heritage, Trill's place was extremely monochromatic—even somewhat sterile, truth be known—with grays and touches of black.

As with Teagan's apartment, everything was military neat, and Nova felt her nerves fray in the deafening silence. She watched Trill as the APS team lead set down Nova's suitcase before she took off her leather jacket and unbuckled her concealed carry holster, tossing the items on the couch. Trill then picked up Nova's suitcase again and strode across the living room to the hallway that would take them to the master bedroom. "Come," she said simply, her tone stern, though not unkind. Trembling, Nova followed her into the master bedroom. Trill dropped Nova's overnight bag next to her dresser then turned and faced the petite femme.

"Do you understand exactly why you are being punished here today, Nova? If there's even one tiny seed of doubt in your mind, you need to let me know right now. It's unacceptable to any of us to punish one of our femmes without making sure she understands exactly *why* she is being punished."

"I understand, Trill." Tears caught in Nova's throat and she dropped her eyes, still trembling and slightly sick from what was about to happen—although she strangely felt the rightness of submitting to Trill.

"Good." Trill's voice didn't alter. "Please remove your jeans and your panties, and then lay face down across my knees. Place your hands at your sides." She sat on the edge of the bed and widened her legs enough to form a stable shelf for Nova to lay across. Nova's tears started to fall as she did what Trill had directed. She whimpered slightly as she positioned herself and waited with bated breath.

Trill didn't hesitate. *Smack*! Nova squealed and caught her breath with how much it hurt. As she automatically moved her hands to cover her rear end, Trill caught her wrists behind her back in one of her own large hands.

"I've allowed you to remain unrestrained during this, Nova, but I will revoke that privilege if you do that again." Trill's tone hardened. "Punishment spankings are *supposed* to hurt." *Smack! Smack!* Nova screamed again from the pain then gasped in a huge gulp of air, but she forced her hands to stay at her sides.

"For *eight years*, you put yourself into a position where you could have been brutalized just as severely as the woman you were trying to help." *Smack!* Nova started to cry. "You could have been beaten; you could have been *raped*. No one was aware of what you'd been doing, you had no protection, your self-defense skills were non-existent, and you put yourself at horrific risk every single time you got involved with a rescue." *Smack! Smack! Smack!*

"No one—least of all, APS—would *ever* judge you for wanting to keep these women protected or to keep their secrets safe." *Smack! Smack!* "But there are ways to go about doing things like this that will keep *you* safe, and you didn't do that. *I. Could. Have. Lost. You, Nova.*" Nova heard the emotion under Trill's stern tone.

"Never *again*, little diva. Do you understand me?" *Smack!* "Despite your intelligence and your cunning, we *all* could have lost you. And you don't *ever* want to know what kind of hell I would have unleashed on this community if someone would have taken you away from me." *Smack! Smack!*

When Trill was finally done, she gently pulled Nova up into her lap, mindful of Nova's tender, burning bottom. Nova continued to cry for a while, struggling to process both the pain and the *fear* she had heard in Trill's voice. *I matter to her*, Nova suddenly realized through the churning haze of her emotions. *I matter to her, and she was afraid for me.* Her sobs slowed after a while and her equilibrium started to right itself.

"I'm sorry." Nova's voice was almost inaudible. She leaned against Trill's chest and went limp in the sinewy arms that had banded around her. "I never meant to cause anyone any worry, Trill." She hiccupped with her emotions. "It was so important to me that I kept these women hidden and safe, that I…I didn't think beyond that."

"I know, little diva." Trill's voice was gentle now as she rubbed her fingers over Nova's tear-stained cheek. "I've already told you I love you for what you did for them. But, going forward, we're going to do this in a way that's safe for *everybody*—most of all, you."

After they'd sat there in silence for a while longer, Nova cuddled against Trill's chest, Trill finally kissed Nova on her temple. "I want you to take a shower while I'm making you something to eat, baby. When you're done showering, I'm going to smear some cream on your bottom, we're going to eat, and then I think it's time to call it a day. You've had a long, very emotional day, and you need to be at peace now.

"I want you to sleep in my arms tonight, where you'll know you're safe. I want you to realize that you're no longer alone. I promise you: I will burn the world down before you have to deal with these kinds of burdens by yourself ever again."

ᘐωᘐωᘐωᘐ

"Jesus *Christ*, Trill. I don't even fucking know what to do with this," Bryn Armstrong said, expressing the sentiments of every single member of the APS management team. The Armstrong twins and the Seven were meeting for their usual six a.m. management meeting. Trill had brought them up to speed with what she'd found out about Nova since the night of Delaney Malloy's rescue.

"You're telling us that Nova MacLeod has been playing clandestine search-and-rescue operative for the last eight fucking years, all by herself, without any training and without any backup?" Blake Seibert dragged an aggravated hand through her hair. "Oh, *fuck* no." She glanced at Trill sharply. "I'm assuming you let her know what happens when an APS femme puts herself in danger, right? Because…because…" Blake made a pissed-off sound in the back of her throat.

The corner of Trill's mouth tilted up without humor. "She now knows *exactly* what punishment spankings are for. I told her I loved her for what she had tried to do for these women. She also knows how much the entire APS team respects her, and that we couldn't be prouder of her determination to keep Delaney safe from that fuckwit Bellwood." Trill nodded at Teagan. "But the way she chose to go about helping these survivors was about as fucking wrong as it's possible to get. I told her there's a better way…a way that will keep *her* safe, as well as keep those women safe, and won't give us a goddamned heart attack in the process."

The team snorted.

Trill explained to everyone what the procedure to help Nova's survivors would be going forward. "Nova knows I understand the intimidation factor that's often present in others when it comes to dealing with APS...*especially* when it's a fragile domestic abuse survivor, even though we try to be as supportive of and non-threatening to these women as we can."

"We all do," Bryn commented. "We work with some of these survivors every single day and our number one goal has always been to first get them safe, and then to provide them with everything they need to heal."

"Exactly. But I don't think it's ever occurred to any of us that a few of them would *deliberately hide themselves from us*." Trill lounged back in her conference room chair and steepled her fingers, a contemplative look on her face. "In our minds, our reputation isn't something that would ever feel like a threat to a woman who's been abused. If anything, she would automatically reach for us as a safe haven, which has always been our assumption.

"Because of Nova, however, we now know there's a tiny segment of women out there who desperately need help, but who've been completely off our radar. These women are in such imminent danger from their abusers, they don't fucking trust *anyone*. Nova has been the only reason they've come forward at all. And fuck if she doesn't get them out, too." Trill rubbed her brow. "How the hell she's managed to do this on her own for eight years without losing a single survivor is beyond me."

"Thank the goddess for Nova," Kenn muttered. "Who knows how many of these women would have stayed hidden in the shadows with nowhere to turn—and, most likely, eventually dead—if it wasn't for her." Her eyes focused closely on Trill. "Please tell me she understands how many lives she's probably saved over the years, even if her way of going about it was fucked up."

"She does." Trill was grim. "She also understands I'll fucking blister her ass a second time if she ever again puts herself in danger the way she has been doing."

"Whatever made her start to do this?" Drew was curious. "I mean, Nov was already building her reputation as a *food stylist* when we were all still in high school. She was funny and talented and snarky as hell, so I don't understand what would have triggered *domestic abuse rescue*, of all fucking things. I mean, what the hell? That doesn't track."

"Her older sister is the one who started it. You all remember Gillian, right?"

The team nodded.

"Nova walked into Gill's room one day eight years ago when Gill was changing her clothes, and Nova told me she vomited right on the carpet when she saw the cuts and bruises and welts on Gillian's body…given to her by some lowlife scum motherfucker Gill was dating."

Teagan made a malevolent sound in the back of her throat.

"He beat the fucking shit out of her and had apparently been doing it for quite some time. He'd also threatened to kill her if she ever told anyone." There was a collective hiss from the entire team. "That's what started it—Gill was Nova's first rescue—and Nova's been doing it ever since. Except now," Trill's smile held no humor, "she'll be protecting herself the way she always should have from the beginning."

"Fuck my life." Casey shook her head then rubbed the back of her neck. She looked at Trill. "I'll make sure that Jess has an accelerated self-defense program put together for her ASAP, cuz. And…Nov may be tiny, but Jess has already said she's smart as hell and has been picking up Krav Maga self-defense moves damn quick. Nova is aware she doesn't have bulk and strength behind her moves because she's so little, so she analyzes *everything* to compensate for her small stature."

The corner of Trill's mouth lifted. "Sounds exactly like a woman who should be involved with a data and technical security analyst then, doesn't she?"

ᘐωᘐωᘐωᘐ

As they were wrapping up for the day, Jaime asked Trill what her next steps were going to be. Then a malicious smile spread across her face. "I think these two fuckers and I," she waved her hand at the Armstrong twins, "delivered a very *pointed* message to that useless scum abuser from Nova's last rescue about keeping his goddamn hands to himself from now on." She quickly brought the rest of the team up to speed.

Riley's smile was dark as she exchanged a look with her twin and Jaime. "I think he got the point."

Trill shut down her laptop, and the team prepared to leave for the day. "Nova's still sleeping," Trill said. "I didn't run with you all this morning because I didn't want to leave her. After we took care of business last night, I had her take a shower, put some cream on her, then scrambled her a couple of eggs. She was exhausted, so I put her to bed after she ate.

"I left her a note and told her to text me when she was awake, but I haven't heard from her, so I'm going to assume she's still asleep. When she's finally awake and has had her coffee, I'm going to bring her to the Recon Room to meet my crew."

Then Trill rolled her eyes and started to laugh as she headed to the door with the rest of the APS management team. "While I'm thinking about it…you probably need to know that Nova is about to start a food-styling contract on a movie that will be filming down on the Gulf beaches for the next two months. Nova and Rowan are already losing their shit because it's starring Isadora Nightingale." Trill chuckled as she walked out of the door with the rest of the team. "Just be prepared for the impending detonation when the rest of our femmes find out."

Chapter 7

Nova paused for a moment after she walked into the glass-walled conference room next to Trill's office in the Recon Room, feeling a bit out of her element. Five pairs of eyes were fastened on Nova's face and five kind, welcoming smiles greeted her.

"Nova!" Kendall Quaide jumped to her feet with a grin, making Nova feel immediately comfortable. "What's up, little diva?" As Nova rolled her eyes, Kendall went over and hugged the tiny brunette and kissed her on the cheek.

Nova hugged Kendall back and then smacked her in her hard abs with the back of her hand. "I see you've been resisting the lure of my ice cream and Delaney's desserts," Nova snarked, smirking. "We'll have to do something about that."

Kendall laughed then faced Trill with her hands on her hips. "I guess we're at her mercy then, aren't we, chief?" The corner of Trill's mouth quirked up as Kendall looked at Nova again. "Nov, can I get you something to drink? Cold water, coffee?"

"I'm up to my eyeballs in coffee this morning, but some cold water would be great. Thank you." A faint flush hit her cheeks as she noticed how closely Trill was watching her.

Trill seated her at the conference room table and sat next to her as Kendall got her water. "Baby, this is my core team, known around

APS as the Geek Crew. The people you see out by the monitors," Nova looked through the large glass partition to look more closely at the collection of associates gathered around monitor screens, "are monitoring our clients.

"APS offers 24/7 security and protection services, and part of that involves monitoring clients who are single or widowed and who may be alone in their homes. Those associates you see are part-time security specialists who take care of that monitoring. These five fuckers, however," Trill laughed as five middle fingers shot into the air, "take care of various other functions. I know you've already met Kendall, but I wanted to introduce you to the rest of the team and let them give you a very brief overview of what it is they do."

When Nova had woken up that morning, she'd realized she was still lying in Trill's arms, unable to believe how relaxed and peaceful she felt. Trill had kissed her on the forehead when she saw Nova's eyes flutter open. "Good morning, little diva," Trill had whispered. "How did you sleep?"

"I slept great." Nova had felt unbelievably safe and warm. "But I thought you told me you had your daily management meeting this morning?"

"Already been, already back, and I already have coffee ready for us. It's 7:20, baby, so you just need to tell me what you want for breakfast."

"I usually only have coffee and maybe a little bit of fruit in the mornings, Trill. I'm not a big breakfast eater…I never have been. What I really, *really* need to do right now, though, is pee like crazy."

With a grin, Trill said, "Then I'm going to go fix our coffee while you're taking care of business and getting dressed. I want to bring you down to the Recon Room today so you can meet my crew and get a better idea of what it is we do in particular at APS."

She'd kissed Nova's temple and then her forehead. "I've waited to wake up to you for a long time, Nova MacLeod, and I plan on doing that until we're both old and gray. Although," she flicked the sleeve of the large T-shirt she'd given to Nova last night after her shower, "I hope you realize you'll be sleeping in my bed naked from now on." Nova had felt her core heat from the predatory look in Trill's eyes.

Now, Nova relaxed in her chair as she listened to Trill talk.

"First of all," Trill slid her arm around Nova's slender shoulders, "everyone, this is Nova MacLeod. Legendary ice cream artisan, one of the best food stylists in the business—from what I understand—and the woman who's now living with me."

"Pay *up*, motherfuckers," a golden-haired butch with twinkling hazel eyes crowed. She grinned mischievously at a confused Nova. "It's so good to officially meet you, Nova. I'm Darcy Leveque. When Kendall told all of us how absolutely fucking awesome you are and how you can hold your own against virtually anyone, I bet that this cold-ass motherfucker," she waved her hand at Trill, "wouldn't stand a chance against you. We already know from Blake that you like to make book with the APS crew, so here we are." Nova burst out laughing with the rest of the team, deciding she adored the Geek Crew already.

"Asshole." Trill rolled her eyes. "Baby, Darce is my second, which means she's the one everyone goes to when it comes to data and technical security questions or concerns if I'm not available. She is a big fucking pain in my ass, but you won't find a better information security analyst anywhere in existence."

Darcy rapidly sobered. "The bulk of my job, Nova, involves making recommendations to improve our security systems, and to decide the best way to advance our overall security, for both APS and for our clients. My main focus is to make sure we protect our digital assets—meaning anything that can be stored and transmitted electronically through a computer—from unauthorized access and mitigate risks before a data breach occurs."

"Do *not* let your head explode, little diva." Trill rubbed her shoulder, immediately sensing Nova's burgeoning unease. "You need to understand we've all studied for *years* to be able to do what it is we do. We have degrees and certifications and all kinds of other shit that help us to do our jobs with data and technical security."

"Nov." Kendall looked at her seriously. "There is positively *no* fucking reason you would ever know any of this. It's not what you do and no one's going to expect you to understand jack shit about it."

A handsome butch with black hair and brown eyes who clearly came from Asian culture spoke up next. "I'm Val Chan, Nova…I'm the APS cyber security analyst. *You*, little sister, should have no worries whatsoever." The rest of the team nodded emphatically.

"Trill's told us just a little bit about the women you've helped over the past few years and I, for one, am in fucking *awe* of you.

"I get why APS hasn't been involved, because of the fear these poor souls have, but I'm extremely happy that Trill is in a position to help you out now. She knows—and now *you* need to know—if there is *anything* we can do to make things a little bit easier for you, you only have to say the word."

"Thank you, Val." Nova was grateful, feeling a bit more at ease. "Do you mind telling me exactly what the job of a cyber security analyst entails?"

"Not at all. In a nutshell, I protect the APS organization from cyberattacks and threats. You would not *believe* how many jackasses there are out there who think they can attack us and our networks, especially when they're looking for information." Val rolled her eyes. "Darce and I worked closely with Remy and Harper from Teagan's telecommunications crew when we were trying to shut that asshole Frank Bellwood down."

Nova nodded in remembered understanding then turned to Kendall again.

Kendall's blue-gray eyes smiled at Nova. "I'm the data analyst for APS, little sister. Basically, I look at the big picture of everything APS is involved with from a data standpoint. I organize it in such a way that the management team fully understands the data at a glance and can use it to make strategic decisions. My education pretty much focused on analytics, computer modeling, science, and math, since I actually straddle both the data and the technical sides of the house."

"Damn." Nova was still feeling a little overwhelmed.

"Seriously, Nov, don't." Kendall was solemn as she shook her head. "You know, I had to go and look up food styling when Trill told us you were a legend in the field. *Because I didn't know what food styling meant*. And, I mean…*damn*, girl. We all need to go out one day after work and grab a beer at Seashells so you can explain more about that shit. I am absolutely mesmerized, and I promise you, these fuckers will freak out."

"Ask her about painting grill marks on steaks using eyeliner." Trill's tone was wry. Nova burst out laughing while the rest of Trill's team looked at her with fascinated eyes. Trill grinned and kissed Nova's temple. "Melanie, you're up to bat next."

"Melanie Reed. Infrastructure analyst." Melanie had extremely short, dark curls, dark hazel eyes, a medium-brown skin tone, and an infectious smile. "My job is to identify any flaws in our infrastructure and make decisions based on the technical analysis. When Jaime Quintero's physical security team breached us during their last pentest because of a weakness Kelly Armstrong found in our infrastructure, I'm the one who's been working with Darcy to fix that. Those assholes." Her eyes twinkled at Nova while the rest of the team snickered.

"And the best gets saved for last." An auburn-haired associate with blue eyes crossed her arms on the table in front of her and gave Nova a devilish grin as everyone else groaned. "It's good to meet you, Nova. I'm Peyton Montgomery and I'm the APS systems analyst." Peyton then grew as serious as the others had. "Systems analysis involves looking at our entire system, breaking it down into parts, and figuring out how each part works with the others in order to achieve maximum efficiency. We have an outside firm we contract with, and they were the ones who actually built all of our systems here when APS first started. But I'm the one who collaborates with them and Trill to maintain that relationship and keep our systems at peak performance."

"Wow. I just…wow." Nova pinched the bridge of her nose. She cast her eyes sideways at Trill. "I know you keep saying not to get overwhelmed, but how can any normal human being *not* be?"

She fixed everyone with a frank look. "You all need to understand that I *never* went to college. *At all*. I got into serious food styling with my mom when I started high school. By the time I graduated, I was making so much money and had so much work, I didn't have the inclination to go. Most food stylists have some type of culinary degree, but my mom started teaching me the business when I was only eight years old, believe it or not. She herself has a culinary degree from the Culinary Institute of America. She fell into food styling on her own, and she is an absolute phenomenon."

Nova sipped her water, then continued. "I never bothered going to school because I learned more from Caprice MacLeod than I would have *ever* learned in any culinary program anywhere. My food-styling education was one long apprenticeship with the best food stylist in the United States…if not the world. Now, at thirty-five, when I maybe could find the time to go to school, I don't really feel any desire. I'm a food stylist and an ice cream artisan."

She shrugged and shook her head deprecatingly. "I love what I do…very much…but it's not exactly rocket science either, as challenging as it can be. It's not *nearly* in this league." She swept her hand around the room.

ə-ωə-ωə-ωə-

"Who says it has to be, baby?" *Fuck it,* Trill thought as she reached over and bodily lifted Nova then sat her on her lap. Nova's eyes grew huge as Trill wrapped her arms around Nova's waist. "You are probably one of the *most* intelligent women I've ever met, Nova MacLeod." There was a faint echo of dominance in Trill's voice. She could see that her woman barely managed to control the shudder that tried to envelop her. "You are *brilliant* in your field. I don't give a motherfuck that it's 'just food styling,' so don't even try it."

Nova sat, frozen, her eyes glued to Trill's.

"Television. Movies. Print ads. Social media. The food-styling industry is a *huge* business, baby. And from every damn thing I've seen, Caprice and Nova MacLeod are two of the ones at the very top." Nova looked around the room and was disconcerted to see that the Geek Crew was staring at her in something approaching awe.

Trill banded her arms even more tightly around Nova's petite body. "The number of fucking degrees someone has doesn't make one goddamn bit of difference. Some of the *stupidest* motherfuckers I've ever met waved their master's degree around like it was some kind of a fucking red cape and thought it made them hot shit…but they couldn't navigate their way out of a paper bag."

The entire room chimed in with murmurs of agreement.

"*You*, however? The fucking powers-that-be of a movie that will be being filmed locally and will star one of the biggest box office draws in existence today wants *you* to do the food styling for it…because the star is playing a chef and they will do whatever it takes to make her look good and to make that set look convincing. *Including* hiring one of the best food stylists in the business."

You could have heard a pin drop.

"Baby." Trill swiped at the two tears that had fallen onto Nova's cheeks. "My crew has been so goddamn excited to meet you, you wouldn't believe it. Especially since that fucker there," she gestured to Kendall, "hasn't shut the fuck up about how awesome you are. And that was even *before* they knew about your reputation in the food-styling business.

"It's not about degrees or certifications, little diva. It's about *knowledge*, regardless of how that knowledge is acquired. That's what's important, and you have a fuckton of knowledge in your field. It's like Kendall said: There's no reason you'd know anything about what we do, because it's not what *you* do."

Nova nodded then drew a shuddering breath.

"Nova…already, just that whole using eyeliner to paint grill marks on steak has me freaked," Val said. "I cannot wait until we all go out, but I'm going to warn you that you are going to be *hammered* with questions. This is too cool."

Trill chuckled. "Wait 'til you hear the one about the jackass on a movie set who swiped his finger through what he thought was pancake syrup and licked it, and it turned out to be motor oil."

The crew roared with laughter.

Nova gave them all a grateful look as she relaxed back against Trill. "Thank you, guys. So much. Unfortunately, I don't know if I'll have a chance to hang with you all before the movie starts filming, though. I have a meeting with the director this afternoon, and there's always a hell of a lot to do in pre-production. We typically work 12 to 14 hours during filming as well, but we'll get together as soon as possible after the shoot moves to LA, I promise. We'll have all the food scenes shot by then, so I won't have to go."

"Kendall's going with you to your meeting, little diva." Nova frowned at Trill in confusion. "She's not going to get in the way, and she'll wait for you outside until you're done with the director, but I'll feel a hell of a lot more comfortable if I have some idea of how this all works."

Nova blew her bangs out of her eyes. "There really won't be much to see, Trill, at least anything that would be of interest to you at this point. This is pre-production." She looked around the table at everyone as she explained. "The movie's been 'greenlit,' which means it has all its financial backing, but pre-production is what happens before the principal photography piece—the actual filming—takes place.

"There are a bunch of people involved in pre-production, like the director, the producer, the cinematographer—if they've even hired one already—but I'll be meeting solely with director Chad Lancaster today. He's also Isadora Nightingale's husband, incidentally. We'll be discussing where I'll put my rig, and he'll give me a copy of the script so I can start figuring out the food needs for the shoot…including feeding the cast and crew. Beyond that, though, there won't be much you'll care about at this point. I'd hate for Kendall to waste her time."

"What do you mean, your 'rig'?" Melanie was curious.

Nova gave them an impish look. "Mom and I have a 17-foot cabover truck we bring to movie shoots. The inside cargo area is actually a full commercial kitchen. We have a six-burner stove, a refrigerator, microwave, grill, freezer, prep tables, storage, and a TV. Oh, and a portable inverter generator, which is a good twenty decibels quieter than a conventional generator. That's important on a movie set.

"The truck has a lift gate and everything inside is on wheels, so I can take it all out and assemble a kitchen right in the middle of the beach." She laughed at the stunned look on everyone's face. "Anyhow, I need to find out from Mr. Lancaster where on the set they want my rig and get the movie script from him. Even if it's still in rough draft form, which they often are at this point, I can get a preliminary idea of the food needs and start to plan."

"That's it. I'm *definitely* going." Kendall was adamant. She grinned smugly at her team, who flipped her off. "Weep, motherfuckers, because this is going to be *epic*."

Trill was amused. "Baby," she said to Nova, holding her even more securely. "Indulge me. All kidding aside, I think each one of us would feel better if someone has some idea of the initial setup. I'll be going myself when the set is more complete and your rig is actually in place." Then she grinned. "No need to ask if you were involved with picking out Delaney and Teagan's catering truck for their marriage celebration then, is there?"

Nova gave her another impish smirk.

"What time is your meeting, Nov?" Kendall asked. "And where is it exactly?"

"In the production trailer, which is already on site on Madeira Beach. That's where the actual shoot will take place. Chad Lancaster will meet us there at two o'clock. One of his assistants texted me the directions."

"We'd better leave around one o'clock then—considering what traffic on the beaches can be like this time of year, even though that's usually only a twenty-minute drive," Kendall said. "Anything else, chief?" She raised an inquisitive brow at Trill.

"I think we're good for now, as far as little diva goes. I want you all to stick around for a few, though, because I have something to discuss with you regarding the whole Frank Bellwood shit show and cyberattacks." She ran a hand up and down one of Nova's arms.

"Baby, I'm sure Kelly's around somewhere. I can ask her to come and get you, so you two can hang out until Kendall is done." One corner of her mouth lifted as she kissed Nova and then helped her up off her lap. She sent a rapid text then took Nova by the hand.

"I'm grateful," Nova said quietly, looking around the table at the five kind, friendly faces. "You've all made me feel so welcome and so much better about things. No matter what you all say, it's easy to be intimidated by a group like you, but I feel like I've been surrounded by a newfound family instead."

Chapter 8

"This is it." Nova jumped out of Kendall's SUV and started toward a lone trailer near the edge of the beach-access parking lot. There were a handful of other cars parked and a few people milling around, but the site was largely deserted. "This lot and part of the beach will be completely transformed in another few weeks or so," Nova told Kendall. "Pre-production means there's a lot of money going out without any tangible returns, so the director and the executive producer will try to keep this part of the process as succinct as possible." Just then, the door to the trailer opened and a man stepped out.

He was about 5'10", with a husky build, thinning hair, and a sparse mustache. He smiled when he saw Nova and came toward them with an outstretched hand and a practiced smile. "Ms. MacLeod? I'm so pleased to meet you. I'm Chad Lancaster, director." He shook Nova's hand and then turned his attention to Kendall. "And who is this, may I ask?" He smiled again, but Nova noticed his smiles never seemed to reach his eyes.

"This is my neighbor, Kendall," Nova said, feeling an unexpected frisson of unease whisper its way up her spine, although she didn't know why. She continued to improvise rapidly. "Kendall was kind enough to give me a ride today since my car is in the shop unexpectedly, but she'll be waiting out here until we're done. That is, if you don't mind, Mr. Lancaster?"

"Not at all, not at all." Lancaster's tone was jovial although his eyes curiously remained flat. "Kendall, I promise not to keep Ms. MacLeod any longer than necessary. This shouldn't take too long anyway since I understand she's the best in her business." Nova noticed that Chad Lancaster's eyes kept flickering down to the APS logo embroidered on Kendall's polo shirt, and she wondered why it kept drawing his attention.

"Take your time, Mr. Lancaster. I am completely at Nova's disposal this afternoon and I was happy to help her out today. Nov, I'll be waiting in my SUV until you're done." Kendall smiled pleasantly, but Nova caught an almost imperceptible edge to her voice.

Nova followed Chad Lancaster into the trailer. She was surprised to see that it was as neat as a pin, with none of the pre-production chaos she was accustomed to seeing. "My goodness," she said politely, looking around. "I don't ever think I've ever been in a production trailer this organized or well-kept before."

Lancaster rewarded her with a thin smile.

"Others may work well in the midst of disorder, but I find it's quite easy to be far less productive in such circumstances. When my lovely wife and I were first married, she was somewhat of an untidy person, but she soon discovered the merits of living a disciplined lifestyle."

Nova couldn't fathom why Chad Lancaster's words raised the hackles on the back of her neck, but her sense of unease deepened.

"Now, Ms. MacLeod. Why don't you have a seat, and we'll discuss what needs to be done for pre-production as far as you are concerned."

Nova sat gingerly on the edge of a chair and cut to the chase immediately, anxious to have the meeting over with so she could remove herself from Lancaster's strangely stifling presence.

"I have a 17-foot cabover truck with a full commercial kitchen in the cargo area that I use for movie productions and other location shoots. I'll be bringing it on location in the next few days, so I will need some direction from you on where you would like it to be parked, if that differs from the location that was spelled out in our contract.

"Really, the only thing I need from you today is a copy of the script. That way, I can start to determine what the food needs are going to be for the actual filming itself. Once you have a full cast and crew list, I'll need to know who those individuals are, along with their contact information, so I can find out what their dietary needs and preferences are."

"The script is not yet fully complete, Ms. MacLeod." Chad Lancaster took a seat across from Nova. She noted that he arranged himself precisely in his chair then straightened the edge of a paper that was almost imperceptibly misaligned on the stack in front of him.

"I understand that, Mr. Lancaster," Nova continued in an easy tone, even though she was suddenly feeling anything but. "Scripts seldom are at this stage of the process. However, there will be enough there for me to start outlining what I'll need to purchase. Once the script has been finalized and the film production shooting schedule has been established, I can then work with my vendors to bring in what will actually be needed."

"I see." Lancaster appeared to be thinking. He steepled his fingers. "To be frank, Ms. MacLeod, I'm not sure I'm comfortable releasing the script to anyone at this point."

Fucking seriously?

Nova felt a prickle of dislike, wondering if Chad Lancaster was attempting to set up an intentional roadblock in the process for her, but unsure why he would do such a thing. What she *did* know, however, was that she wasn't about to let this fool make her job harder than it needed to be, no matter what his motivations were. Her eyes chilled.

"To be equally frank, Mr. Lancaster, the terms of my contract state I could expect to receive an advance copy of the script at our initial meeting." Nova's voice was crisp. "I don't know how the other food stylists you've worked with in the past operate, but that is a necessity for me to be able to do my job properly. If that will be an issue for you, however, then I suggest we void our agreement so you can find another food-styling resource whose philosophy is more in keeping with your own." She couldn't help the faint acerbity that colored her voice.

Chad Lancaster looked at her with thinly veiled dislike. "I'll be honest with you, Ms. MacLeod. The only reason you were even offered this food-styling contract is because my wife absolutely insisted on it. Plainly speaking, you would not have been *my* choice. I have a food stylist of my own with whom I usually work, and his performance has always been quite satisfactory."

HIS performance? Suspicion took root along with Nova's unease. While there was certainly nothing preventing a male food stylist from signing a client contract—and there were, in fact, several very good ones in the business—this, coupled with Lancaster's insufferable attitude, made for a highly unusual and questionable situation. Was the director some kind of misogynistic bastard who hated women and refused to work with them unless absolutely necessary?

Lancaster continued, arrogance underlining every word. "I am the director, and my word is final on *every* decision that is made on my films…but Isadora actually went so far as to say she would not star in this film if you were not the food stylist who was chosen for it." *Was that actually RAGE she heard behind his words?*

Nova thought she was starting to understand the issue. Chad Lancaster was a controlling asshole who always expected everyone around him to automatically comply with his edicts. He was livid because his wife hadn't automatically fallen into line as far as his staffing choices went. He'd also clearly taken an instant dislike to Nova when, in his mind, she wasn't properly deferential and obsequious to him. Now he was determined to make them both pay as their punishment.

Oh. *Fuck*. No.

No matter what his issue was, Nova was done playing around with this presumptuous prick. By all appearances, Isadora Nightingale was determined to have Nova work on this film—and Nova would not disappoint her—but Mr. Chad Lancaster was going to understand right fucking now that Nova's world didn't revolve around him and his imperious ass. With an arctic smile, she rose to her feet and moved to the trailer door.

"If I haven't received the script and directions to the location for my rig by the end of today, I'll assume that your intentions are to void our contract and bring in your own resources. My contact info is listed in the contract. Please be advised there will be a fifty percent cancellation fee should you choose to take that route."

Nova paused, her hand on the door handle. "I don't know what your issues are with me, Mr. Lancaster…because, to my knowledge, we've never met before today. But you were right when you stated I was the best in my business.

"You should understand, therefore, that I will compromise neither my professional reputation nor my personal high standards for *anyone*. Should you choose to continue on with me and my team, I'm sure you will agree that it would probably be more comfortable for both of us if you would designate a contact person from your side to manage all production communications going forward. Good day to you, sir." Nova exited the trailer without a backward glance.

Kendall's brows lowered when Nova climbed into her SUV, spots of color burning on her pale cheeks and hellfire simmering in her eyes. "That motherfucking prick," she spat vehemently, yanking on her seatbelt. "Who in the *fuck* does he think he is?"

"Do I need to go out there and beat the shit out of him, Nov?" Kendall asked as she stared through the windshield at Lancaster, who had also come out of the trailer and was looking after them—obviously in a temper with his arms crossed belligerently on his chest.

"Just get me the fuck out of here, Kendall, before I beat his motherfucking ass bloody myself." As they were driving back to APS, Nova told Kendall about everything that had transpired in her meeting. "I don't know what his goddamn problem is, Kendall, but he needs to back off before he buys himself a shit ton of trouble. Trust me, I've dealt with Hollywood types long enough to know that some of them can be real assholes. But, *Jesus*...Chad Lancaster takes the cake."

Kendall touched the comm in her ear. "Chief, little diva and I are on our way back. ETA, about fifteen minutes. She's here with me and she's safe, but some weird fucking shit went down during her meeting with Chad Lancaster that we need to tell you about."

When they reached Trill's office, Trill immediately pulled Nova into her arms and took possession of her mouth. Nova collapsed against Trill and kissed her back fiercely, letting the heat of Trill's mouth absorb the rest of her anger. After Trill raised her head, she brushed Nova's bangs out of her eyes with one hand while running the other soothingly down Nova's back. "Talk to me, little diva," she murmured soothingly.

After Nova had explained the story a second time to Trill, the APS team lead looked at Kendall, who was lounging against the door jamb. "Are you thinking what I'm thinking, cuz?"

"I'm fucking thinking," Kendall was grim.

"Thinking what?" Nova looked back and forth between the two, not understanding.

Trill sat down in one of her office chairs with Nova in her arms then gestured to Kendall at the other chair. When they were all settled, Trill said, "Baby, I know you are very familiar with what we do here at APS. Especially with what you yourself have done over the past eight years. What you're probably *not* extremely familiar with, however, is how to actually recognize a potential abuser when there's no visible evidence…just hunches and gut feelings."

Nova's skin started to crawl.

"You get panic calls from desperate women who are in fear for their lives and are already at the very end of their rope. That's what triggers a rescue for you. You've never had to play detective and dig out a story, solely based on your gut instinct and your observations, until your hunch turns into tangible facts."

Trill brushed Nova's bangs out of her eyes again. "You come in at the tail end, little diva, when things are already on fire. But you need to understand that, based on what you and Kendall have told me about what happened in your meeting today, Chad Lancaster has the core characteristics of a domestic violence abuser."

ௐ҈ௐ҈ௐ

Nova sat beside Trill in conference room 2 of the APS headquarters complex, surrounded by the Armstrong twins and the rest of the Seven. Before they'd left Trill's office, Trill had brought Kendall up to speed on the new honeypot Val and Darcy were working on. Kendall left immediately for the Bullpen—the large, shared office used by APS associates who were not members of the management team—and told Nova she would most likely see her in the morning.

"What's a honeypot?" Nova had asked curiously while she was walking with Trill to the conference room.

"It's a decoy system, designed to look like a real system that's been compromised and is vulnerable to cyber attackers," Trill explained. "Theoretically, a 'honeypot' will lure bad guys in so we can log their network capture then squash them. In this particular case, we'll do our own threat attack to see if there are any system vulnerabilities remaining. Val is a damn beast when it comes to shit like that."

She stopped in front of a door that was just down the hall from the Recon Room and pressed a series of numbers into the keypad that was set into the door frame. The indicator light turned green and Trill opened the door, ushering Nova into the conference room.

"That fucker there," she pointed at Jaime Quintero, who was already in the room, "and her physical security team breached our headquarters recently because of a small weakness Kelly Armstrong found in our infrastructure." Jaime grinned as Trill flipped her off. "Val and Darcy are developing the honeypot so we can use it to run a final test on the system corrections we've made. Since Kendall was with you this afternoon, I needed to bring her up to speed."

"*Mi hermana.*" Jaime stood up and went over to Nova then hugged her and kissed her on the cheek. "Before you beat my ass, that means 'my sister' in Spanish. I'm rapidly finding out that non-Spanish speaking femmes get a bit miffed when they don't understand what a Spanish-speaking butch is saying."

"Well...*yeah*, Captain Obvious," Nova snarked with a lifted brow and a smirk. Jaime grinned again and went back to her seat. The door opened and more of the APS management team filed in. Nova had known the Armstrong twins and the Seven since she'd moved to Whimsy when she was in the fifth grade. She hugged and kissed everyone, happy to see them, then settled back in her chair next to Trill when the full management team was assembled.

"It's good to see you, little sis." Then Bryn drilled her with her eyes. "I know you and Trill have straightened everything out, but you have to know we weren't real happy when we found out what's been going on with you. No more giving us heart attacks, Nov, okay? You've been ours—especially Trill's—since grade school, and we'll lose our shit if anyone ever hurts you."

Nova nodded, looking around the conference room table with soft eyes.

After everyone was seated and had settled, Trill started. "The reason I wanted us to get together is because I think Nova may have a potential abuser situation on her hands with this movie production she's working on."

The team's eyebrows lowered.

"You're all aware that Nova usually comes in *after* an abusive situation has caught fire and she needs to move rapidly. Therefore, she isn't as well-versed in identifying the warning signs of a probable abuser when there isn't as much of an immediacy to the circumstances. In her world, things have always progressed far beyond that point already."

"Right," Casey agreed. "Nov, I hope you realize no one here expected you to understand that piece of it either. What's going on?"

"I had a meeting this afternoon with the director of the new film I'll be working on. The one starring Isadora Nightingale?" Aggravation started to glimmer in Nova's honey-brown eyes. "This director, Chad Lancaster, is also married to Isadora. And he is a fucking *tool*. By the time I got back to Kendall's SUV, I was ready to beat the shit out of that arrogant son of a bitch. I'd never met him before today and I sure as fuck wasn't missing anything." Nova snorted in disgust.

"The thing is, though…When I got back to APS headquarters and told Trill and Kendall what had happened in my meeting, Trill said that Chad Lancaster has the hallmarks of a domestic violence abuser."

Thunderclouds hit the faces of the team around the table.

"Trill wanted us to sit down with you and have me tell you exactly what happened so you can discuss it. It's like you've already said…I'm not necessarily going to see these kinds of warning signs because I've never had to deal with them before. The only thing I do know is that Lancaster is probably one of the biggest fucking dicks I've ever met in my life. And I've met some Hollywood jackasses in my time, trust me."

"Why don't you get started then and just talk," Riley said. "We'll stop you, interrupt you where we need to, ask for some points of clarification as we go along, things like that. Don't worry about being perfect, little sis. The details will come the more you talk about it."

Nova nodded. "All right then. When I first got there, Lancaster initially was perfectly pleasant. Shook my hand, said it was great to meet me, blah blah blah. The usual mannerly shit. Then he noticed Kendall and his eyes kind of went flat. It was a bit eerie, the way his mood shifted on a dime. I improvised really fast, telling him that Kendall was my neighbor who'd given me a ride because my car went into the shop unexpectedly, and I hoped he didn't mind."

"That was smart thinking," remarked Drew.

"I noticed his eyes kept flickering down to the APS logo on Kendall's polo and he seemed a bit…I don't know…strange, I guess you'd say. He gave every indication he recognized the logo, but I thought that was weird. I mean, APS is famous in west-central Florida and fucking *everybody* knows who you are here…but why would a movie director from *California* recognize you?"

"He wouldn't," said Blake. She tapped her pen thoughtfully on the table. "There'd be no reason in the world he should have the first fucking clue who we are. Nor care."

Nova continued. "When I went into the trailer, I was kind of freaked out because it was so damn neat. Almost military neat, like Trill and Teagan's apartments are. All of yours are like that, I would imagine, even though I haven't seen most of them. If you've ever been in a production trailer, however, you know the last thing they are is neat. There are scripts laying around, schedules, casting information, just a ton of shit. Even if the director and the producer aren't slobs, there's no way in hell a production trailer ever has that level of orderliness.

"Even freakier, when Lancaster sat down at the table, the top paper on one of the stacks was very slightly misaligned, and he made a big deal about straightening it out until it was perfectly in alignment."

"Did you mention it to him at all?" Kennedy asked.

"I did. I told him I had never before seen a production trailer that was as orderly as that one was. And he made this really prissy comment…he said that he found it much easier and more productive to be orderly." Nova hesitated for a moment. "Then he said that Isadora had been untidy when they'd first met, but she'd discovered what he called the 'merits of a disciplined lifestyle' with him."

"Fuck." Teagan scrubbed her face with her hand. "I am not liking where this is going at all, just so you know."

"He made me uneasy, and I literally felt the hackles on the back of my neck stand up after he'd said that," Nova told them. "I didn't know why though."

"This is where shit started going south. He asked me about my pre-production needs. I told him I needed to confirm where to park my rig and that I needed a copy of the script. That's written into my contract, because I need to get started on figuring out the food needs for the shoot as soon as possible. That's something that's pretty standard when it comes to food styling on a movie production anyway. Productions like this one take a *ton* of food supplies and the sooner you can begin your planning, the better."

Nova's brows lowered. "But Lancaster told me the script wasn't finalized and he didn't feel he could release it yet. And I'm thinking, *what the fuck*? That was *highly* irregular, because this is how all food stylists on a movie set work. Scripts are very rarely past the rough draft stage by the beginning of pre-production. We expect that, it's never a surprise to us, but there's still more than enough completed on the script to get us started, so it's not a problem.

"When Lancaster told me that, I was extremely irritated…and I decided I was *done* with that motherfucker and whatever game he was playing with me. It's a great contract, but I don't have the time for penny ante power play bullshit from some jackass. I was getting all sorts of bad vibes from him anyway, so…I told him he could either pony up a copy of the script as it was by the end of the day, or he could void the contract and I would charge him a fifty percent cancellation fee."

"Far fucking *out*, little sis." Jaime and Blake high-fived each other, their expressions gleeful.

"Yeah, well…then the condescending bastard informed me that I hadn't been *his* choice for this movie, that he had a food stylist under contract with whom he usually worked, and he'd always found his work to be 'quite satisfactory,' as he called it. Which kind of flipped me out right then and there. I mean, not that male food stylists aren't in the business, because they definitely are, but you need to understand this is a *vastly* female-dominated space.

"For a male food stylist to be under permanent contract to a bigwig Hollywood director like Chad Lancaster? It doesn't fucking compute. I started suspecting I was dealing with some misogynistic bullshit right there. Lancaster then tells me the only reason I had been signed is because Isadora Nightingale had flat-out said she wouldn't do the movie unless I was the food stylist that was brought on board. And he was *pissed*…I mean, you could tell without a doubt he was in a fucking rage about it."

"Not something that would typically send a Hollywood director into a rage, I take it?" Riley mused. Nova shook her head.

"Not at all. However, in a nutshell…I told Lancaster that either he sent me a copy of the current script and a location where I could park my rig by the end of the day, or I would take it to mean he was going to void the contract and he could expect to pay the cancellation fee. Then I walked out. When I got back to Kendall's

SUV, I made it clear to her that we needed to get out of there and get back here before I beat the shit out of that pissant. I was *so* fucking mad.

"The asshole was standing there glowering at us when we pulled off. I told Kendall what had happened, and she did that comm thing you all do to give Trill a heads-up and let her know we were on our way back."

Trill rubbed her arm reassuringly.

"When we got back here to APS headquarters, Kendall and I told Trill what had happened. When I was done, she said Chad Lancaster has all the hallmarks of an abuser, and we needed to talk to the APS management team as soon as we could. So, here we are."

"Jesus, little sis." Kennedy's face was tight. "I am so fucking sorry you had to deal with that moron. You did awesome, though."

Bryn's voice was arctic as she looked at the diminutive brunette. "I am having one hell of a wild thought right now, Nov. Is there *anyone* at all you can think of who would have known about your secret rescue efforts? No matter how stupid or inconsequential it might seem to you?"

"No way, Bryn. It's a very closely guarded secret, and I have never breathed a word about it to anyone." Nova paused for a moment, thinking, then decisively shook her head. "Only my sister knew, and Gill wasn't about to say jack shit to anyone. And of course, the women I rescued would have known about it…but that's *it.* Not even my parents know, and I never keep *anything* from them."

"Well, some way, somehow…I have a big fucking suspicion that the information about you and what you do has reached Isadora Nightingale's ears."

Nova's eyes widened as she looked at Bryn, uncomprehending.

"That's exactly my suspicion, too." Trill squeezed Nova's hand and Nova turned to face her, clearly taken aback. "Baby, from everything you've told us, I think Isadora is being abused by that jackass husband of hers. I also think she's found out about you and the battered women rescue you do—somehow, some way, as Bryn said."

"When she found out she was being offered the lead in this movie," Drew was grim, "and that it was being filmed on location in west-central Florida—where Nova McLeod lives—she decided she was going to do whatever she fucking had to do to make sure Nova was the food stylist who was contracted for it."

Blake was still tapping her pen. "That has to be why Lancaster was so fucking pissed off when Isadora said she wouldn't do the movie unless Nova was the food stylist. I mean, the dude is a fucking tool anyway, but for her to defy him like that and refuse to work with his pet food stylist? I'm betting that's not something that's ever happened before and he lost his shit."

"I also bet that's why he was such a fucking prick to Nova." Trill's light brown eyes darkened. "He was probably wondering who this bitch was who could make his usually obedient wife step out of line like that."

"Little does he know who she is," Casey muttered as she and Kenn exchanged looks.

"In Lancaster's mind, Isadora's misbehavior was already Nova's fault, even before they met," Trill continued. "He likely pulled that bullshit with the script just to see how Nova would react. When Nov *didn't* fall into line and bow to his male superiority—as he expects every female he comes in contact with to do—he turned nasty and it was on."

Casey crossed her heavily muscled arms and leaned back in her chair. "I'm thinking Isadora likely argued with Lancaster about using his pet food stylist and said it didn't make any sense to not take advantage of Nova's close proximity to the location. She could have told him she wanted another Oscar or Golden Globe award, and that hiring Nova was the way to do it because of Nova's reputation in the field of food styling."

"But…what Isadora is *really* seeing by working with Nova is the opportunity to get the fuck away from him once and for all," Riley speculated. "What do you want to bet Ms. Nightingale's *never* alone? That Lancaster has her locked down so tight, she's never had the opportunity to seek help anywhere before? No one would find it suspicious that he'd keep a close eye on her under the guise of 'protection,' because she's such a big star."

Riley and Bryn looked at each other.

Bryn finished her twin's thought. "But now, Isadora is starring in a movie where the food styling is critically important and Nova is the food stylist. The one woman outside of APS who can get her out, and who will be in the perfect position to do it."

"You guys are forgetting one small detail," Nova finally said in a calm voice, although it was clear she was anything but. "This is *not* what I do." She leaned forward seriously. "*At all.* I don't know how to do this. I help women who have come to me because they don't have anywhere else to turn. They're scared, they're alone, and they're convinced beyond a shadow of a doubt that they are about to lose their lives.

"We're at critical mass by the time I hear from them. And forget about the fact that this is all pure speculation at this point. We don't know that she's planning on approaching me, or if our hunch is even correct. But let's pretend for a minute this is all proven and this is what she's planning." Nova fidgeted.

"Isadora Nightingale is one of the *biggest* damn box office stars in existence today. Parties, galas, film premieres, award ceremonies—*three* Academy Awards, I think, plus the same number of Golden Globes. She goes *everywhere* and knows *everybody*. Why in the hell would she put her life into the hands of a small-town food stylist—okay, so I have a reputation there, but whatever—and believe I'll be able to get her out from right under her husband's nose?"

Trill slid an arm around Nova's shoulders. "Because you're you, little diva. Because you're smart and you're cunning and you're tenacious as hell, but you fly under the radar. And I'm betting she is quite aware of that. Lancaster doesn't like you simply because he thinks you're a mouthy woman who won't bow to his male superiority, fucking misogynistic prick that he is. But he doesn't know who or what you *really* are."

Bryn spoke up. "Trill's right, Nov. If I was Isadora, I'd be thinking that's *exactly* why I'd want you, in addition to your reputation. She'll have every reason to talk to you frequently on set without rousing any suspicion if you're the film's food stylist and she's playing a chef. That will piss Lancaster off, I bet, *but*…he's the film's director. I don't know shit about the film industry, but I assume he will have a fuckton to do during filming, so he can't have his nose up your asses 24/7."

"True," Nova said slowly. Then the corner of her mouth quirked. "He also knows he pissed me the fuck off with his high-handed attitude and I won't give a shit if he doesn't want me to talk to her. I'll do it just to spite him."

"Change of subject for a minute." Teagan was staring off into space, thinking. "What kind of crew do you usually have for something like this, little diva? Besides yourself?"

"For something like this? There will be me, an assistant food stylist, a prop stylist, a shopper, a dishwasher, and a combination driver/roadie." Nova smiled at their astonishment. "People assume that roadies are only used for music productions, but that's not necessarily true. There's often a ton of equipment that needs to be moved around for a food production. I have my rig, so my needs are a lot less because of how Mom and I designed it, but there's still a decent amount to do."

"Good. Peyton's hired, then." Trill nodded at Teagan, understanding what she had been getting at, then caressed Nova's arm. "We can't use Kendall because Lancaster already knows she's APS—which is going to piss Kendall off, unfortunately—but Pey is an unknown and won't raise any suspicion. Put her on your staff, I don't care where, and that way we're all happy that you have protection while you're dealing with that asshole. Maybe she can be your driver and your roadie for the job, unless you already have someone you regularly use."

Nova gave Trill a wicked smile. "Well, gee. I was thinking dishwasher," she snarked with a raised brow. Everyone burst out laughing and Blake chuckled. "I would pay serious money to be there to see her face if you told her that, little sis."

"Speaking of which, she *will* get paid for this," Nova said. "Salaries are built into my budget, which is written into the contract." Her mouth curled up into another wicked grin. "We'll let that motherfucker Lancaster pay for the privilege of Peyton guarding my ass." There was another round of laughter.

"The assistant food stylist and the prop stylist I like to use, Esmeralda Graves and Kathy Amadon, have worked with me and my mother for about a million years. They are both beyond amazing and a lot of fun. Susie Carfagna has only shopped for me for about five years, but she is incredibly competent.

"It's summer, so I'll contact one of the local high schools and ask if they can recommend an incoming senior drama student who might be interested in being the dishwasher. It's hard work, and there are a fucking ton of dishes that need to be done constantly, but most high school girls are so thrilled to be on a movie set and near the cast, they don't mind the work.

"Peyton can be my roadie because I don't have anyone I regularly use. Roadies aren't often in town because they're on tour with a band, so I kind of hire whoever happens to be around at the time wherever I am. In this day and age of kickass GPS, Kathy, Susie, and Esmeralda have always preferred to take themselves wherever they need to go, so we very seldom ever use a driver."

Trill was pleased. "That's perfect, then. I guess our next step is to see if that jackass motherfucker actually sends you the script tonight, although I'm betting he will. You can get your crew together, little diva, and we'll let Peyton know that starting tomorrow, she's full-time assigned to you." Trill looked around at the rest of the APS management team. "I guess that's it for now, fam, and we'll keep you posted. Nothing's going to happen until Isadora is on set anyway and that's at least two weeks away."

"Don't forget we got you, little diva." As everyone got up and prepared to leave, Drew came over and held Nova gently by the shoulders. "Whatever you need, you tell Trill or you grab one of us if she's not around. None of us are about to play around with this jackhole."

"No, we're not." Trill took Nova's hand after Drew had released her. "We're going to figure this out, baby. If Isadora Nightingale *is* being abused, we're going to be at your back while you make sure that fucking prick *never* puts his hands on her again."

Chapter 9

Nova curled up in Trill's lap and rested her head on Trill's shoulder as the two of them sat together in a big, comfortable armchair in Trill's living room. It was late by the time their meeting with the APS management team had broken up, so Trill had ordered dinner from the Pier House Grill and arranged to have it delivered to her apartment.

While they were waiting for their food, Nova and then Trill had showered, and Trill promised she would clean out a couple of dresser drawers the next day so Nova could put some clothes away. Nova had smirked when Trill had handed her a large envelope with a "Blue Moon Studios" logo on it that had been hand-delivered to Caprice MacLeod.

When Nova told Trill that her mom had texted her about the delivery, Trill had immediately arranged for a courier to pick it up. "That pussy," Nova had snarked, rolling her eyes at Trill, who'd grinned.

When they were done eating—a medium-rare ribeye for Trill and crabmeat-stuffed shrimp for Nova—they cleaned up then collapsed in the big chair together. Trill kissed Nova's temple as she gently ran her hands over Nova's small body. "Alone at last, little diva," she whispered, a dark, seductive note running through her voice. Nova shivered at the sound then moaned as Trill took her mouth and kissed her deeply.

Trill moved one hand behind Nova's head to hold her still, while her other arm wrapped around Nova's waist, her hand coming to rest on Nova's hip. Nova had never felt so intimately held, and she shuddered with her desire as Trill's very dominant nature flared to life.

"Little diva," Trill growled softly when she had released Nova's mouth, the tiny brunette already flushed and trembling from Trill's kiss. Trill cupped Nova's cheek then lightly traced Nova's mouth with her tongue, flicking at the seam of her mouth, until Nova felt a gush of liquid pour out of her to soak her panties.

"I want you, baby. And I have every intention of having you tonight." Trill nibbled on the side of Nova's neck while sliding her hand down to clasp her nape. "I know you want me too. We've wanted each other for a long time, Nova MacLeod, and I've already told you that you belong to me. Consider yourself captured and claimed, my little diva. *Permanently*. Because I have no intention of ever letting you go."

Nova shuddered again as Trill stood up effortlessly with Nova in her arms. She strode into her master bedroom then gently lowered Nova onto the pale gray comforter, climbing onto the bed and straddling Nova's delicate body. She leaned down and ran her mouth down Nova's jaw. "You should know I'm a Dominant by nature, baby. However, I don't practice formal dominance and submission. I don't have rules and safe words, nor do I expect to be addressed as Master. Nothing like that.

"But when you're in my bed, I expect you to defer to me in all ways." She slid two strong hands under Nova's T-shirt and cupped her braless breasts. "There are times when I'll be gentle, and there are times when I'll be rougher with you, depending on what your needs are at the time. And I'm very, *very* good at reading a woman's body, baby." She ran her mouth down Nova's throat with a wicked smile. "You can also be sure I *always* know exactly what a woman's screams mean."

Nova felt a huge flood of moisture slide out of her at Trill's words.

"If something is too much for you, you simply say 'stop' and I stop. I may try to push you a little further at times, like when I have my mouth on that delicious pussy and I'm eating you until you're screaming for mercy." That brief, wicked smile crossed Trill's face again. Nova moaned, unable to help herself.

Trill flicked her fingers over Nova's nipples then lightly pinched the sensitive buds. "I don't ever want you to be afraid when you are with me, little diva. As with a traditional Dominant, your safety and your happiness are the most important things in the world to me."

"Trill," Nova whispered, overwhelmed with being in Trill's bed after longing for the handsome butch for so long. "The night of Delaney's rescue, I knew you were coming after me. And all I wanted was to spend one night in your bed with you, to be taken and claimed like I've seen you do with so many other women through the years. But I thought I couldn't let myself have even that one night with you because of the women I was helping. They had to be my priority, because they don't have anyone else. But, oh…how I've wanted you all these years." She drew in a long, tremulous breath.

Trill wrapped one strong arm around Nova's back and raised her up so she could hook her fingers at the bottom of Nova's T-shirt to pull it over her head. "When I saw you that night at The Phantom Kitchen after Delaney was safe, I knew you'd given me the perfect excuse to finally claim you. You were mine, but you'd been hiding things from me. You put yourself into danger for these battered women for more years than I care to remember, so you were fucking going to learn what a punishment spanking was first…if I had anything to say about it."

Trill leaned down and licked the stiff peak of one pale, beautiful breast. Nova's breath caught and she whimpered from the hot, wet heat of Trill's mouth.

"After I spanked you and I was sure you understood that you would *never* put yourself into danger like that again, I wanted you to know that *You. Were. Mine.* You were going to be mine forever and it would be over my dead body that anything would ever hurt you." She brought her face back up to Nova's and licked the slow tears that had started trickling down.

"And, then," Trill looked directly into Nova's tear-filled eyes, "I was going to fuck you until I branded you everywhere. That's where we are now, my little diva. I want to make you scream as your body explodes for me. I want everything you can give to me, until you don't have a drop of energy left. I'm going to wring you dry, Nova MacLeod."

A firm hand slid down Nova's body until Trill had hooked her fingers in the waistband of Nova's shorts and eased them down her shapely legs. She smiled as she leaned down and drew the scent of Nova's arousal into her lungs then slid Nova's drenched panties down her legs as well. Trill looked at the beautiful, naked femme she was straddling, and Nova quivered at the look of dark desire in her eyes.

"My little pocket-sized Venus," Trill said softly, running her hands over Nova's pale skin. "So tiny. So perfect. So made for love and passion and possession." Then she smiled slightly, a smile filled with hunger and wicked intent. "*My* love and passion and possession, little diva. Mine alone…because I will *end* anything that ever tries to take you away from me."

Nova was shaking from the primitive, possessive tone of Trill's voice.

Trill trailed her fingers down over Nova's belly to gently touch the dark curls between her legs. "So, so pretty," the handsome butch whispered, rubbing her fingers between Nova's legs with a featherlight touch. Nova whimpered, feeling yet another gush of her arousal escape her body to soak the bed beneath them. "I can't wait until you flood like that in my mouth," Trill purred. A low, satisfied laugh filled the room as Nova's body drenched Trill's hand at the words.

"Open your legs for me, little diva," Trill's dark voice commanded quietly. Nova flushed as she did as she was told, coloring from being so exposed.

"Mmmmm. Look at this pretty pink pussy. So wet for me." Trill gently parted Nova's pussy lips until her hot, wet channel was open to Trill's gaze. With another slight smile, Trill bent down and lightly licked Nova's clit. Nova shrieked from the jolt of electricity that hit her between her legs. Trill continued to lick her with barely-there strokes of her tongue until Nova was crying out. She tried to close her legs to get away from Trill's insidious tongue, and Trill gave her pussy a sharp, corrective slap. "Nuh uh, little diva," she reprimanded Nova.

"Do that again and you'll find yourself restrained on the bed with your legs tied open and a vibrator buried in your pussy at a very slow speed. I'll leave you there for hours until you've learned your lesson about pulling away from me."

Unbidden, Nova's pussy gushed even more at the threat.

"Ooh, you *like* that," Trill murmured with a low, sinful laugh. "Well, well. My baby is just full of surprises now, isn't she?" Nova mewled, half in protest, half with a blade-sharp craving she couldn't resist. Trill explored the peaks and valleys of Nova's pussy with her fingers, avoiding her clit until Nova thought she would lose her mind.

"T-…T-…Trill," she stammered then gasped as Trill teased the entrance to her body. "I…I…oh, *please*," she cried, digging her fingers into Trill's hard thighs. Trill bent and licked the side of

Nova's neck while she stopped teasing Nova's pussy and slid her hands back up Nova's quaking body until she cupped her soft breasts again. Trill massaged them firmly then blew her hot breath over the stiff peaks.

Nova choked when Trill circled first one rigid nipple and then the other with her tongue. "Why are you teasing me like this?" she whispered, her voice faint. She clutched Trill's dark blonde fade with her hands, burying her fingers in its softness as Trill devoured her breasts with her mouth. She felt lightning hit her core, which seemed to catch fire with the wicked ministrations of Trill's tongue.

"So, so sweet," Trill murmured as she skimmed her tongue down to Nova's belly button for a moment. Then she sat up and pulled her T-shirt over her head before raising her body to slide out of her shorts.

Nova's breath caught when Trill was naked, thinking she had never in her life seen anyone as perfectly flawless and hard-muscled as Trillian Dacanay. Her job as the head of the APS Geek Crew clearly had no impact on her fitness. Although Trill was the smallest of the APS management team, she was still fit and sinewed, with broad shoulders, a flat six-pack belly, and lean, muscular legs.

"Like what you see, little diva?" Trill asked an awestruck Nova with a small tilt to her lips.

Nova gulped and nodded. "I've never seen anyone who looks as perfect as you do, Trill," she breathed almost inaudibly. "I've dreamed about you for such a long time, and…my dreams haven't come anywhere *near* to the reality of what you really are."

"My tiny beauty." Trill captured Nova's mouth once more. "You are just as perfect to me. And now, I am done playing because I need to have you and make you mine, once and for all."

Nova melted into Trill's hard body before her legs fell open as Trill moved down Nova's petite frame one more time. Nibbling her way back down, Trill sank down even further, until her mouth licked and nibbled Nova's shaking thighs. Finally, her hot breath hovered over Nova's core. "Mine at last," Trill whispered fiercely. "Mine *forever*." She lowered her mouth and ran her tongue all over Nova's sopping wet center before starting to devour her.

With a shriek, Nova felt her pussy spasm and her hips jerked in a reaction she couldn't control as Trill's mouth and tongue consumed her. Suddenly, Trill's strong hands banded her wrists and held Nova's hands immobile to her sides so she couldn't move as Trill continued to feast on Nova's helpless body.

"Oh. Oh, *Trill*," Nova wailed as she struggled against the handsome butch's relentless touch. "I c-c-can't…I d-don't…" She screamed as she felt her whole body seize, hovering just on the edge of orgasm. Trill sucked her pussy even harder and faster, and Nova struggled even harder against the restraints of Trill's strong grip. Trill's broad shoulders kept her legs separated so she couldn't close them, and Nova screamed for mercy as her whole body coiled toward an explosive orgasm.

When it hit, it was as if a tsunami flooded Nova's body at the same time as it detonated in the most explosive release Nova had ever had in her life. Nova shrieked and fractured into a million pieces as Trill continued to draw out her orgasm, until Nova screamed one last time and everything went dark.

When she groggily came to, Nova found herself curled up in Trill's arms, held gently against that powerful body. The sheets were clean, Nova had been bathed, and her long brown waves had been pulled back loosely into a hair tie. Tears pricked as Nova realized how carefully Trill had taken care of her while she was out.

Trill nuzzled her jaw. "There's my baby. How do you feel, my little diva?" Without waiting for an answer, she helped Nova to sit up and then held a bottle of water to her lips. Nova drank deeply then sighed as Trill laid her back down and wrapped herself around Nova once more.

"Trill?" Nova's voice was quiet as she caressed Trill's hard abs. "What about you? I want to touch you, to make you feel just as wonderful as you've made me feel. I'm not a pillow princess, not by any stretch of the imagination.

"I know there are some butches and femmes who are into that, and that's totally fine for them if it makes them happy. But I don't think I could handle never being allowed to touch you."

Trill kissed her forehead. "Oh, you'll get to touch me, little diva. No worries there. Although I have to be honest with you and tell you that someone going down on me has never done much for me." Nova felt rather than saw the slight smile that touched Trill's mouth. "I'd rather eat than be eaten, baby. But you can touch, stroke, play and please to your heart's content, I promise. Just not tonight."

When Nova's eyes narrowed at her, the corner of Trill's mouth quirked. "Baby, you've had one hell of a day. Truthfully, I probably shouldn't have touched you myself, except I was too impatient and couldn't wait to have you any longer. I wasn't going to be able to sleep until I knew I had made you mine. Now you're in my bed, all soft and warm and drowsy and satisfied, and I'll be able to sleep like a baby with you in my arms."

"Okay." Nova's brows smoothed out and she squelched a yawn, determined to stay awake for a moment. "I don't…I don't want to freak you out by saying this, Trill. I don't ever want you to feel like you have to give me anything you're not ready to give." She ran her fingers down Trill's cheek. "But I think you should know just how much I care about you and how long I've crushed on you, Trillian Dacanay. My heart would go ape shit when I saw you in the halls at school." She grinned when Trill chuckled.

"I'm not saying that because I'm expecting some sort of undying declaration of devotion or anything like that from you, Trill. But I do care about you, a whole hell of a lot, and…and I thought you should know that."

"Nova MacLeod." Trill's voice was soft as she brushed Nova's bangs out of her eyes. "I have been in love with you since high school. Hell, even before that. Probably since fifth grade when you moved to Whimsy."

Nova gasped and her eyes grew huge.

"When we were in elementary and middle school, I made every excuse I could think of to sit near you. Whimsy Elementary and

Whimsy Middle are small schools, so it wasn't hard." Nova heard the amusement in Trill's voice. "When we got to high school, we were on two totally different career paths—even though we were in the same grade—so I didn't have any classes with you anymore. I still managed to finagle the same lunch period as you, though."

"Trill." Nova's voice was astonished.

"When all of us enlisted in the Marines after we graduated from high school, I knew we would be doing four years of activity duty. After that, we would still have to serve four years of inactive duty…but it's rare you ever get called back in peacetime, so we all headed to Gainesville and the University of Florida to start college when our tour was up.

"We had dreams and plans, baby." Trill caressed Nova's face. "APS was already a reality for us in our minds—had been since high school—and our goal was to get done with college as fast as possible so we could get started. I was taking such an intensive course load trying to get through college and graduate school in half the time, I never came home to visit. Mom and Dad and Zaph always came to visit me." Just like Trill, Zaphod Dacanay had been named by Trill's quirky Hitchhiker's Guide to the Galaxy-obsessed mother.

Then Trill laughed. "Mom was always under strict orders to bring me the latest news about you when she came up to Gainesville." Nova's eyes grew even bigger. "And I think you might want to have some words with your own mother, little diva…because I'm pretty sure Alice Dacanay and Caprice MacLeod were in some serious cahoots with each other back then."

Nova giggled, unable to help herself.

"I've been in love with you for a very long time, Nova. My heart tells me you've been in love with me for just as long."

Nova nodded, tears beginning to slip down her face.

"I'm sorry," she gulped. "I know you don't like it when I say unflattering things about myself. I also know you've always been my friend, Trill, and you've liked me a lot. All of you have since I moved here from Jacksonville at the beginning of fifth grade.

"But I never dreamed that someone like you would be interested in someone like me…because for years, I just didn't feel like I was up to your level. Why would be the smartest butch in seven counties be interested that way in a femme who never went to college at all?"

She held up a finger as Trill started to speak with a stern warning look. The handsome butch subsided when she saw that Nova had more to say.

"Despite that, you and your crew have done a lot to make me understand that education and knowledge aren't always the same thing." Nova saw Trill start to relax at her words. "You all showed me that a person can accumulate a ton of knowledge about something, even if they've never stepped foot in a classroom. That's still a brand-new concept for me and it will take me a little while to get used to it, but I'm not feeling intimidated by you like I once did. Which is a good thing…because I'm in love with you too, Trillian Dacanay."

Trill kissed Nova deeply. "We have a lot to talk about concerning our future together then, baby," she said softly when she raised her head. “But I’m not in any rush and neither should you be. You’re here in *our* apartment, we’re together now, and those are the most important things. We need to get Gillian’s stuff packed and shipped out to her in Albuquerque as soon as she and her boyfriend are settled and ready. We need to pack all your stuff and get you moved in here. But that conversation and those plans can wait for now.

“You’re exhausted, little diva.” Trill kissed Nova’s forehead and pulled the diminutive brunette into her arms. “Sleep now, my beautiful woman, and know that I love you with everything in me.”

“I love you too, Trill. More than you could ever imagine.” Nova’s drowsy voice faded as she snuggled peacefully into Trill’s arms, feeling safe, warm, and protected. “Thank you for being everything I’ve ever wanted. You are my dream come true.”

ঌωঌωঌωঌ

On the other side of the country in southern California, however, another woman was feeling anything but peaceful, safe, and protected—her dreams long ago scorched to ashes until they had turned into a horrific nightmare she lived every single day.

ঌωঌωঌωঌ

Smack! "You worthless *cunt.*" Chad Lancaster knew the deep red mark on his wife's cheek would fade before the glamorous Hollywood film premiere they were attending the next evening, so he wasn't worried about smacking his useless whore of a wife around a bit tonight. "The *fuck* is wrong with you, you ignorant bitch?" *Smack!* Isadora Nightingale fell to her knees.

"You had to insist on that goddamn shrew as the food stylist for this film, because you think you're too fucking good for Craig Acosta? You high and mighty piece of shit."

Isadora, on the floor and holding her cheek, was frozen in place. Chad grabbed a handful of Isadora's long, pale blonde hair and yanked her to her feet. He twisted the long strands painfully around his fist and pulled her face close to his.

"You dared, *dared* to defy me and actually had the fucking *nerve* to tell me you wouldn't do my film unless I hired Nova MacLeod as the food stylist? Let me tell you something. I met with her today before I flew back here to California and I swear, that goddamn bitch is going to be nothing but trouble for me, Isadora. She's a mouthy broad who already thinks she can tell me what to do.

"You'd better hope and pray she learns her place, bitch, or I'll take every fucking ounce of trouble she causes out of *your* worthless hide." He shook her roughly by her fisted hair then cruelly pinched the flesh under her right breast. Isadora whimpered, having learned to never shriek or cry when he put his hands on her because that would only spur him on.

Lancaster harshly thrust her away from him and Isadora staggered, barely able to keep her feet. "Take yourself from my sight, cunt," he said, sneering. "I don't want to see you or hear you for the rest of the night. I suggest you put some cream on that cheek, unless you want my staff to know you earned yourself yet *another* correction tonight. Now, get the fuck out of here."

Isadora fled up the stairs of the Malibu Colony Beach mansion and escaped into the isolation of her master suite. She quietly shut her bedroom door—since slamming it would send Chad into a towering rage—and walked into her master bathroom, seating herself at her vanity. Finally alone, she let the tears flow down her cheeks and she stared at the wan, all-but-broken beauty in the mirror, a look of despair on her delicate face.

Chapter 10

Isadora silently wept, covering her mouth with her hands so that her sobs wouldn't escape. Her shoulders shook as she tried in vain to bring herself under control…then resigned herself to the fact that her body clearly needed to purge some of the pain, grief, and anger that was a constant part of her daily existence.

At thirty-one, Isadora was one of the biggest movie stars of her generation. When she had burst onto the Hollywood scene at age nineteen, unbelievably winning her very first Oscar in her debut role, the world had realized there was far more to Isadora Nightingale than just the pale, flaxen hair, huge spring-green eyes, and delicate frame that was her signature look.

Chad Lancaster had been the director, a man already well established in Hollywood circles, and whose name was often mentioned with other commercially successful directors such as Steven Spielberg, Peter Jackson, and Ron Howard. When the young, starry-eyed, fascinated Isadora had found herself under the direction of the older, more sophisticated Chad in her debut film, she'd turned in a performance that critics had called "transcendent" and "Oscar-worthy"—a performance for which Chad took complete credit.

Young, ignorant actresses, he had explained succinctly to Isadora, *are only as good as the director they are with. Often, there is raw talent there—as there is with you—but it takes a brilliant director to mold that talent into something praiseworthy.*

Chad's controlling personality had evoked feelings of security in Isadora—at first—since Chad knew how to expertly navigate the Hollywood scene. Isadora had felt relief at finding a mentor like Chad so quickly. After her debut film's release, Isadora had found herself inundated with scripts, all of which her agent had urged her to look at. With the Oscar buzz being generated, she'd found herself confiding in Chad when he'd called her, asking him what he thought she should do.

As swift as a striking snake, Chad had fired her agent, installed one of his own people as her new agent, and assembled a group of individuals whom he referred to as her "safety net" team. Surrounded by Chad's handpicked staff, she'd felt protected, especially when Chad had asked her to marry him almost immediately.

"With my reputation as a director and your talent as an actress," he had told her when they were at dinner one evening, "we will become Hollywood's power couple in short order. I've already selected the script for your next movie, and I have no doubt that it will become just as big of a success as your debut was."

Her second movie was subsequently scheduled to be released three days before Isadora and Chad's wedding, and a wild mania had swept through the country. Moviegoers couldn't get enough of Hollywood's princess and her knight in shining armor, and the plans for their extravagant $1 million wedding—in conjunction with their movie release—had sent the public into a frenzy.

Isadora had become increasingly uncomfortable with all the attention, however, and she had asked Chad why all of the extravagance was necessary. It was the first time he had snapped at her—in a vicious tone of voice that had frightened her—and she had backpedaled quickly, telling him she was just nervous. She had dismissed Chad's behavior as stress from the wedding and the movie's release, and then had forgotten about it.

After their wedding and the film's premiere—Isadora's performance again generating Oscar talk—they'd settled into Chad's $42.5 million Malibu Colony Beach house. Isadora had hoped they would be able to return to a quieter existence now that all the insanity from the movie's release and their wedding was over.

They had been married for about two weeks when Chad had struck her for the first time. Isadora had been arguing with him about a film script he had wanted her to look at, which Isadora hadn't thought was right for her after she'd read it. When Isadora had continued to stubbornly insist she wasn't interested in taking this particular role, she had been stunned when Chad had hauled off and struck her right across the face. Holding her cheek, she had stared at him in shocked disbelief, then had cried out when he had grabbed her long blonde hair and yanked it hard.

"You listen to me, you spoiled little bitch," he had gritted, his eyes aflame. "Your behavior has been absolutely *appalling* over these past months. I am here to tell you that things are going to change, starting *now*. From now on, you will obey me and do *exactly* as you are told, or more corrective action will be in your future."

"Ch-...Ch-...*Chad*!" Isadora had stammered, trying unsuccessfully to free her long hair from his gripping fist. She'd shrieked when he had smacked her across the face again and fell to her knees, wailing, from the pain in her scalp when she thought Chad was going to rip her hair out by its roots.

"Shut *up*! Shut up, you little cunt! I don't want to hear any more noise out of you, Isadora! At. *All*." A boot had then made contact with Isadora's head and, when he'd let go of her hair, she'd fallen completely to the floor, almost insensible. Chad had grabbed one of her arms and roughly dragged her back on her feet, smacking her across the face a third time to bring her attention back to him. Isadora had whimpered but kept silent, afraid of provoking him further.

He had leaned down to look directly into her eyes with a hateful glare. "This is *my* house, *my* staff, *my* life that I have graciously agreed to share with you, Isadora. You were *nothing* when I found you, just an ignorant child with a modicum of talent…and you would have continued to be *nothing* without me."

Isadora couldn't breathe.

"And this? This behavior is how you repay me? After everything I've given you and done for you, you think you're going to disrespect me like this?" He had grabbed her other arm, and Isadora had tried not to scream as he'd squeezed her biceps so hard, she'd known she would have massive finger-shaped bruises.

"I expect you to *always* obey me without question. You will go where I say you will go, wear what I tell you to wear, eat what I tell you to eat." He had shaken her. "And you will fucking *accept* the movie scripts I *tell* you to accept! What do you think a stupid bitch like you knows about picking a movie script?"

Then he had shoved her away. "Go to your bedroom, Isadora. You will stay there until you have my permission to leave. The staff here has been instructed not to speak to you and to report to me if you even attempt to speak to them. If you do, I will have to take more corrective action." He had turned his back on her but then had glanced back toward her one more time. "You will have a good life with me, Isadora, if you're obedient and realize *I'm* the one who's in control. *Not* you."

Isadora had dragged herself upstairs—in pain, in shock, and shaking so hard, she thought her legs were going to give out. When she had reached her master suite, she'd shut the door—not daring to lock it—then had staggered to her bathroom and sat down at her vanity.

She had originally been upset when she'd found Chad's Malibu Colony Beach mansion had two master suites and they wouldn't be sharing a bedroom. For months, she'd thought it odd that Chad would never spend the night with her in her small rental or that he never invited her to sleep at his house before their wedding—saying only that he didn't want to give the paparazzi any excuse to invade their privacy.

Their quick couplings at Isadora's house had been fast and uninspired. She had excused it away, telling herself that Chad was an intensely private man and that things would be totally different after they were married. And they were—because Chad's mask had dropped and she got to see the vicious, abusive man he really was.

Isadora had never been so thankful to have her own bedroom as she had been on that night, when her dreams had gone up in flames and she had been faced with the harsh reality of what it really meant to be Chad Lancaster's wife.

ܣ૭ܣ૭ܣ૭

Isadora tore herself away from her reminiscing to focus on cleaning her face and doctoring the dark red marks on her cheek. After twelve years of marriage to Chad, she was an expert at taking care of her wounds herself by now. Even if there was some residual color left—although there wouldn't be any actual bruising because Chad was far too careful about leaving marks on her where other people could see them—her makeup artist would erase the evidence.

Her makeup artist, her hairdresser, and her personal wardrobe stylist were all gay men whom Chad had personally chosen to be part of "her" staff. They were all incorrigible gossips, but Chad paid them handsomely to keep their mouths shut and to ignore any evidence left on her body from Chad's rampages.

Her contracts always specified that Isadora would not only use her own staff on any movie shoots, but she would also not do any nude scenes—nor would she assume any role or do any promotions that called for her to be “immodestly clothed.” No one except her personal stylist ever saw her naked—and Harrison Blackridge was a man too focused on his own reputation and advancement in the film industry to worry too much about any bruises that had formed on Isadora’s body.

Her face cleansed, Isadora carefully applied a healing salve to her cheek then brushed her hair and loosely braided it, wincing at her tender scalp. When she was done, she undressed and wrapped herself in a robe before going out onto the balcony that overlooked the Pacific Ocean.

She sat on a large chaise lounge to listen to the crashing waves below and then finally—finally!—let herself think about the incredible secret she’d been keeping to herself for the past several weeks.

The month before, Chad had informed her that they were going to film a movie about a woman—a chef—who had inadvertently overheard a plot to kill a local politician. Chad stated it would be shot on location on the Gulf beaches in Florida and a fairly elaborate set would be built for it, since Isadora’s character owned a beachside restaurant where much of the story took place.

Isadora had felt her heart give a great big *thump* at his words.

Over the winter, she and Chad had taken a trip to Indian Shores, Florida—an extremely affluent neighborhood on Florida’s Gulf shore—to visit Chad's old college roommate, Andrew Matheson. Andrew was the Florida head of the entertainment law firm used by Chad's production company, and Isadora could only assume Chad had had business that needed to be discussed with him in person. It would have never occurred to Chad to pay a visit to someone "just because," especially someone who lived clear across the country.

Andrew's third wife Brandi was somewhat of a ditz but still quite personable, and Isadora had enjoyed her company. On their second day, she and Brandi had been sitting out on the large lanai next to the crystal-clear pool while the men were inside having another "meeting." Brandi had been gossiping about a scandalous local drama involving the mysterious disappearance of a prominent woman who, it was whispered, was being physically abused by her husband. As Isadora's face had drained of color, Brandi had then told her about another local woman who supposedly helped these women in trouble—although nothing had ever been proven.

"Maybe you know her, Isadora?" Brandi had asked. "She is this *crazy* popular food stylist who lives in Whimsy, which is only about thirty minutes from here. I guess she does *bunches* of print and film work, and they say she and her mother are the best. Nova MacLeod?"

"Nova MacLeod?" Isadora had repeated slowly. "No, I don't think I do." Then she had forced herself to laugh. "Chad has his own food stylist who's under contract to him and we've never needed anyone else. I guess Ms. MacLeod will have to remain a mystery!"

She deliberately turned the conversation back to an earlier bit of gossip and Brandi was off, Nova MacLeod forgotten.

But Isadora *hadn't* forgotten. She had filed away Nova's name in the back of her mind, wishing there was some way she could contact this woman without Chad finding out—certain that Nova was just the person for whom she'd been praying. Chad, however, had an advanced tracking app installed on Isadora's phone that let him monitor her incoming and outgoing phone calls, texting, emails, and her internet history remotely. It also monitored her GPS location, contacts, and calendar as well. Since she wasn't allowed to go out by herself either, there'd never been an opportunity for her to get a second phone that Chad didn't know about.

Now sitting on her balcony in California, she shivered at how everything had come together almost magically and opened a path for her. Understanding what she had to do, she had openly defied Chad professionally for the very first time in her married life, even going so far as to refuse to do the film if Nova MacLeod was not hired as the food stylist on it. *She needed the best*, she had insisted stubbornly, earning herself a couple of beatings for her defiance—but in the end, she had gotten her way. Chad was livid tonight because of Nova MacLeod, whom he had called a "mouthy bitch," but every strike Isadora had been given would be worth it.

Because…she and Nova MacLeod were *finally* going to be in the same town, working on the same film. And Isadora Nightingale was going to do everything in her power—even risk her own life—to escape the evil viciousness that was Chad Lancaster and expose him for what he truly was…if it was the last thing she ever did.

Chapter 11

"That should do it." Nova looked around the cargo area of her cabover truck with satisfaction. "We can pull everything out to get it all together and then check the final setup as soon as we're sure that douche canoe Lancaster is done with his juvenile games." She rolled her eyes. "I expected trouble from him…but what I *wasn't* expecting was for him to pussy out and put his personal assistant in the line of fire instead of facing me himself. Coward."

When they had arrived at the production location, Peyton Montgomery had meticulously backed the food-styling rig into the spot designated for them in their contract. Nova had no sooner jumped out of the truck's cab and started toward the rear lift gate of the rig when a thin, supercilious man had appeared. "Ms. MacLeod," he had harped, scampering over to Nova. "You simply *cannot* park that…that *monstrosity* there."

He had sniffed with disdain, then looked down his nose at Nova, who had paused as her crew climbed out of their own vehicles after parking next to them. "I'm sure I don't know what you're thinking, taking up that amount of room on the lot. It simply won't do."

Nova had slowly turned around then gave the man a slight smile. "And you are?" she inquired pleasantly, brushing her bangs out of her eyes.

He drew himself up and raised his receding chin. “I am Morton Hanneford Osgood the Third, first assistant to Mr. Chad Lancaster.” Osgood sniffed again. “Mr. Lancaster is very particular about his location shoots, and everything needs to be just so. As I’ve already so *clearly* stated, this won’t do.”

“I see.” Nova arched an eyebrow then crossed her arms as she faced him full on. “And *I* am very particular, Mr. Osgood, about my time and the efforts of my team being needlessly wasted. *That* won’t do. I suggest then that you let your boss know my rig is parked according to the exact details of my contract, and *here* is where it will stay.

“If he has an issue with that, I further suggest he come out here and address it with me *himself*. If I don’t see or hear from him within the next fifteen minutes, I’m going to assume he no longer feels the need to make any last-minute adjustments to the contract—for which, you might want to remind him, there will be an associated fee. Good day to you, sir.” And Nova turned her back on him.

There was silence for a full minute, the only sound the stomping of Osgood’s feet as he stormed away. As the stomping faded, Nova’s crew burst into laughter.

“*Hooey*, that was one mad little white boy.” Esmeralda Graves slapped her thigh, cackling with glee. Her dark brown eyes shone. “How’d you manage to piss off the director already, Nov? That’s gotta be some sorta record, even for you.”

A tall woman in her sixties with short hair dyed a flaming red elbowed Esmeralda. “Twenty bucks says Osgood is gone with the wind and we won’t see him or the director for a while.”

Esmeralda snorted.

“You think I throw my money away, Amadon? Nova, you tell Kathy here that my mama didn’t raise no fool.”

Susie Carfagna, who rounded out Nova’s core team, snickered. “That jackass is going to learn right quick that pissing off women with attitudes and sharp knives is never a good idea, especially when you have vulnerable dangly bits.” As Esmeralda and Kathy hooted, Susie leaned forward in a confiding manner.

“Before I joined your team, Nov, I was the food shopper on another film Lancaster did with his wife. Craig Acosta, his permanent food stylist, is one big fucking tool, just like Lancaster is.” Susie rolled her eyes as Nova arched an eyebrow.

“Isadora Nightingale is the sweetest thing, but she was completely railroaded by the dudes on set…and Lancaster let *every single one of them* order her around like she was a nobody.” Susie huffed in disgust. “She’s one of the biggest box office stars in existence today and they treated her like a fucking gofer. I will never in my life understand why she simply didn’t walk. Someone like her doesn’t need to take that kind of shit from *anybody*.”

Nova kept her mouth shut, although she felt the hair on the back of her neck stand up. “Well, at least Ms. Nightingale doesn’t need to worry about anyone treating her like a piece of trash on *this* set…from a food-styling perspective, anyway.” She checked her watch. "Douche canoe's fifteen minutes are up, and I don't see hide nor hair of either his Gucci loafers or those of his limp-dicked assistant. I think we can pull everything out, then do our setup."

"Peyton!" She hollered toward the front of the truck. "Come on, roadie, we've got shit to do." A grinning Peyton Montgomery, who had been waiting for Nova's cue at her request, swung herself out of the driver's seat. As she sauntered toward the back of the truck, the eyes of the food-styling crew widened when they got their first full head-to-toe glimpse of the APS systems analyst.

"*Lawddd* have mercy…who is *this* fine-looking specimen?" Esmeralda fanned her face with her hand. Nova burst out laughing, knowing that while Esmeralda was both straight and happily married to her husband of forty years, she was an incorrigible flirt.

"This, ladies, is Peyton Montgomery. She's taken, Es, so keep your drawers on." Peyton was an incredibly handsome butch, standing about 5'8" tall, with dark auburn hair, blue eyes, and the same muscled frame shared by all the APS associates.

Peyton's grin broadened as she took Esmeralda's outstretched hand then bowed over it and kissed the back in a courtly gesture. Nova rolled her eyes as Esmeralda swooned. "It's a total pleasure…Esmeralda, is it? And who are these other lovely ladies, Nova?" She turned to the diminutive brunette and winked, the corner of her mouth quirking.

"Nova MacLeod, I think you've been holding out on me all these years, girl." Esmeralda stuck her hands on her plump hips and raised her eyebrows at Nova. "You've been keeping this kind of eye candy to yourself and not sharing with your crew? For *shame*," she scolded, only half in jest.

Nova couldn't help it; she burst out laughing again. "Peyton and I only met a short while ago through mutual friends, Es. When I found out she was going to be in town at the same time this movie shoot was happening, I snapped her up and asked her how she felt about being a roadie on a film set. She was game, so here we are." Peyton's eyes twinkled at Nova's skillful, technically truthful introduction.

After all the introductions were over with—with Esmeralda, Kathy, and Susie all insisting on giving a delighted Peyton a big hug and kiss on the cheek—Nova and her team got busy pulling the kitchen elements out of the truck so they could assemble them outside. They were a well-oiled machine who worked together like perfect clockwork, their banter rapidly taking a back seat to executing their setup.

Peyton was a fast learner, as well as amazingly strong, so they had everything unloaded and put together in no time. To Nova's surprise, Peyton was dressed casually in jeans and a plain T-shirt, with no evidence of the concealed carry holster every APS associate typically wore. It left Nova a bit puzzled, knowing that no APS associate would be caught dead unarmed on the job.

When Peyton caught Nova trying to figure out how she was armed, she gave Nova a slight smile and casually rubbed the waistband of her jeans through her untucked shirt. Nova immediately realized Peyton was wearing an inner waistband holster and gave the APS associate a slight, imperceptible nod in understanding.

"Well, I'll be damned. It's an actual working kitchen." Peyton put her hands on her hips in amazement as she looked at the setup when they were done.

Durable 3' x 3' dance floor panels had been snapped together to create a "kitchen floor" at the edge of the parking lot where they had been instructed to park. The entire floor was securely anchored down with an 8-foot-high overhead canopy sunshade, as well as a three-sided windscreen that rose about 32" from the floor base and protected the actual assembled kitchen from traffic and wind.

Next to the kitchen stood a huge beach cart with balloon wheels that would prevent the cart from sinking in the sand. Nova and her crew would use the cart to bring their assembled food dishes onto the set for filming. Smiling at Peyton's awestruck expression, Nova snapped some pictures with her phone and stored them in a folder she had created specifically for this particular shoot. Then she grinned at Peyton and sent the photos to Trill and the Geek Crew.

The response was instantaneous. "You fucker, Montgomery!!!" Kendall's text screamed. "That is the *coolest* thing I've ever seen." A text from Val was hard on its heels. "Are you sure you don't need any cyber work done, little diva? I can be there in twenty minutes."

"The hell those assholes are going to crash my party," Peyton muttered to Nova in a low voice. She shook her head and let the volume of her voice become normal. "Seriously, Nov, you and your crew are fucking incredible. I've never seen anything like this."

"We got skills, yo." She grinned as Esmeralda stopped unpacking supplies from the portable cabinets. Arms akimbo, she huffed as Nova, Kathy, and Susie cracked up at the expression on her face. "You may have skills, white girl, but your street talk sucks." She shook her head in mock disgust and went back to unpacking the cabinets.

Just then, a group of men and one lone woman approached them. Nova recognized Chad Lancaster and Morton Osgood among them, but the woman and the remaining three males were unfamiliar to her. The woman had beautiful pale blonde hair pulled back into a loose bun, ivory skin, spring-green eyes, and a delicate frame that reminded Nova of a wood sprite or a fairy. She was being marched along by Chad Lancaster, who gripped her elbow firmly as he made his way to the edge of the portable kitchen.

This, Nova realized with a very slight widening of her eyes, was the legendary Isadora Nightingale, Chad's wife and the star of the movie. She was a thousand times more beautiful than her pictures, although her demeanor seemed a bit standoffish. She kept her eyes slightly downcast, refusing to look anyone directly in the face.

Nova felt a lump rise in her throat as she recognized the evasive stare of many abused women. Afraid of being exposed, they would usually avoid the gazes of others so they wouldn't trigger any questions or suspicions—trying not to draw any attention to themselves. Isadora was also meekly allowing herself to be led to wherever Chad wanted her to go, in a clear bid to avoid upsetting or angering him.

This cock-sucking motherfucker, Nova thought to herself in a burst of unexpected rage, *is going down if it's the last fucking thing I ever do in my life.* She drew in a deep breath in an effort to calm and center herself.

"Ms. MacLeod." Chad Lancaster stopped in front of her. "This is my wife, Isadora Nightingale. You will be working with her during the course of the location filming to prepare all of the dishes that will be needed as specified in the script. This," he nodded at the three gentlemen Nova didn't know, "is Craig Acosta, my permanent food stylist. Next to him is Lenny Beasley, the first assistant director, and next to him is Chet Gillespie, my property master." The three men stared at Nova with equally snotty looks on their faces.

He raised his eyebrow at Nova and continued with a sneer. "Mr. Acosta will be supervising your work on this film. Anything you need from my wife should go through him. For all intents and purposes, Ms. MacLeod, he will be your boss on this production and will have the final say on everything you do and everything you produce."

Craig Acosta looked at Nova with a superior smirk on his face.

These asshole pieces of shit, Nova fumed to herself as she decided she was putting a stop to Lancaster and his idiot games *right fucking now*. He thought he had her over a barrel and that she would have no choice but to comply with whatever he said—but she was about to teach this bastard jackass who *really* held the power in this situation.

"I see." She kept her expression passive despite the river of rage that flooded her entire body. "Peyton." Her voice was level. "Please work with Esmeralda, Kathy, and Susie to start breaking down our setup and packing it up."

Lancaster's eyes widened, obviously dumbfounded over this unexpected reaction from Nova.

"Sure thing, *boss*." Peyton's pointed words and cold voice wiped the smirk off Craig Acosta's face, as well as dampened the superiority of the other two men. Nova heard her crew begin to tear down the setup behind her, although she didn't turn around.

Nova regarded Lancaster icily, her arms folded across her chest, before she addressed him with an equally frosty tone. "My office will be sending you the bill for cancellation of our contract, Lancaster. I am exercising my right to declare this contract null and void because of your indisputable violation of our terms. The fact that Mr. Acosta here thought it was acceptable on *any* level for another food stylist to open her techniques and proprietary information to him—not to mention allow him to *supervise* her work—shows how very little he and you know about how *real* food stylists work on a film set."

Craig Acosta flushed red with anger, which Nova ignored.

"I'm sure the food stylist community will be quite interested to know about my experience with you, and I will make sure they heed my caution to avoid contracting with you on any level in the future." Nova then looked expressionlessly at Isadora Nightingale for the first time. "I'm sorry, Ms. Nightingale. I've been a fan of yours for a long time and was very much looking forward to fulfilling this contract. But I hope you understand the unacceptable actions of this film crew have made it impossible for me to continue on, as much as I thought I might have enjoyed working with you."

Nova knew she was taking a huge risk and that Chad Lancaster might well call her bluff—but she was willing to bet that he needed her too much to let her walk away. It was quite clear from his reaction that he had never in a million years thought she would be prepared to nullify the contract and turn her back on this production. There was a long moment of silence except for the noise behind her as her team continued disassembling their setup.

"Now, you hold on for just a minute," Lancaster finally sputtered, his face red and his eyes angry. "You can't just walk away from this contract, Ms. MacLeod. People *don't* walk away from the opportunity to work with me. Or Isadora," he added, almost as an afterthought.

Nova gave him another chilly smile. "Oh, but I can and I will, Mr. Lancaster," she said vindictively. "You want me to stay? Then you will abide by the exact terms of the contract *in full*—the same way I'm prepared to—without any more of your nonsense. Mr. Acosta will remove himself from my proximity. Your other associates will do the same." She cut her icy eyes toward Lenny Beasley, Chet Gillespie, and Craig Acosta for a moment before focusing back on Lancaster.

"Ms. Nightingale is the only person on this set who has the right to be around my setup, with the exception of Mr. Gillespie—on *rare* occasions—as he is the property master on this set. During those times, he will work with Kathy Amadon from my team since she is my prop stylist. There is no need for him to interfere in what the rest of us are doing, or to disturb Ms. Nightingale when she is collaborating with me."

Suddenly, Nova dropped her icy facade and let her anger burn bright. Chad Lancaster actually dropped Isadora's elbow and took a full step back from Nova as she pointed an accusing finger at him, her wrath evident on her face.

'I have *never*—in all my years of film work—been subjected to this level of juvenile behavior." Nova held up her hand, cutting off an angry Lancaster as he was about to speak. "I assure you, Lancaster, this is the last time I will *ever* consider working with Blue Moon Studios. I expect the same professionalism and respect from my clients that I give to them…and this has been so far removed from that, I am virtually speechless."

Nova folded her arms over her chest again. "What happened today was strike two, after your first strike with the script games you tried to play with me. Three strikes, I walk for good, and the entire production can go to hell as far as I'm concerned. I'm far too busy and in too much demand to have to put up with this kind of idiot game-playing from *anyone*. Consider yourself warned." Nova turned her back on Chad Lancaster, his wife, and his team, and walked away without a backward glance.

As much as she wanted to send a wide-eyed Isadora a look of reassurance, Nova didn't dare. Better to have Lancaster thinking

Nova lumped Isadora in with the rest of the production staff, rather than to risk Isadora taking another beating because Lancaster thought Isadora was the one person exempt from Nova's outrage.

"We're going to hold off for now and put everything back together," she calmly informed her crew as she walked around the wind screen to the portable kitchen opening. The corner of her mouth twitched as she saw the team had only disassembled areas that could rapidly be reassembled. How fucking well they knew her.

She watched Lancaster and his minions depart, furious but with their collective tails between their legs. Chad Lancaster once again gripped Isadora's elbow roughly as he hauled her off, and Nova's mouth tightened as she saw Isadora silently wince.

Peyton, who had been sending a text, slid her phone into the back pocket of her jeans and prepared to help the rest of Nova's crew finish reassembling the kitchen. "I just updated Trill on what's been going down," she said in a low voice so that no one else could overhear her. "Other than the fact that she's ready to come down here and pound Lancaster into the ground like a peg herself, she said it sounds like you have everything well under control. She wants us to go directly to the Recon Room when we're back."

"I hope so, Pey. This whole goddamn place is like House Frey, and I almost lost it more than once." Nova, a Game of Thrones fan, felt her anger still simmering. "I think I need to let Trill know my impressions of Isadora as soon as I get back. I am about as sure as I can be that motherfucking douche canoe Lancaster is abusing her, and I frankly don't know where we go from here."

"Nov…this is what your buddies in APS *do*, little diva." Peyton hugged her. "We'll get your girl out. When it comes to women, Trillian Dacanay is the most protective son of a bitch I know—and so goddamned smart, Lancaster is going to look like an even bigger drooling idiot than he already does by the time it's all over. We just need to keep Isadora safe until she comes to you, little diva, because you know she will. You *know* it."

"I know." Nova hugged Peyton back fiercely then stepped back. "I guess the only thing we can do is get ourselves ready and wait until production starts. I have a couple of things I want to talk to Trill about, a few ideas that have occurred to me." She sighed and huffed her bangs out of her eyes as she started to help Peyton secure the prep island again.

"There's no telling how long she's been abused, Pey," Nova whispered, the distress clear in her voice. "She and Lancaster have been married for twelve years, and I can only assume the abuse started shortly after their wedding, after the deal was sealed.

"I spent a lot of time looking at photographs of her online last night—and in every single fucking picture, there is a deep sadness in the back of her eyes that you won't see unless you're really looking for it. She may be one of the greatest actresses in the world, but there's no hiding that kind of pain from anyone who knows what they're looking for." Nova discreetly dashed the tears out of her eyes.

"Hang on for just a little while longer, little diva." Peyton hugged her again before she went back to re-securing the prep table.

“We’re here now and we’ve got her. Chad Lancaster is going to rue the day he *ever* raised his hands to Isadora Nightingale by the time Trill Dacanay gets done with him.”

Chapter 12

Nova curled up in Trill's bed, tired from both her emotional day as well as the demanding, passionate sex she had surrendered to when she and Trill had gotten home.

At the end of the work day, Nova and Peyton had met Trill and the rest of her team in the Recon Room. There'd been some huge grins and high-fives after Peyton had described how Nova had "shown that jackass Lancaster up for the chump he is." Their smiles had disappeared, however, as Peyton had gone on to talk about Isadora Nightingale, her demeanor, and Chad Lancaster's treatment of her.

ᘐωᘐωᘐωᘐ

"I *know*, without a shadow of a doubt, that the motherfucker is abusing her," Peyton growled wrathfully and looked around the room, her gaze settling on Nova. "Isadora has all the classic signs of an abused woman. She won't make eye contact with anyone. She let Lancaster haul her around without resistance, like she was some fucking bag of laundry. She was folded in on herself, as if she was trying to escape notice. That woman is one of the *biggest* box office stars in the world. Why else would she do that, unless she was trying to stay unnoticed and off Lancaster's radar?"

"She wouldn't," Trill said calmly, although it was apparent she was angry. She leaned over and kissed the tears that had started to drip down Nova's face. "Baby, from what you've told me, production is starting very soon, and you'll have Isadora under your umbrella before you know it. I doubt very much she's going to wait very long before she tries to connect with you.

"You can set the stage for that. Tell her how thrilled you are to be working with her, apologize for needing so much of her time during production, but you want to make sure she has what she needs to play her chef role. Actresses spend a lot of time in their trailers between takes, don't they? Suggest she spend that time with you and your crew instead."

"That's exactly one of the things I want to talk to you about, Trill." Nova sniffed then visibly pulled herself together. "First of all…Delaney is a formally trained pastry chef. She can join my crew and teach Isadora how to make professional knife cuts, things of that nature, that will give Isadora an air of credibility for her role. If Teag is okay with it, that is. I truly doubt there's any way Lancaster could know Delaney is the wife of one of the APS Seven, but I understand if Teagan would be a bit skittish…especially with what Del went through with that dick, Bellwood."

Trill brushed Nova's bangs out of her eyes. "Peyton will be right there with you all, so Teag will be just fine." She and Peyton nodded at each other. "That's a good thought, little diva. It will be one more layer of protection for Isadora while you're on the set."

"Second," Nova continued, looking around the table, "I want to hire Alyssa Riker as my sketch artist."

"Sketch artist?" Val Chan frowned and leaned back in her chair, folding her arms. "I'm not tracking here, Nov. This is a movie production where Isadora Nightingale plays a professional chef, not an artist. Why would you need someone like Alyssa?" Everyone on Trill's team was equally puzzled.

A wily smile spread across Nova's face. "Sketch artists always draw storyboards and set elements at the direction of the film's art director during pre-production before they finalize the design and actually start building the sets. I already know I'll most likely have some pet douche of Lancaster's to deal with…probably the art director himself.

"But because I have complete autonomy over *anything* that has to do with the food on set, that means I can hire my own sketch artist if I feel it's necessary." The corners of Nova's mouth tipped up. "And for some reason, I feel it's necessary." Broad grins hit the faces of Trill's team as they started to understand where Nova was going.

"Besides," Nova then grew pensive, "we'll need to sweep for bugs or other listening devices each day. I'm about as sure as I can be that motherfucker Lancaster is going to have my setup bugged, trying to keep his thumb on Isadora. Although I'm pretty sure Trill has already thought of that." Trill squeezed her arm in acknowledgment after Nova raised one eyebrow at her in question.

Turning back to the team, Nova said, "Bringing Alyssa on board, however, gives Isadora another means to communicate with us. I already know Isadora draws, because the few times I've seen her from afar with Lancaster and his douche patrol, she's always been carrying what looks like a sketch pad. Seeing that gave me an idea.

"Isadora and Alyssa can communicate graphically with each other, under the guise of working on the food setup for the shoot. Lys is a damn good art therapist, which means she can interpret fucking *anything* anyone draws. Her regular therapy students aren't artists and some of them can't draw a straight line…so figuring out what someone is trying to say graphically won't be anything unusual for Alyssa. She does it all the time in her work.

"Isadora can therefore be a little cryptic if she needs to be and Lys will still catch it. Plus, the sketchbooks will be *Alyssa's*. Lancaster won't have any right to take them from Isadora or even look at them because they aren't technically hers, which will also keep Isadora protected."

"Fuck my life." Darcy ran a hand over the top of her head then gave Melanie, who was sitting next to her, a high-five. "Nova, I swear you and your girls are fucking brilliant."

"You're just figuring this out, Darce?" Nova snarked then burst out laughing as Darcy rolled her eyes. "Also, Alyssa is not an APS wife or girlfriend like Delaney is, so I won't have to worry about another APS bad ass breathing down my neck while she's on the production set. Thank the Goddess."

"She might want to discuss that with Jaime Quintero," Kendall muttered quietly to Melanie, who chuckled under her breath.

Nova drummed her fingers on the conference room table. "I've already talked to both Lys and Delaney, and they are fired up to help out. Sweet Expectations isn't open yet, so Del said she could leave almost everything in Rowan and Darius's very capable hands for a month or two with no problem. Ro and Darius are all in to pitch hit for Del so she can do this.

"Alyssa has her regularly scheduled art therapy classes, but Brooke Marino said she's more than happy to fill in for Lys for a while as well. Brooke is a graphic artist just like Rowan, with her own business in the craft brewery industry. She's assured me her schedule is totally flexible…plus, Brooke has filled in for Alyssa before when Lys has gone out of town for a conference or sat for a certification or whatever. We're good.

"Although," Nova coughed into her fist, "I can't promise that Lancaster or his minions of darkness will still have their dicks attached when all's said and done. My girls are just a tad bit pissed at what a huge movie star like Isadora has had to deal with over the past ten-plus years. Even our sweet Rowan and Delaney are *seething*. They're totally ready to take those fuckwits out themselves."

"Fierce." Melanie shook her head as a slow grin tipped up the corners of her mouth. "For some reason, I'm thinking the APS femmes are not a group of women you ever want to fuck with."

"Right?" Val rumbled, her arms folded across her chest in amusement.

"Baby, I think we're all in awe of you and your posse." Trill lifted Nova into her lap. "You've thought this out, you have a solid plan, and I don't give a motherfuck that you've never done anything like this before. Because you know how the food-styling industry works, how movie sets operate and, most importantly, how an abused woman thinks and feels and reacts, I can't think of anyone who is in a better position to get Isadora Nightingale out than you. And that's including every single person at APS."

Nova's tears started to fall again. "I just want her to finally be safe, Trill," she whispered, burying her face in Trill's throat. "I can't even fathom how she must feel, being one of the most visible and sought-after celebrities in our society today…yet feeling so totally alone and isolated.

"How in the hell has she survived all these years? How many women out there are so envious of her life because they see what she has—including the adoration of millions—but they have absolutely no fucking idea Isadora would probably give it all up for just one single day of peace, security, and safety?" Her voice broke.

"Baby." Trill settled Nova more firmly in her lap and held Nova's head to her chest with one hand. "If it's the last thing we do, we're going to give that to her. Chad Lancaster is a powerful man, and I'm sure he has contingency plans to discredit Isadora in the event she leaves him or says anything about his abuse of her.

"He's not about to let her destroy his reputation. But as soon as Isadora steps foot on that lot, the very first thing you and Alyssa need to do is communicate to her that you know about her situation…that you not only know about it, but you have an army at your back who's going to help you to get her out. That alone may well give her the strength to hang on for a while longer. How long before she's on set? Two weeks or so?"

Nova nodded.

"Then let's pull the girls in and have a meeting with everyone together to formulate our game plan. We'll make sure we're ready for her the minute she comes on the set. Chad Fucking Lancaster may think he has the advantage here because of who he is, but he's about to find out APS and their femmes are not anyone you *ever* want to fuck around with."

ᘛᘚᘛᘚᘛᘚᘛ

In the present, Nova idly drew tiny circles on Trill's hard abs as they rested in bed together. "I know we can get Isadora out and away from that fucking douche fairly easily, Trill," she said with a sigh. "That's not the problem. The problem is, how do we do it without destroying Isadora's reputation and career at the same time, or have him leave her destitute?

"Lancaster may be a tool, but he's also a very powerful man in Hollywood. He'll ruin her, just out of spite and revenge. He has a bunch of ass lickers on his payroll who will do or say whatever he wants them to say to cover his own ass. Good luck trying to prove he's nothing more than a lying sack of shit because of that. His asshole minions will lie, cheat, and steal to win his favor, especially when they think it might advance their own careers."

Trill kissed Nova and wrapped her arms more snugly around her woman. "One thing at a time, baby," she said. "First, we get Isadora on set and let her reach out to you. Second, we then make sure she understands that you've got her, that you and your girls are there for her, and she doesn't have to be alone anymore. The more I'm thinking about it, the more I believe the most effective way to handle this will be to let Lancaster shoot himself in the ass." Trill was contemplative. "We can make sure his abuse of Isadora is caught red-handed on tape and then leaked, so that both Hollywood and the public light the fuck up with it.

"We'll have Jaime and her crew duplicate a pair of Isadora's earrings, but these will have a tiny spy camera hidden inside one of them that records everything." Nova's eyes grew huge. "We can send any recorded film of Lancaster's domestic violence anonymously to every news station you can think of and watch as Lancaster fucking implodes.

"I *despise* the thought of Isadora taking another beating from that piece of shit," Trill growled menacingly, "but we will let *her* make that decision. She may well feel that being subjected to one final physical confrontation with her husband is worth it to get incontrovertible proof of his abuse, just so she can put an end to the nightmare her life has become over the last twelve years."

Trill nuzzled behind Nova's ear.

"Like I said, though, we'll let *her* decide. I suspect she's going to say that asshole motherfucker regularly throws her beatings for perceived infractions anyway, so she might as well use one of them for her own benefit."

Nova growled in turn.

"When everything's on fire, baby, we can get women's domestic violence groups involved to pour even more gasoline on the flames," Trill went on. "Even if Lancaster tries to put a spin on it and talk his way out of the situation, it's likely his minions will scatter rather than risk going down with a sinking ship. The fuck any of them are going to put their cocks on the line for Lancaster in a situation like this.

"Everyone and their mother will be desperately trying to get an interview from Isadora when everything explodes, but she won't have to say a word. It will actually do more for her credibility if she keeps silent and refuses to talk to anyone. In the meantime, she can stay safely hidden with one of us, and I'll ask Mama Armstrong to be her official spokesperson."

Despite the seriousness of their discussion, Nova giggled at the thought of Rosi Armstrong dealing with the Hollywood press. "Mama A will fucking torch those vultures if they so much as dare put a foot wrong."

Trill chuckled then deeply kissed Nova one more time.

"I texted the management team to tell them we wanted to get everyone together early tomorrow morning—before you have to be on location—to work on our plan," she said when she had released Nova's mouth. "Everyone will make sure their number twos are there as well. I also let Peyton know, and Kelly was going to tell the girls. We'll have everything planned out and in place by the time Isadora gets on set.

"We've got her, little diva. Isadora will be safe very, very soon…and Chad Lancaster won't know what the fuck hit him by the time we're done with him."

ᘛᘚᘛᘚᘛᘚᘛ

Ten days later, Nova and her food-styling crew were putting supplies away from a huge shopping trip that had been made by Susie Carfagna, when Chad Lancaster and his crew came stomping up to her again, Isadora's elbow gripped firmly in Chad's hand once more.

Nova's jaw ticked. "Lancaster," she said flatly, an impassive look on her face. She stopped what she was doing long enough to turn and face Lancaster with an arched brow.

Chad Lancaster sneered at her and pushed Isadora toward her. "We start filming in two days, Ms. MacLeod. I certainly hope that's enough time to teach Isadora what she needs to know to act as a professional chef. I brought her here for instruction, no matter how hopeless I think it might be." The look of contempt on his face deepened. "Then again, I don't think teaching someone how to cut up a chicken breast is all that mentally taxing."

Delaney Malloy, who was on set as Nova's professional chef resource, smiled sweetly. "No worries, Mr. Lancaster. It's quite difficult for lay people like yourself to understand the intricacies of the food world, when top-level chefs like Wolfgang Puck and Anne Burrell make it look so easy to the *untrained* eye. I can assure you that Ms. Nightingale will receive everything she needs to make her role in your movie a success."

Nova's lips twitched as she caught Delaney's subtle insult.

Lancaster's brows lowered. "I expect Isadora to be taken back to her trailer when her instruction here has been completed each day. There is no need for a star like Isadora to have her time wasted by a bunch of *food stylists*." He sneered again.

"Isadora, you know what is expected of you. In spite of Ms. MacLeod's insistence that none of my people be in attendance while you are working with her, that does not mean you can conduct yourself as you please. On second thought, however…" he paused for a moment then continued arrogantly, “I will be along to collect you myself at the end of the work day.” With one more stern look at Isadora, Chad Lancaster stomped off with his entourage.

Despite her anger, Nova smiled pleasantly at Isadora. “I am extremely pleased to meet you, Ms. Nightingale. I’ve been a fan of yours for a very long time. Rest assured, my associates and I have made sure there is no way for anyone to interrupt our work or interfere with anything we talk about here today.” She gave Isadora a meaningful look, hoping that the actress caught it.

Before they had come to the set earlier that week, Jaime Quintero had given Nova and Peyton a small piece of equipment she said was called a bug sweep. “This is an electronic bug sweep, *mi hermana*,” Jaime had told her as she’d handed Peyton a small device that looked like an old-fashioned transistor radio. “Bug sweeps look for bugging devices and other electronics that are capable of either transmitting data or storing data that can be retrieved by an eavesdropper.

“You can bring this to your food-styling rig and we’ll test it to make sure any eavesdropping devices on the set are blocked. It has a 24 GHz radio frequency range and will eliminate any telephone line bugs, covert hidden cameras, or wiretaps. There is also other equipment we’ll use in conjunction with the bug sweep, as well as additional steps we’ll take that you won’t need to worry about, little diva…including jamming any video surveillance.

“Just know that Lancaster and his minions of darkness won’t be able to get all up in your business while you’re on set.” Jaime had smirked. “He also won’t be able to say anything to you without admitting he tried to have you bugged and monitored either, which should piss him right the fuck off. Sucks to be him, doesn't it?"

Now, Nova continued. "Let me go ahead and introduce you to my crew, Ms. Nightingale. This is Esmeralda Graves, my assistant food stylist; Kathy Amadon, who is our prop stylist; and Susie Carfagna, who is the production's food shopper. Peyton Montgomery is our roadie, Delaney Sedgwick will be handling all the professional chef instruction, and Alyssa Riker is our sketch artist." Nova deliberately avoided using Delaney's married name as a precaution.

"You and Lys will be working closely together to graphically communicate what you'll need to accomplish as far as the finished dishes go. I hope you understand, but any sketchbooks will have to stay in Alyssa's possession at all times. I'm afraid we're a little particular about our proprietary information and who has access to it."

"Please. It's Isadora." The petite blonde's low, sweet voice reminded Nova of Rowan. "And I completely understand, Ms. MacLeod." Her eyes fastened intently on Nova's face. "Actresses are not eager to give up their trade secrets either, I can assure you. I believe you said there isn't anything that can interfere with our work here today? No one can see what we're doing?" Her tone was casual, although her question was anything but.

Alyssa Riker responded in a kind tone, giving Nova a chance to collect her stunned thoughts because of what Isadora was already asking. "All of us here are on a first-name basis, Isadora. We've worked together for a very long time, and we're eager to make you an unofficial part of our crew." The barely hidden gleam of hope in Isadora's eyes clearly wrenched at Alyssa's heart.

Back on an even keel again, Nova said, "Before you get started with Delaney, Isadora, I'm going to suggest that you and Lys make some sketches of the anticipated finished dishes based on the script. I believe I saw you with a sketch pad when you were on the other side of the lot before we met you the first time. It sounds like you draw?"

Isadora nodded.

"Good, that's excellent. If you two will do that, Delaney can then have some idea of where she needs to start with her chef instruction. Sound good?"

Isadora nodded again as a very small smile crossed her face.

"I also have all the artist supplies we will ever need, Isadora, so you don't have to worry about having anything of your own," Alyssa told her. "Nova and Esmeralda have a very detailed list of all the dishes needed in the film already put together, so it's just a question of us starting at the top and working our way down."

Isadora still appeared a bit hesitant, however. "You're sure no one will see our sketches except for you and me and Nova…and the rest of the food-styling crew?" It was evident the movie star had little in the way of trust for others, especially given the perils of her life.

"Isadora." Nova didn't dare place her hand over Isadora's, even with any possible video surveillance being blocked, but she made sure the inflection of her voice carried everything she wanted Isadora to know. "We are a very *protective* crew. We protect each other and we protect those who are important to us at *all* cost.

"It's like I've already said: You are now an unofficial part of this crew, and we're going to look out for you just as much as we look out for each other. We've got you, honey. We're going to make sure we do everything in our power to make this production a success in every single way you can think of."

"Okay," Isadora whispered, blinking until the miniscule glimmer of moisture in her eyes disappeared and the tension in her shoulders eased a bit.

"Personally, I think there's no time like the present for us to get started." Alyssa's voice was crisp, although extremely gentle. "Give me ten minutes to get set up and we'll start sketching at the top of Nova's list, Isadora. Del can give us her input as we work, because she's a chef and she knows what these dishes are supposed to look like when they're done. Once we're happy with the sketches, she'll then have a really good idea of what she needs to teach you in order to make your role look authentic. Nova, are you ready, my homegirl?"

"I'm ready."

ঞ০ঞ০ঞ০ঞ

"He's been beating her since she was nineteen." Tears poured down Nova's face. A pissed-off APS management team, as well as anyone else who had been involved in Nova's anticipated rescue of Isadora Nightingale, was in the Bunker of APS, regrouping at the end of the day. Curled up in Trill's lap, Nova had been bringing everyone up to speed on what had happened on location that day. She'd managed to stay calm until she'd reached the point where Isadora had started to open up to her, Alyssa, and Delaney.

"She told me she had found out about me through the wife of her husband's entertainment lawyer. Isadora and Chad were in Indian Shores last winter because Lancaster apparently had business with this dude. When Isadora and the lawyer's wife were talking, my name had come up as someone who helped rescue women from domestic violence situations…because of an abused woman this lawyer's wife knew who had disappeared from the area. This woman is a huge gossip, Isadora said, and this was the latest scandal in the area that she had been eager to share with Isadora.

"The wife then wanted to know if Isadora knew me because I did food styling for the movies in addition to commercials and print ads, she said. Why this bitch knew so much about me, I don't have the first fucking clue. Anyhow, Isadora pretended to be completely clueless and changed the subject, telling this woman that Chad had his own food stylist under contract, but she filed my name in the back of her head." When Nova started to cry, Trill hugged her tightly and stroked her hands up and down Nova's arms in an effort to soothe her upset femme.

"It turns out the two of them had been in Indian Shores so that Lancaster could talk to his lawyer about this particular production. When Isadora found out she was going to do this movie and that it would be filmed on location on the Gulf beaches here, she saw her chance. She told Chad she absolutely refused to do the movie unless I was the one who was hired as the food stylist for it.

"He," Nova hiccupped before she went on, "he beat this *shit* out of her a couple of times because Isadora would not work with Lancaster's pet food stylist, Craig Acosta. She said she kept insisting she wanted another Oscar or Golden Globe for this movie, and hiring me was the way to do it with a role like this one. She told Lancaster flat out she wasn't going to get there with Acosta."

Alyssa dashed the tears from her own cheeks. "While we were pretending to sketch food dishes, Isadora was graphically detailing her life with Lancaster. It was all I could do to pretend that things were fine and we weren't doing anything but sketching storyboards, but I thought I was going to throw up from what she was drawing for us."

Then she snorted. "At the end of the day, that fuck of an art director showed up and insisted he wanted my sketchbooks…everything that Isadora and I had done that day. I basically told him to go suck his own dick—they were proprietary, they were mine, and he had no right to ask me to turn them over.

"To cover Isadora and divert any suspicion away from her, I told that fuckwit she'd already asked me to give them to her so she could take them to Chad and I'd told her *no* as well." Alyssa was startled when Jaime Quintero, who was sitting right next to her, reached out and captured her hand, squeezing it in a show of support.

"It's bad." Delaney's voice was quiet and filled with angst. Her head was resting on Teagan's shoulder from her perch on Teag's lap. "I can't figure out how in the world she's managed to survive all these years…all alone like she's been and without anyone having one single clue about what she's been going through in that time." She took the handkerchief Teagan handed to her with a kiss and dried her wet eyes. "Nova and Lys also have the sketchbooks for you to look at."

"You three have done one absolutely amazing job so far." Riley's voice was dark even as she praised the APS femmes. She kept massaging Kelly's shoulders in an effort to calm her livid wife down. "Jaime, how did the bug sweep and the surveillance blocking go?"

"Like silk." Jaime still refused to let Alyssa's hand go. "We couldn't see or hear a thing. The girls did a stellar job pretending to simply be talking about the food dishes for the shoot. If Lancaster has any suspicions at all, it's only because he's a paranoid son of a bitch, not because they did anything to trigger him."

"Isadora also indicated that Lancaster's abuse lessens when they're on a film set…because it's a lot harder to hide the marks of his beatings when they're filming," Nova mused with a small hiccup, getting her head back in the game. "It's not that he doesn't at all—and Christ knows those queer fucking bitches who work for him don't give a shit what he does to her—but there are too many other people involved in the production for him to take a chance of getting caught doing anything overt."

Alyssa snorted again with narrowed eyes. "All of you can take care of Lancaster's skanky ass before this is all over with, but those tools on Isadora's staff are *mine*. I'll be whacking their tiny little dicks the fuck off before we're done. Asshats."

"Easy, *mia fogata*," Jaime murmured before the corner of her mouth quirked and she squeezed Alyssa's hand again.

"What are our next steps?" Blake asked, absent-mindedly playing with the pen in front of her as she absorbed everything about which they'd been talking.

"Now that the communication channel between Nova and Isadora is open, I think we need to tell her about our proposed plan." Trill rapidly explained the trap they were considering for Chad Lancaster to everyone in the room. She looked at the entire crew solemnly when a dark look hit the assembled faces.

"Nova and I discussed this at length, and we're not one fucking bit happy that we'd be asking Isadora to put herself in Lancaster's crosshairs again. But I'm certain the most effective way to shut him down is to catch him red-handed in the act of beating Isadora. We need to get his abuse clearly on film.

"Jaim, we're going to get you photos of a pair of Isadora's favorite earrings and have you make a duplicate pair with a tiny camera hidden inside one of them. Nova…you, Alyssa, or Delaney need to find out from Isadora what her favorite pair of earrings are, the ones she's the most prone to wear that wouldn't rouse any suspicion."

The women nodded their understanding.

"Most of all, Isadora needs to understand that this is *her* decision alone, fam. We'll support her either way, no matter what she decides…although I have a deep suspicion she's going to agree to this. If this is something she doesn't think she can do, however, then we'll just figure out an alternate plan. No matter what, though…Isadora Nightingale is going to understand she is no longer alone, and it will be a cold goddamn day in hell before that piece of shit motherfucker *ever* keeps her a prisoner of his sick abuse again."

Chapter 13

"I'm hungry. I didn't make any plans for dinner because I didn't know how late it would be before we got home, but there's a decent bunch of stuff to cook." Nova peered into the refrigerator. "What do you want to eat, Trill? I know you're probably starving, too."

Trill wrapped her arms around Nova from behind and nuzzled the side of her neck. "I am the undisputed champion of stir-fry, little diva, so why don't we collaborate in the kitchen and see what we can come up with together?"

Forty minutes later, Nova leaned over the large skillet and sniffed deeply. "My God, Trill, this smells incredible. I think we make a good team." While Trill had cut boneless chicken breast into thin strips and quickly diced bell pepper, zucchini, snow peas, and scallions, Nova had whisked together a finishing sauce made from minced fresh garlic, freshly grated ginger, dark soy sauce, toasted sesame oil, and Chinese five-spice powder. The entire apartment was filled with hunger-inducing smells.

"We do, baby. Let's get some plates and go eat because I am now rabidly hungry after smelling what we've done."

After dinner, both of them replete, they moved over to Trill's big armchair and collapsed in it together. "Leave the dishes for now, baby. I'll get them in a little bit," Trill said lazily as she held Nova to her and nuzzled her neck again.

Nova turned and kissed Trill for a long minute before she pulled away and cast her eyes around the room. "I've noticed you seem to like plain, monochromatic colors, Trill," she observed, looking at the grays and blacks of Trill's apartment. "Your office at APS is the same way." She thought about her and Gillian's apartment, which had exploded in a riot of color.

"Baby, I've never had time for any decorating shit. My mom has volunteered on more than one occasion to brighten things up, but I'm so busy at work, it's just never been a priority. Frankly, for as much as I'm usually home, it's never been worth the trouble.

"But you live here now, so I'll be home a lot more often and I want you to be comfortable. I'm thinking you and Mom can get together and do whatever the fuck you want." The handsome APS team lead ran her hands down Nova's petite body. "Just don't put any pink shit on the walls, okay?"

Nova snorted. "Dude. Seriously? Do I look like some kind of fluffy, pink tutu chick to you?" She sank into Trill as she felt the rise of Trill's dominance in the strong hands that wandered over her body, redecorating forgotten.

"I need to take a shower," she whispered after Trill had lifted the hard, commanding mouth that had taken possession of Nova's for a long minute. "I can help you clean up real fast and then go do that."

"Baby, I said I would get the dishes." Nova shivered at Trill's stern, implacable tone. "I would hate to spank that gorgeous little ass because you're being stubborn. I'd much, *much* rather play with you tonight. And I'm really looking forward to my dessert." A gush of wetness escaped Nova's body and soaked her panties.

After going into the bedroom, Nova pulled her long waves into a messy bun and took her shower then went into the bedroom wrapped only in a towel. She was pulling a clean pair of panties and a tank top out of her suitcase—which still had yet to be unpacked, they'd been so busy—when Trill came into the bedroom. The corner of Trill's mouth lifted in a humorless smile.

"You aren't going to have clothes on long enough to matter, little diva." Trill flipped off the overhead light so the only illumination came from a soft night light by the bed.

"Come here, baby." Trill's voice, while soft, made it clear that she expected Nova's full cooperation. Her heart thundering in her chest, Nova moved closer to the dominant butch. "Tonight, we're going to see how well you follow direction, little diva. I'm also curious to see how well you tolerate restraints."

Trill reached up and freed Nova's hair from her bun so that the long waves fell down her back. "How do you react when your arms are bound up over your head? Does your pussy spasm when your legs are held open and restrained so that nothing is shielded from my gaze? What happens when I lick and nibble and suck your clit then slide my tongue into you while you can't move?"

Nova's nipples hardened and she felt moisture running down her legs as she whimpered. Trill reached out and pinched one of Nova's nipples through the towel until she gasped. "How do you react when

I slide my cock into you and fuck you, bound, until you lose your voice because you've screamed for so long and so hard? What happens when I make you come over and over and over again until you're pleading, *begging*, for my mercy?"

"Trill." Nova's voice barely had any strength.

"Nuh uh, little diva. I did not give you permission to speak."

Nova drew in a shocked breath and her eyes grew huge.

Trill wrapped her arms around the diminutive brunette. "My strong, beautiful femme. I would like your permission to play with you, Nova. I would also like to know that you are ready to extend your trust to me right now…and that you know I will keep you safe and respect your boundaries always. I told you before, I am not a formal Dominant. But I would like to play with you tonight as a Dominant often plays with her submissive, that you obey me fully while we are together tonight…but you also trust that if you say *'Stop'* because something is too much for you, I will honor that and stop."

Nova was shaking and aroused and a little scared, but she also knew she had never before trusted anyone in her life the way she now trusted Trillian Dacanay.

"I trust you, Trill," she whispered as she planted her face into Trill's chest. "I'm so nervous and scared right now…but I also know you would never, *ever* hurt me. I want…I want to make you happy. I want to *please* you, oddly enough. The biggest thing I'm worried about is that I'm afraid of disappointing you, because I don't know what to do."

Trill lifted her chin and kissed her gently. “Thank you for your trust, little one,” she whispered back to Nova. “There is no way you could *ever* disappoint me, unless you weren’t honest about what you really wanted and needed. The only thing you need to do is follow my direction implicitly, baby. Do what I tell you to do when I tell you to do it, and everything will be just fine. You have my pledge and my promise.

“I’m going to take you to heaven tonight, Nova MacLeod. And know that by the time this night is over, you will be irrevocably bound to me as mine forever—body, mind, and soul.”

ϑωϑωϑωϑ

Trill then disengaged herself from Nova’s arms and stepped backward. “Drop the towel, little diva,” she instructed calmly. Nova took a deep breath and let the towel wrapped around her slide to the floor. She trembled slightly as Trill’s intense brown eyes slid over her naked body. “Exquisite,” Trill murmured. Those intense eyes met Nova’s.

“As I’ve already said, you need my permission to speak, Nova. Although I don’t typically use them because I don’t practice formal dominance and submission, I also think allowing you to pick a safe word tonight would be a good idea since this is the first time you’ve ever done anything like this.”

Nova looked at her, uncomprehending.

"This kind of play is something new to you, so I need to make sure you feel absolutely secure in my ability to understand your needs and boundaries. Okay?" Nova nodded before Trill continued. "By picking a word you can say during our play that will *one hundred percent* guarantee everything stops if you become too overwhelmed, you'll know without a shadow of a doubt that you have a way to halt *everything* if it gets to be too much for you. Because things are going to get very intense, Nova."

Trill's eyes softened and became kind. "Feel free to speak now so you can tell me what word you'd like to use, little diva. Something easy to remember, but not something that you might be prone to yell out anyway if things get fierce, such as *'No!' or 'Stop!'* Many formal submissives use the word *'red'* as a safe word."

Nova thought for a moment. "Can we use the word 'gelato'?" she asked, uncharacteristically shy.

"Baby, we can use whatever word you'd like. *Gelato* it is." The corner of Trill's mouth quirked up before her eyes became stern again. "Now, I want you to climb on the bed and kneel, facing the headboard. Hold onto it with your hands then widen your legs so that your pussy is open to me. Then wait for my command."

Shaking like a leaf, but more aroused than she'd ever been in her life, Nova did as she was told.

She'd never before felt this vulnerable and exposed to anyone, yet she couldn't deny the excitement Trill had already aroused in her just from her words alone.

She heard Trill moving around the bedroom, a drawer opening and closing, then Nova felt the mattress sink as Trill climbed up in the bed behind her. Nova's thighs were already soaking wet from the arousal pouring out of her, and her heart thundered in her chest as she waited to see what Trill would do next.

A featherlight touch slid up the inside of her wet thighs. "So drenched for me already,'' Trill murmured. Nova jumped as she felt a long, strong finger ease its way through the soft hair at the juncture of her legs. "Widen your legs as far as they will go and hold tightly to the headboard, Nova." Trill's entire hand then began to rub Nova's exposed, wide-open pussy after Nova had done as she had instructed. Nova whimpered harder, her pussy clenching in a desperate effort to capture Trill's teasing fingers. Nova cried out as Trill slid one of her fingers inside of her. The handsome butch added a second finger and began to stroke them in and out of Nova's needy body. Nova ground her pussy down onto Trill's fingers in response, feeling her peak rise faster than it ever had.

Just before the fastest orgasm of her life hit her, Trill stopped and pulled her fingers out of Nova's body. "No-o-o-o!" Nova wailed, letting go of the headboard, her body rebelling against Trill's denial. A strong *smack!* echoed through the bedroom when Trill slapped her ass and Nova drew in a deep breath at the sharp correction.

"I did not give you permission to either speak or to let go of the headboard, Nova. Resume your position and be thankful I don't fully spank your ass for your infraction." At Trill's uncompromising words, a flood of arousal poured out of Nova's body. She grabbed the headboard again, whimpering softly, and tried to ignore her painful need.

A low, sinful laugh reached her ears and Trill felt her gush of arousal. "I'm beginning to think you want a spanking, little diva. You know, there is a big difference between a punishment spanking and an erotic spanking." A strong hand caressed her ass.

"Punishment spankings hurt without any type of pleasure involved because they are meant to teach a lesson. With an erotic spanking, however, spanking and playing are alternated so you feel both pleasure and pain. By the time your Dominant lets you come, you'll be screaming so hard from the intensity of the release, you'll actually lose consciousness in many cases."

That low laugh again. "Well, the way *I* give an erotic spanking, anyway."

Nova felt movement on the bed behind her again. "Let go of the headboard and move backward into the center of the bed, little diva. Keep your legs spread, rest your upper body down on your elbows, and raise your ass into the air. And *don't* move." When Nova was where Trill wanted her, she screamed when Trill gave her three sharp smacks on her ass then mewled when she felt Trill's hands separate her pussy lips. Nova choked as Trill's mouth then started to devour her from behind, her tongue and lips licking and sucking her until she thought she would lose her mind.

When Nova was shaking so hard she thought she was going to collapse, Trill flipped her over on her back and rapidly ran a soft rope around her wrists. She tied Nova's hands firmly to the bedposts then did the same thing with her legs so that Nova was spread-eagle and completely open to Trill. Clad only in a sports bra and a pair of boxer briefs that had a hard bulge in them, Trill then tied a blindfold around her eyes.

Nova gasped in deep breaths, all but out of her mind, and tried to squirm against her restraints. She felt Trill check her bindings to make sure they weren't too tight…then, the dominant butch came down over Nova, caging her beneath her hard body.

Nova gave a shuddering, helpless moan as she felt the tip of Trill's strap-on cock at the entrance to her body. Another surge of moisture escaped Nova's body. "I'm going to fuck you, little diva," Trill said softly with a growl. "You're tied down, you're blindfolded, and you're *completely* helpless. I can do anything I want to you, can't I?" Nova felt Trill's cock penetrate into her an inch and a scream started to build in the back of her throat. "You. Are. *Mine*, Nova MacLeod. My partner, my equal in all things…the love of my life."

Nova felt her heart stutter in shock even as Trill sank another inch into her needy body.

"When we are in bed together, I take care of everything. I take care of *you* and your needs. You obey me in everything when you are in my bed because I am the one in charge here. But everywhere else? Everywhere else, we stand side by side. I protect you while you kick ass like you always have, beautiful." Trill sank the whole way into Nova and planted herself as far as she could go. Nova cried out, feeling so full, so captured, so dominated by her butch lover…but also cherished in a way she couldn't explain.

Then, Trill began to move, slowly at first, and then harder and faster. She leaned down and captured Nova's mouth and kissed her hard as Nova kissed her back just as ferociously. "You're mine forever, little diva," Trill whispered when she had released Nova's mouth, driving decisively into the diminutive brunette. "You are my sun and my moon and my stars, and I will love you forever." A flood of tears cascaded down Nova's face at Trill's passionate, romantic words, even as she felt her orgasm build and her desire reach a fever pitch.

"Come for me, Nova," Trill commanded, her powerful thrusts bringing Nova right to the precipice. Nova screamed as she exploded, the combustible heat of her release sending her spiraling into the stratosphere. She continued to scream as Trill planted herself inside of her one more time and groaned as she came with her.

Vaguely, Nova felt Trill untie her bindings, and she blinked in the dim light when Trill gently eased off her blindfold. She sighed, a sob catching in her throat as Trill pulled her into her protective arms and said, "I love you, Nova," as she kissed Nova's forehead. A hazy gray film then fell over Nova's eyes as a sense of peace flooded her being…and her last conscious thought was that she would love Trillian Dacanay forever as well, before the darkness took her.

Chapter 14

A short while later, Nova woke to find herself still nestled in Trill's arms. "There's my baby," Trill whispered, nuzzling Nova's cheek. "How are you feeling, little diva?" Nova's heart contracted when she realized that Trill had once again bathed her, changed the bed linens, and tied her long hair back while she was asleep. She looked at Trill as tears started to run down her cheeks, so overwhelmed with what she was feeling, she wasn't sure what to say. In the end, there was only one thing she *could* say.

"I love you too, Trill." Nova's voice was faint as she sniffled. "For as many years as I've had a crush on you, I never in my wildest dreams believed that you felt the same way. That we would end up here, together. I don't think you'll ever, *ever* understand just how much I really *do* love you, Trillian Dacanay. And I will love you forever, too."

Trill leisurely kissed her cheek and wrapped her arms more tightly around Nova's petite frame. "Enough to marry me, little diva?" she asked softly. Nova drew in a sharp breath, shocked at Trill's unexpected words.

"I want you to be my wife, baby. I want the world to see a ring on your finger and to know that you belong to someone. That you are loved and cherished, and that there's someone in this world who has staked a claim on you.

"I don't care if you want a big wedding like Bryn and Rowan are going to have. I don't care if you want a casual beach wedding like Riley and Kelly did, or if you want to sneak off like the Malloys. *I. Don't. Care.* I just want to marry you so I can shout from the rooftops that Nova MacLeod Dacanay is *my* wife. Say *yes*, baby…please."

Nova burst into tears. "Yes," she choked then threw herself on Trill and covered her face in kisses. Trill laughed at Nova's unbridled reaction and rolled over so Nova was caged beneath her. "How many years I've dreamed of this." Trill's voice was still soft as she nuzzled Nova's neck. "I want you to come with me to pick out your ring, baby. I suspect that between your food styling and your domestic abuse rescue, you're going to want something simple…but a ring that's unconventional too, I suspect. Then we'll get matching bands for our actual ceremony.

"Mom and Dad want to meet us out for lunch this weekend, and Zaph and his wife want to come as well. I think we should invite your parents too and break the news to everybody at one time. The moms will probably cause a scene of absolutely ridiculous proportions, but hopefully the dads will keep them from destroying the place."

Nova laughed through her tears.

"You know what I'd really like to do for our wedding, Trill? I want to ask Wade Jimenez if he'd let us take over the Pier House

Grill for an entire day. We can get married out in their back gardens because it's beautiful out there then set up the entire reception buffet on their veranda. It's huge but cozy, and it will feel just a little more serious than what Kelly and Riley did…but not as crazy formal as Bryn and Rowan are going to do."

Nova snorted as she snuggled more closely into Trill's arms. "Forget about getting away with anything like Teag and Delaney did, though. Your mom and my mom would kick my ass so hard I'd be feeling it for the next two months."

Trill threw back her head and laughed.

"Sold, little diva. It sounds like a plan to me. Now, what about timing? Teagan and Delaney are going to Ireland in August, and then Bryn and Rowan are getting married at the end of October."

Nova smiled as she lifted her eyes shyly to Trill. "I always thought if I ever got married, I'd like to get married at Christmas time, believe it or not, when everything is decorated in red and green. Not only is red my favorite color, but in Chinese culture, the color red means fortune and happiness. Chinese brides usually wear a red wedding dress and I'd like to do the same, even though I'm not from that culture."

"If that's what you want and if that's what will make you happy, then that's what we'll do. Val will lose her fucking mind at the thought since she is of Chinese descent, and I know her mom would be happy to answer any questions you might have. Mrs. Chan is awesome. And I don't mind waiting a little while until we get married."

She smirked as she caressed Nova's face. "Bryn has been squawking like a little bitch because she has to wait until the end of October, but the fuck anyone's overriding what Rosi Armstrong has decreed."

Nova giggled.

Trill kissed her again. "Go to sleep, little diva. You're exhausted, and you have to deal with Lancaster and his idiot minions again tomorrow. In the meantime, we'll start kicking around ideas on how to extract Isadora without risking her reputation or irrevocably harming her career.

"I love you, my precious almost-wife." Trill kissed the tears that had started to slide down Nova's face again. "You made me the happiest butch in the universe tonight. And I vow to you with everything in me that you will be as safe, happy, and cared for as you deserve to be for the rest of our lives together."

ə·ωə·ωə·ωə·

"A tropical wave has started to form out in the Gulf, about sixty miles north of Cancun." Kenn was tapping rapidly on her phone. "Spaghetti models have the forecast track all over the place right now. Some take it straight north to New Orleans, some have it making landfall in the Florida Panhandle or the Big Bend area, some have it turn to the east before it hits the west coast of the state somewhere.

"Right now, the National Weather Service does not foresee this system developing into anything greater than a weak tropical storm, maybe 40 mph sustained winds. You know both the APS complex and our apartments were built to withstand 155 mph wind speeds, which are Category 5 hurricane-level winds. No worries there. As usual, our families and close friends will just shelter with us because it's doubtful the state will call an evacuation for something like this."

"This fucking early in the season? Jesus." Casey rolled her eyes. "I personally want to know how that dick Lancaster and his minions are going to handle this. I'm sure that from what Trill and Peyton told us, all Nova has to do is break down her shit, stash it in her rig, and drive away. Boom! She's out of danger.

"I don't know the first thing about how movie sets are constructed though, so I don't know what it would take to break one down…or even if it has to be broken down at all. I mean, how sturdy are they? Nova said it went up pretty fast."

"According to little diva, they're pretty sturdy. Set designers usually have some kind of training or degree in architecture as well as design." Trill was perusing her laptop screen. "Lancaster might be a fucking douche and his set designer probably kisses his ass, but that doesn't mean the set designer doesn't know what he's doing.

"Lancaster's movies gross a ton of money and that doesn't happen with a shoddy production, no matter how appealing the star is. I'm betting the set designer has already accounted for the possibility of inclement weather and has made plans accordingly. If this really is a weak tropical system, they'll have to secure the small design stuff, but the set itself should be fine."

"What I want to know," Drew leaned back her chair and interlaced the fingers of her hands on the back of her head, "is what else we can do to get Isadora away from Lancaster, without him ruining her reputation or destroying her career…or without putting her into harm's way, like we've already discussed.

"Some might think it sounds stupid to be worrying about shit like that when Isadora is already being physically harmed, but that's who we are. And that piece of shit has taken enough from her without her having to give up her career as well because he's a vindictive dick. But deliberately putting a woman in the path of an abuser like that, even when it's for a solid reason and she is totally on board with the plan? That fucking makes me want to *puke*."

"Agreed." Riley was darkly contemplative. "Kelly and I talked about this more last night ourselves. My wife is beyond pissed at the thought of Lancaster putting his hands on Isadora again. We all are. But…Kel also said by taking herself out of the situation and looking at it without emotion, it makes sense to work with Isadora and lay a trap for him that way.

"She says that when it comes down to it—even though we all fucking *abhor* the thought—*that motherfucker beats Isadora.* He always has, and he always will until he's stopped for good. She said we would *not* be asking her to deliberately provoke him…just to make it possible for her to record his violence when it happens.

Because we all *know* it's going to happen again sooner or later, no matter what."

"Then we can nail his balls to the wall." Jaime's voice was as dark as Riley's face. "I'm in the process of getting the recording earring ready for Isadora, and I can complete it as soon as I get the photos of her favorite earrings from Nova. Kelly's right, unfortunately. We know it's just a matter of time before we'll have his abuse caught on tape, even if we fucking hate the thought of what Isadora will have to endure to get it.

"I really think we need to focus on what we're going to do with that tape once we have it. How do we release it to cause him maximum damage and to protect Isadora the most?" Jaime turned and looked at Bryn. "Same plan we used when we fucked up Dino Coravani for Rowan? Explode it across all the major news stations and let the news wires pick it up from there?"

"It worked to expose that son of a bitch, so there's no reason to believe it won't work for Lancaster either," Bryn replied. "The minute that tape is released, Mama is going to hide Isadora. Riles and I have already talked to her and filled her in on the situation." The corner of her mouth quirked up and the twins gave each other ironic looks. "Sometimes, Mama's reactions make us almost feel sorry for the shitheels who put themselves in her crosshairs. *Almost*."

"Lancaster is still unaware that any of us know about what he's been doing to Isadora all these years." Trill's light brown eyes darkened until they were almost black. "All I know is that the fucking piece of shit is also going to pay for every single ounce of worry he's caused my fiancée throughout this whole goddamn ordeal." There was a moment of silence as the twins and the rest of the Seven registered the impact of what Trill was telling them.

"Dude! Fucking A! You're *engaged*? Outstanding!" Blake jumped up, followed immediately by the rest of the APS team. Broad grins, back slaps, and tight hugs from the entire team came from all sides as everyone put aside the seriousness of their conversation for a moment to congratulate Trill.

"You have been *fascinated* by Nova MacLeod since the day she walked into the Whimsy fifth-grade classroom." Kenn smirked, crossing her arms over her chest. "On one hand, we had you…all serious and a total brainiac even when we were ten, then in walks this tiny thing with enough balls and snark for a girl three times her size."

"That fuckwit Brian Bonaire is lucky the twins were the ones who took care of him for bullying Nova her first week there, not me." Trill raised an eyebrow. "I would have done a lot worse than glue his skanky ass to a toilet seat."

Everyone grinned at the memory.

"When's the wedding?" Casey wanted to know.

"Nova wants to get married around Christmas and I don't mind waiting until then." Trill shrugged. "That way we're past all this fucking bullshit with that tool Lancaster and she can relax. Well, inasmuch as she'll *ever* relax, because domestic abuse rescue isn't anything she'll ever give up."

"You tell little sis that whatever she needs to keep doing what she's doing, we'll make it happen for her." Blake was uncharacteristically solemn. "Where is she anyway? I would have thought she'd want to be here with you to break the news."

Trill snorted. "She said the last thing she fucking needed was to deal with a bunch of emotional butches and told me I could tell you all myself." Trill burst out laughing at the look on everyone's face. "She's still as goddamn snarky as she was in grade school, and I predict she's going to be spending a lot of time over my knee in the coming years."

The APS management team began laughing in turn.

"Life will never, *ever* be boring with Nova MacLeod at my side, that's for sure."

&ω&ω&ω&

"It's something you need to think about very, very carefully, Isadora." Nova kept the look on her face bright for the benefit of any onlookers in the area. "There is absolutely no way Chad will be able to find that transmitter…but you also need to understand it will be on 24/7 if you decide to do this. The only way to totally keep your privacy will be to take that earring out of your ear."

Alyssa had the script open next to her and Isadora, looking back and forth from the script to her sketch pad as if she was sketching a dish on Nova's list from the script. "We need to know exactly what your favorite earrings look like so that Jaime Quintero, one of the APS management team leaders, can have them perfectly duplicated. She's already working on it. Do you have a pair you wear often when you're not dressing up for a role or going out in public?"

"As a matter of fact, I do,'' Isadora said slowly. "If you look on the front page of my website, there is a candid of me there…I'm standing next to Chad in an emerald-green blouse, and my hair is pulled back into a ponytail. I have my favorite earrings on in that photo, and you can see them very clearly because my hair is out of the way."

Nova reached for her phone and casually pulled up Isadora's website under the guise of making a note. "That's perfect, that's exactly what we need," she said when she saw the photo. "I'm going to lift the photo and send it to Jaime so she can get started."

"But wait…all the photos on my website are protected. I don't know how they did it, but they made it impossible for anyone to take any photos from the site. Even if you try to do it with a simple screenshot, it will gray the picture out."

Nova snorted. "You have absolutely no idea who I'm dating, Isadora." Then she smirked. "Trillian Dacanay of the APS Seven is the most brilliant butch in seven counties when it comes to data and technical security. This will be child's play for her." Nova rapidly sent Trill a text with the link to Isadora's website. "Did that motherfucker give you any trouble last night? Over not being able to get Alyssa's sketchbooks?" Nova smoothed out the slight frown that had formed between her eyebrows at the thought.

"Surprisingly, no." The relief in Isadora's voice was clearly evident. "I guess Dale told him Alyssa had refused to give him her sketchbooks…then he told Chad I had tried to get them as well and she had turned me down, too. He…" Isadora hesitated for just a brief moment, "he told me I was nothing but a useless bitch, but that was all."

"Maybe I'll change my mind," Alyssa murmured as the strokes of her pencil quickened. "Maybe I'll call dibs on the pussy minions *and* Mr. Thinks-He's-Hot-Shit and take them both the fuck out by myself. Those useless motherfuckers have wasted enough of the planet's oxygen."

"Girl, Jaime will freak right the fuck out if she thinks you're going to do something that will put yourself in danger…and there's no telling *what* she'll do if you actually step in some shit. Pissing off an APS bad ass is *not* recommended. Trust me, I know from personal experience."

Alyssa rolled her eyes. "Oh, please. Jaime Quintero is the *last* person in this world that I'm afraid of, MacLeod. Besides, I am *not* hers. She doesn't get to tell me what I can and cannot do."

"That's what you think," Nova muttered. She glared in Peyton's direction as the APS butch looked at her with a broad grin on her face. Just then, Nova stopped what she was doing as she saw Chad Lancaster and his group of minions heading in their direction. She sighed in exasperation. "Incoming," she snarked, not bothering to lower her voice or stop what she was doing. "The heralds of sweetness and light approach."

Alyssa snickered.

"Ms. MacLeod!" Chad Lancaster's strident tones reached her ears. "Ms. MacLeod, are you not done with wasting my wife's time with your inane instruction yet?" He glanced around, noting that Delaney was not present. "Where is the other one? The one who was supposed to be teaching my wife how to properly handle a knife for the film? You are costing this production money by deviating from the schedule!"

"Ms. Sedgwick's presence was not required today." Nova's voice was equally forceful. "Until Ms. Riker has sketched all the finished food dishes that will be needed for actual filming, there was little need for Ms. Sedgwick to be here. She will be on hand to show Isadora how to properly execute them once that's completed."

"That's Ms. Nightingale to *you*, Ms. MacLeod!" Lancaster was outraged. "How dare you act as though you have the right to speak to her as a peer? You're nothing but a food stylist! And *not* one who was *my* choice, may I remind you!" He glared at Isadora, who put her head down and seemed to fold in on herself.

Nova's temper hit the stratosphere as she decided once again that she was *done* with this prick. "Ms. Nightingale was apparently gracious enough to overlook any impropriety in my interactions with her, which is *far* more than I can say for *you*. You are *arrogant*, you are *rude*, and any delays stemming from our part in this production can be laid at *your* feet." Nova breathed fire into Lancaster's red face as she let loose.

"Now, I very strongly suggest you leave, take your minions of darkness with you, and *let us do our jobs*. If you continue to interrupt me with your useless prattle and cause me to go off schedule, you'll be speaking to my lawyer. I am *done* with you, your useless underlings, and your attempts to cause constant interruption and chaos on this production." She met Lancaster's livid face with a wicked look of her own.

"I think perhaps the executive producer needs to know exactly what his director has been doing to deliberately force disruptions and why. You may be Mr. Big Shit Hollywood Director, Lancaster, but I doubt he'd be pleased to find out you've jeopardized a very lucrative contract with one of the top food stylists in the country—one that could potentially cost him a boatload of money if it's canceled, incidentally—and have greatly lessened the possibility of turning this production into something Oscar-worthy with your antics. And trust me…I will be *more* than happy to have that conversation with him."

In the interest of protecting Isadora, Nova then said, "Now, I think you and your lackeys need to get back to work and stop interrupting mine. Stay out of my way, Lancaster, or I *will* be having that conversation with Tony Girardi. Your wife also needs to understand that I don't want to hear her defending your poor choices and making excuses for your behavior anymore."

She turned to Isadora. "I'm sorry if I offended you by using your first name, Ms. Nightingale, and I apologize if you didn't feel you could correct my personal interactions with you at any time. I also hope you understand there is a serious conflict between Mr. Lancaster and myself, and I would appreciate it if you would refrain from trying to 'clarify' his behavior in the future."

Isadora nodded with an impassive look on her face.

"Goodbye, Lancaster. My crew and I have work to do and you are keeping us from it." Nova turned her back on Chad Lancaster and started to send a text.

"This isn't over, Ms. MacLeod." Chad Lancaster's voice was low and poisonous. "I will see to it that you are ruined in Hollywood if it's the last thing I *ever* do."

Nova looked over her shoulder and smirked at the irate director. "I truly doubt that. If there's one thing I've figured out about Hollywood, people will do whatever it takes to win recognition and awards. If it comes down to a choice between either making a presumptuous prick like you happy, *or* winning an Oscar because they've had assistance with their food-styling needs from me or my mother? I think I know which option they'll pick." Nova turned around, dismissing him once again, and went back to her text.

The minute the sounds from Chad Lancaster's noisy and clearly angry departure had faded and he was out of earshot, Nova immediately looked at Isadora. "You do know that was to protect you, don't you?" she said quietly to the actress.

"I know." Isadora's tones were equally subdued. She looked back down at her sketchbook. "He really, really has it in for you, Nova. I'm worried for you. Chad is a very powerful man and if he's decided he's going after you, there's nothing that will stop him. I've seen him destroy more people than I can count in the last twelve years."

"Honey, you have *no* idea who my fiancé is. As a matter of fact, you have no idea who Armstrong Protection Services is in general, let alone how Trill fits into the overall scheme of things…but I think it's about time we have that conversation."

"*Fiancé?!*" Voices rose collectively in a shout at the same time as shock hit every face at Nova's words and everyone started talking at once. "Girl, I suggest you tell us *exactly* what's going on before I knock you out." Esmeralda planted her hands on her hips and glared at the tiny brunette. "What did you do, Nova?" She whirled on Peyton. "How long have *you* known about this?"

"I'm just finding out about it myself." Peyton crossed her muscled arms across her chest and stared at Nova with an arched brow. "As Esmeralda has already said, we suggest you start talking, little diva. You and Trill are *engaged?* When the hell did this happen?"

"Last night." Nova burst out laughing at the absolute bewilderment she saw on the faces surrounding her. "She still needs to get me a ring and we probably won't actually have the wedding until Christmas time, but yeah. We're engaged." Nova could not prevent the broad, happy grin that spread across her face. She squealed as Alyssa threw her arms around her.

"My bitch! You're going down just like Rowan, Kelly, and Delaney did! What in the hell has gotten into our water supply? It's like some kind of damn wedding pandemic has come to Whimsy." After Alyssa had hugged her tightly and kissed her fiercely on the cheek, she let her go so the rest of the group could give her hugs and congratulations, too.

As everyone was hugging and kissing Nova, chattering madly, Alyssa quietly stepped back to Isadora's side. "Armstrong Protection Services—or APS—is a protection and security company geared toward the needs of women. It's located in Whimsy, Isadora. They are famous on this coast for what they do, and they have the respect of every law enforcement and military organization you could ever possibly think of. Trillian Dacanay, Nova's new fiancé, is one of the nine owners and is in charge of what they call their 'Geek Crew'—the team that's in charge of their data and technical security."

Alyssa smiled gently at Isadora. "They are hellbent on helping Nova get you out and away from that jackass bastard you're married to…but they're trying to figure out the best way to do that so he doesn't go after you and destroy either your career or your reputation. Plus, you already know what Nova herself does, and she is about two seconds away from ripping that douche canoe's balls right the fuck off his body."

Isadora's eyes grew huge as Alyssa's smile broadened.

"Do you date one of them also, Alyssa? If you don't mind my asking?"

"Oh, no. No, no. I love them all to bits, but they are a little too Neanderthal for me." Alyssa rolled her eyes, but her gaze grew distant for a moment before she shook it off. "The Armstrong twins and the 'Seven,' as they're called—that's the seven team leads that run APS with the twins—all grew up in Whimsy, the same as I did. I've known them for practically my whole life.

"I don't know how familiar you are with the queer community since you're straight, but a lot of us here in Whimsy—which has a heavily gay population—belong to what is known as the butch/femme part of the community. 'Butches' are females who are more masculine in their thinking and their behaviors, and 'femmes' fall more on the feminine side of the scale."

Isadora nodded her understanding.

"The vast majority of the associates at APS belong to the butch dynamic—*especially* the nine who make up the management team. There are varying degrees of butch identity—from soft butch to stone butch—but the APS butches belong in a class all by themselves. They are protective as hell when it comes to women, and I personally wouldn't want to be on the wrong side of any one of them. They're fantastic and very kind to others in the community, but they can also be some mean motherfuckers if anyone threatens what's theirs."

"I'd like to meet them someday." Isadora's voice was shy.

"I'm pretty sure they want to meet you too." Alyssa reached out and laid her hand on Isadora's arm. "I'll be honest with you though, honey. They're gunning for your husband…and if I was Chad Lancaster, I'd make sure I had a lifetime supply of Depends around. Because he's gonna need them when the APS management team finally gets hold of him."

ఞωఞωఞωఞ

"Your eye and your aim have improved incredibly, little diva," said Trill as she removed her ear and eye protection. She smiled as a glowing Nova removed hers as well. "I think you're done for the day, though. You've had one hell of a hard one, and I don't mind telling you I'm half tempted to go and find that fuckwit Lancaster and introduce him to my fist." Her brows lowered.

"We haven't had a chance to talk about it ourselves yet, but Peyton filled me in earlier. She said she stayed calm because she didn't want to scare Isadora, but she really didn't start getting back on an even keel until you told them all we were engaged. That stupid motherfucker should count his blessings because Pey was ready to fuck his ass up." Then Trill smirked.

"She texted me after the excitement had died down and she said you're lucky Esmerelda didn't stick her foot up *your* ass."

Nova grinned.

When they had cleaned up and Nova had disarmed herself properly, they walked out of the shooting range. "By the way, where's Kenn?" Nova asked curiously. "She's always here and it's odd that she wasn't around today. She's okay, isn't she?"

"She's fine, baby. She's doing a few things in her Cage because of this tropical system that's developing out in the Gulf, even though she said the National Weather Service still doesn't know what it's going to do. You should know that both the APS headquarters complex and our apartments were built to withstand 155 mph wind speeds, so we're nowhere near being in any type of danger. Kenn said this will be a weak tropical cyclone at best, maybe winds of 40 mph or so if we're lucky.

"Then when she's done here," Trill started to laugh, "she's going to go across the street and see if our new neighbor Piper needs any help securing her new office."

Nova stared at Trill, astonished.

Trill caught Nova's hand as they headed for the entrance. "We can talk about everything more at dinner, baby. No cooking for either one of us today. We're both tired and a medium-rare rib eye from the Pier House Grill sounds like just the ticket as far as I'm concerned. I know you're not much of a red meat eater, but maybe some shrimp or pasta…or, what's that other thing Wade does that you love? Lemon chicken with artichokes and sun-dried tomatoes?"

Just then, Nova's phone went off. She frowned slightly as she looked at the display then answered the call, halting in the middle of the hallway. "Nova MacLeod."

She listened for just a brief moment before she swiftly said, "Are you safe where you are?" The hair on the back of Trill's neck stood up on end as she realized this was an at-risk woman making contact with Nova for the first time. Trill veered to the right and quickly pulled Nova into Conference Room 2 so the diminutive brunette could have some privacy.

"What area of Tampa Bay are you in and do you have regular access to a phone? How much time do we have to talk right now?" Nova listened to the voice chatter on the other end of the line for another minute. "Okay, here's what we're going to do.

"You're right in Pinellas Park, so you're not too far away from me. It sounds like you have a bit of freedom to go to the grocery store and things like that on your own, yes?...Uh huh. When is the next time you think you can call me?...Saturday afternoon then. Fine."

Trill pulled out her phone and rapidly started to capture notes from Nova's conversation.

"You know that little Qwik-Mart on U.S. 19 north right before the on-ramp to get to I-275?" Nova continued then paused for a second to listen to the voice on the other end. "Okay. Can you get there on Saturday afternoon?...Good. Saturday morning, I'll go in there and I'll leave you a prepaid cell phone he can't track in the back of all the laundry detergent—because you won't always be able to borrow someone else's phone like you did today.

"I guarantee you store clerks in places like that are too lazy to move those heavy bottles to clean and no one will find it before you can get to it…Right. When you have the phone, get somewhere where you can't be overheard and call me. We'll figure out our next steps from there."

Trill saw Nova's honey-brown eyes darken as the phone chattered again for a couple of minutes.

"It's all right, honey. I promise you, we're going to get you out. You need to be brave for just a little while longer, okay?…Okay. Take a deep breath and I'll talk to you on Saturday…You take care and don't forget you're not alone anymore." Nova ended the call then took a deep breath before closing her eyes and pinching the bridge of her nose.

Trill wrapped her arms around her clearly agitated fiancée and pulled Nova's head into her chest. "Talk to me, little diva," she said softly, nuzzling Nova's cheek.

"She's an older woman. It sounds like she's early fifties or so. No kids at home." Nova lifted her head and her eyes flamed as she stared at Trill. "Her left wrist is currently in a cast because that piece of shit she's married to broke it two weeks ago when he got drunk and kicked her down the stairs in a rage. She said his drinking has gotten completely out of control and she's afraid for her life."

Trill made a malevolent sound in the back of her throat.

"She's only been married to him for about a year, and she's originally from Salt Lake City." Nova blew out a deep breath. "She moved here with this prick after they got married because he said he wanted to come back to his hometown. He started beating her shortly after. He's a raging alcoholic and she didn't know that until they were here in Florida.

"She's had no way to contact her sister and brother-in-law back in Salt Lake because he has everything monitored, even her phone conversations with them. She told me she just wants to get away from him and go home. That's what I'm going to do, Trill. I'm going to get her home. She's able to go to the grocery store and places like that by herself because his useless ass is usually lying drunk in a bar somewhere during the day."

"She didn't dare take the risk of contacting anyone even when she was alone before because she was afraid he would find out and kill her. But now the situation has turned supercritical and she no longer feels she has a choice if she wants to stay alive," Trill guessed correctly. She blew out her own breath in turn. "Sometimes, it's the same on our end of the world, little diva. What do you need me to do to help you?"

"I need to purchase a prepaid cell phone for her before Saturday, and you heard the plan up until then. Honestly, I think if I purchase enough clothes for a couple of weeks, some toiletries, maybe some other stuff we can ship out to her sister's, she'll be in good shape initially.

"I'll give her some money so she won't be completely broke when she gets there, although she told me she could definitely get her old job back when she gets home. That's a big help right there, because usually these women are starting from ground zero…plus, I often have kids to worry about. By the grace of the Goddess, I don't in this rescue. Just her.

"I'd like to fly her out there if that's okay with you, although I usually purchase train tickets because they're a lot less expensive." Nova rested her forehead on Trill's chest again. "Thankfully, this one won't be a difficult rescue, but we do need to get her out of there immediately. Abusive alcoholics are unpredictable as fuck, although I'm sure I'm not telling you anything you don't already know. If she feels the situation has reached critical mass, then we need to move."

"You are not to worry about the money, little diva." Trill stroked the back of her head with a gentle hand. "We'll buy her what she needs, ship it out to her sister, and get her on a plane as soon as we can. Is the car she's driving hers or his?"

"Ummm…I didn't specifically ask her that question, but from the way she was talking, it's his. I can ask her for sure on Saturday. Why?"

A wicked, malicious smile curled Trill's mouth. "If it is his, you and your new friend can prearrange a place somewhere in St. Petersburg where she can park it, then she can leave with you to go to the airport when it's time for her to go. I'll grab Jaime to go with me to get it as soon as you two are gone. You can have your friend leave the keys in the ignition for me, and you can tell her someone you know will be taking care of the car for her. I assume the registration will be in the glove box, which is where most people keep it, but you can find that out on Saturday as well."

That wicked smile deepened. "I'll drive it to the most crime-ridden neighborhood we know of in Tampa, as far as vehicular theft goes—pocket the keys, but leave the car unlocked, and drive away with Jaim. That fucker loves shit like this, so I know she'll be all in. I'll throw the keys down a sewer grate somewhere over there in Hillsborough County and we're done. That car will be stripped within an hour."

Nova stared at her, astonished.

"What?" That wicked smile grew deeper. "It's not illegal. I was given tacit permission by the owner's wife to drive it, but it was unfortunate I parked it in such a risky area and forgot to lock it. And that's in the very, very unlikely event I'm connected to the car in any way in the first place.

"It certainly isn't illegal for his wife to drive it nor park it in such a dangerous place while forgetting to lock it…foolish maybe, but not illegal. I certainly hope Mr. Asshat is smart enough to keep his mouth shut, because I'm sure the lady will be *more* than willing to talk to the Tampa police about his abuse of her once she's safely back in Salt Lake City with her family. Consider this payback for every time that fucker put his hands on her and hurt her."

Nova burst out laughing.

"Oh, you're evil." Nova couldn't help the broad smile that covered her face as she lifted her hand and ran them over Trill's deep dimples. "I love you, Trillian Dacanay. I think we're going to make one hell of a team, don't you?"

"Undoubtedly." Trill kissed her deeply. "Since we can't do anything else tonight and you have a couple of days before your friend goes to the Qwik-Mart to pick up her new cell phone, I'm still taking you out to dinner tonight. You need to relax and eat before I take you home and show you all the ways you excite me beyond belief. I love you too, Nova MacLeod, and I will always do whatever I need to do to make sure these women are safe, right along with you."

Chapter 15

"Damn, bitch." Nova swiped her sweaty bangs out of her eyes. "What's with the fucking She-Ra shit? You need to slow that roll down, girlfriend." She and Alyssa were in Hades practicing their self-defense.

Alyssa smirked then called a timeout. She went over to the ledge that ran around the huge APS gym and took a long gulp from her water bottle. "You pussy," she taunted Nova with a playful arch of her eyebrow when she was done. "I'm not that much bigger than you, so get your scrawny ass moving. Your honey wants you to know how to defend yourself the best that you can…and after being exposed to that asshat Lancaster myself, I can't say I blame her. At the very least, this will make it *much* easier for you to stick your foot up his ass."

Nova rolled her eyes, the corner of her mouth quirking up.

A grinning Jess Evanston pushed herself off the wall where she had been lounging. "Come on, little diva," she said, uncrossing her heavily muscled arms then nodding at Casey, who was observing from the other end of the mat. "I think part of your challenge is that you don't really want to hurt one of your posse, even as much as you two snark at each other the way you do. It makes you hold back.

Alyssa is not much better…she was also holding back—she was just moving faster than you were so her strikes looked harder."

"What Jess said." Casey came up behind them. "Alyssa, I want you with Jess, and Nova, you'll be with me. We're going to practice the Krav Maga routines you've been learning over the past weeks, and I want the two of you to go *hard* at us. I promise you, you won't hurt us. We won't be hitting back, just defending against your strikes and coaching you as we go. We want to make sure you will be as efficient as possible if you ever find yourself in a position to have to defend yourself."

"If they ever do, you can be sure there are some soon-to-be-dead motherfuckers out there who will find themselves in the crosshairs of some very pissed-off APS bad asses." Two new voices joined them. Nova and Alyssa turned around to find Trill and Jaime standing at the edge of the mat, arms crossed decisively over their chests.

Nova gave Trill a droll look. "The best part about being this short is that you can punch an asshole right between the legs and send his nuts up into his throat without too much effort, Trill. It's all good."

Trill burst out laughing as she looked at Nova with heat in her eyes. "I don't doubt that one bit, baby," she responded dryly, "but let's let Casey and Jess do their thing so I feel more comfortable about turning you loose on the general population."

Casey and Jess chuckled as they got into position.

For the next hour, Nova and Alyssa listened seriously to their instruction as they learned how to put all the maneuvers they had practiced over the past several weeks into a viable defense strategy. When Casey finally called a halt for the day and the two tired, sweaty femmes walked over to their water bottles, Jaime and Trill burst into applause.

"The more you two kept going, the tighter and more efficient your moves grew," Jaime praised. "I thought *mi hermana* was going to take this fucker's head off at one point." She waved a hand at Casey, who shot Jaime the finger as the APS physical security crew chief chuckled.

Trill gave them both an approving look. "It is clearly evident you both just keep getting better," she said. She looked at Alyssa with raised eyebrows. "For someone who gave Jaime such a rash of shit at the beginning of all this, I think you're on board now and doing a stellar job."

"Yeah, Lys. Femme domination and serious ass-kicking, remember?" Nova looked at everyone with a sly face as the APS butches snorted. The two women grinned as they gave each other a high five.

Just then, Kenn came into the gym, followed by Blake. After hugging both Nova and Alyssa and kissing them on the cheek, Kenn turned to the APS crew.

"That tropical wave has strengthened into a tropical depression, and the whole system has jogged a bit to the east. The National Weather Service still doesn't expect it to strengthen into anything beyond a very weak tropical cyclone, however, and it's still at least five or six days out. I'm going to hit our comm in a minute, but since

Blake and I were walking by, I figured I'd just pop in here and tell you in person."

"Isn't that news fucking special?" Casey rolled her eyes. "Jess and I will make sure there's room in here for any extended family to throw sleeping bags down on the floor, in case they want to shelter with us. Even though it doesn't sound like this storm is going to amount to much, there are still some low-lying areas here in Whimsy, and flooding is always a concern.

"I know Delaney's brother and sister-in-law and their family sometimes stay with us…although I think it's less of a concern about safety as it is an excuse for Delaney's niece and nephew to play with Jess."

Jess grinned.

"My mother told me Del's mom and dad are up north for a while and probably won't be back until August or September, so they aren't a worry. Everyone else knows the hurricane and tropical storm procedures for the complex since we've been doing this shit for ten years now. We've got this."

"Brooke Marino usually went to her brother's in Ocala in the past if there was a tropical system that was going to strike this area, but her brother and his family moved to North Carolina for his wife's job last winter." Blake's tone was casual. "That's a bit of a hike for a little tropical storm, so I'm going to persuade her to come here instead."

"And our new neighbor Piper lives in Shore Acres…you know how that place is a fucking flood zone." Kenn was equally casual.

"I'd already promised her she could use the shooting range here at APS as soon as she was settled, so we might as well kill two birds with one stone. I can practice with her while the storm is going on, assuming it even hits here."

Nova felt the hair on the back of her neck stand up on end.

Delaney had shared with her the remarks made by Mrs. Santoras, the elderly proprietor of KitchenWorks, the housewares shop in downtown Whimsy. Mrs. Santoras had been convinced beyond all doubt that the Goddess of her beliefs would send a mate to each one of the nine APS owners—to lend them strength as they did the Goddess's work, she said. Delaney said it had sounded a bit silly at first, but the more she had thought about it, the more it had started to make sense.

Nova and Delaney had known the entire APS management team since they were all students together in grade school. As they had gotten older, none of the butch best friends had ever evinced the slightest interest in finding a serious girlfriend, let alone a wife—although each of them had topped the charts when it came to following a dominant, predatory lifestyle after they'd matured.

When the Armstrong twins had met the Holland sisters, however, they each knew within ten minutes of meeting them that these femmes were theirs for life. Teagan Malloy and Trillian Dacanay had secretly carried torches for Delaney and Nova for years, although they had been convinced nothing between them was ever meant to be because of what they did…and how they were positive it was not a life any good femme would ever want.

As much as she loved Mrs. Santoras, Nova hadn't been sure what she believed, but…Bryn and Rowan. Riley and Kelly. Teagan and Delaney. Now, her and Trill. By the looks of things, Jaime Quintero had Alyssa Riker in her crosshairs, and a few others in the management team seemed enticed by the possibility that maybe there was someone out there just for them as well. Nova was contemplative as she thought about the feasibility.

She shook herself out of her reverie as Trill wrapped her arms around her. "Where did you go, little diva?" Trill asked softly as she nuzzled Nova's neck.

"I'm just thinking, honey. We have a lot going on right now and I'm trying to sort it all out in my head." Nova tilted her head to give Trill better access to her neck. "Are you sure you want to be doing this while I'm so sweaty?"

She felt the smile that curled Trill's mouth. "I certainly don't mind the sweat that pours off you after I've fucked you. Why should this be any different?" she whispered throatily in a low tone. Nova felt herself turn scarlet at Trill's provocative words.

"All right, you two." Alyssa cast her eyes heavenward as she picked up her water bottle and backpack. "Get a room." She laughed as Nova shot her the finger. "Seriously, I will see you all later. I have an art therapy session in twenty minutes with Brooke. I need to bring her up to speed on everything that's going on since she's taking over for me for a little while. Thanks, you guys."

She poked her forefinger in Nova's direction as she headed toward the entrance to Hades. "I'll see you on the set first thing in the morning, okay?" Then with a cryptic glance at Jaime, she was gone.

"I have some paperwork stuff to do tonight, honey," Nova said as she pulled back from Trill's hold then turned to look at Casey, Jaime, and Jess. "You all are awesome, but duty calls and I need to get back to work.

"Alyssa has sketched the first dishes for the film according to the script, and I need to start getting the shopping list together with the supplies that we'll need for the shoot concurrently. Esmeralda is taking care of finding the dietary needs and preferences of everyone on the cast and crew—because we're in charge of feeding them as well—and Susie is standing by to start shopping the minute we give her a list. I'm thinking about sending Peyton with her to help, although," Nova arched her eyebrows skeptically, "I'm not exactly sure I should trust the two of them together. Susie is a fucking troublemaker, and Peyton has that whole deceptive innocent butch thing going on, which means there's no telling the shit they'll step in if I turn them loose without supervision."

The crew laughed.

"I have your laptop in my office, baby, so I'll grab it and we'll head on home. You can take a shower while I fix us something to eat, and then you can get to work. I cleared out some room for you in my home office, although we'll have to change the whole setup and give you your own permanent office space in there. You should have more than enough room to do what you need to do tonight, though." Trill banded her arms around Nova's waist again.

"I should also warn you that I called Mom about redecorating our apartment and she's like a kid in a candy store now. Don't be surprised if she attacks you at lunch tomorrow, between this and finding out about our engagement."

Nova had always loved Alice, Trill's unconventional, quirky mother, and her kind, quiet father, Donato. "Is the weather still going to be okay? I noticed the breeze was picking up a bit this afternoon."

"It's going to be fine. Kenn is on top of it and says it's still only forecasted to be a weak tropical storm, even though it looks like the Tampa Bay area is in the cone now." The "cone" in tropical cyclone weather terminology was the probable track of the center of the storm. "We're still good to have lunch with our parents tomorrow, though…this storm is still too far away to worry about yet. Zaph and Daphne will be there too, but the kids have a playdate with their cousins, so we'll catch up with them another day. We're meeting everyone at Tapas at noon and Calliope Radcliff is ready to roll out the red carpet, she said."

"Okay." Nova rested her forehead against Trill's for a moment before she straightened up and stepped back. "Thanks again, everyone. I'll see you next week for another episode of 'Femme Fun While Kicking Butch Ass'." A mischievous smile tilted up the corners of her mouth as she caught Trill's hand and headed out of Hades amid more laughter.

ಎωಎωಎωಎ

"I cannot believe you two are getting married. *Finally!*" An exuberant Alice Dacanay gave Caprice MacLeod a triumphant high five. "How many freaking years have we been waiting for this, Caprice? Over twenty? You have no idea the mooning Trillian did over this girl while they were growing up. I was waiting for that whole Shakespeare dying of unrequited love thing before it was over with."

Trill rolled her eyes at her mother and snorted.

"Oh, really? *I* have no idea? Then explain to me why the covers of Nova's school notebooks were always covered in hearts and the initials 'TD'. It was beyond pitiful." Caprice smirked at her daughter as Nova's jaw fell open in disbelief.

"Mom!" she growled menacingly. Then her honey-brown eyes narrowed.

"They still make chocolate-flavored Ex-Lax, you know, Caprice. Wouldn't it be something if I developed a laxative-based ice cream for the Dream Creamery and oops! forgot to tell you when I gave it to you to test?" Max MacLeod and Don Dacanay, along with Zaphod Dacanay, howled and slapped each other's backs.

Caprice grabbed her daughter into a huge hug, chuckling. "Funny girl, I hope you realize your dad and I couldn't be happier." She reached across the table and caught Trill's hand to squeeze it. "I've adored you forever, Trillian Dacanay. Seriously, in my mind I could never picture Nova with anybody but you.

"I know you were gone for a long time because of your service and all of your schooling, but—without being snarky here—I want you to realize my daughter has waited for you. There was never going to be anybody else good enough for her or more suited to her than you."

"And," Max broke in, uncharacteristically serious himself, "I think maybe it's time Nova also realizes her mom and I have always known about her domestic violence survivor rescue."

Nova's jaw dropped open again and her eyes grew huge. Max gently took Nova from Caprice and wrapped her in his arms.

"Gill told us what happened to her, baby girl…not long after you got her out. She told us how you pulled her away from that son of a bitch and everything that you did to make sure his ass went to jail. I hope he doesn't see the light of day again for a long, long time.

"Then she told us you were still helping women escape bad situations. Your mom and I talked about it, and we decided not to say anything because we knew you would come to us if you needed us. When it became apparent that Trill had started helping you recently and you finally had some solid protection at your back, we breathed a sigh of relief.

"We know what Trill and her people do, kiddo. There isn't a person who lives in Whimsy who doesn't know." His mouth quirked up. "But for what you yourself have done over years, your mother and I couldn't *ever* be prouder of you than we are, pipsqueak. You are one of a kind."

Tears flowed down Nova's face as she rested her forehead on her dad's shoulder.

Alice wiped her own eyes. "The Armstrong twins and the Seven are like my own kids, Nova. They are brave, they are strong, and I am humbled by their commitment to the women in this community."

She nodded at her husband. "Trillian takes after her dad because Don is a *brilliant* data analyst. That's where she gets it from. And because Don was the one who taught Trillian that being impeccable with your word and refusing to put those you care about at risk by betraying secrets, the APS management team trusts my husband implicitly. I don't know any of the details and frankly, I don't care to know…but I *do* know he's worked with them a lot over the years, helping in their efforts where he can."

Trill looked at her father with eyes that clearly reflected her closeness to him as Don slid his arm around Alice and hugged her to his side.

"And I was the typical pain in the ass little brother." Zaph smirked and threw his napkin at Trill before rapidly growing serious. "We had the usual sibling squabbles growing up…but if there's one thing I always knew, it was that if I was ever in trouble, I could go immediately to Trill and she would take care of it. My kids love her like crazy, too—always have and always will.

"I don't think I've ever met anyone with as much integrity as she has in my whole life." Then Zaph rolled his eyes. "Now I, for one, think this lunch party has gotten too damn maudlin and deep considering we're supposed to be talking about a wedding…but if there is a point to all of this, it's that the MacLeods and the Dacanays are finally where they need to be. Welcome officially to the family, big sister. Like Mom said, finally!"

Nova laughed through her tears as everyone applauded—Zaph hooting like a maniac—and straightened up in her chair after giving her father a kiss on the cheek. "We're going to get married at Christmas time and have the wedding and reception at the Pier House Grill. Like I told Trill, something a little less casual than Kelly and Riley did, but not as crazy formal as Bryn and Rowan are going to do."

She sighed with happiness as she settled in her fiancé's arms. "All I know is that I want to marry her." She looked with love into Trill's eyes. "I told her that if you two wouldn't have killed me, I would have eloped with her the day she asked me."

"Yeah, no." Caprice frowned as Alice's eyebrows shot into her hairline. "Kathleen Malloy was perfectly fine with Teagan and Delaney doing what they did, and so was Marsha Sedgwick, but not in *this* family. We. Are. Having. A. Wedding. Please don't make me play the 'mom' card over this, Nov. I hate the 'mom' card."

"Alice can wield that bad boy like a scythe, so let her do it instead, Caprice," Don said dryly as Max snickered. Trill and Zaph burst out laughing as Alice shook her head in amusement at her husband.

Trill spoke up after she had flagged down their waiter and given him her credit card to pay the lunch bill. "Nova still has a lot of work to do for this movie shoot she's doing, so I think we're going to take off so she can get busy. I have to tell you that watching this process is fascinating. I never really thought about it before, but I'm just astounded at how damn much there is to do in a movie production."

"What's Isadora Nightingale like in person, Nova? Good Lord, she's beautiful and such a talented actress." Alice pulled her purse off the back of her chair as they all stood up to go.

"Quiet. Shy. As sweet as she can be." Nova and Trill had already agreed beforehand they weren't going to say anything about Isadora's abuse by Chad Lancaster to anyone else quite yet. "I'd like to talk her into meeting all of us out at Seashells for a drink one night before she goes back to LA…and I think she'll go, if at all possible. She admires Alyssa, Delaney, and my crew already, likes Peyton a lot, and she really wants to meet Trill…but we'll see what Lancaster has to say." Nova didn't bother to try to hide the contempt in her voice.

"Ah. One of those egotistical Hollywood jackasses, I take it?" Max took Caprice's hand. "And isn't that poor woman married to him?"

Nova snorted. "Unfortunately. That piece of crap she's stuck with could be the poster child for a big old braying donkey."

Zaph laughed uproariously, clearly delighted by his new future sister-in-law.

"You've dealt with Hollywood types before," Caprice reminded her daughter as they all moved toward the exit. "You're supposed to be done by mid-August, so just grit your teeth and hang in there, baby. You'll be done before you know it and you won't ever have to work with him again if you don't want to."

"Yes, but how much longer can Isadora hang on?" Nova whispered worriedly to Trill as they walked outside. "I'm getting nervous, Trill. Lancaster is volatile as fuck, and I don't know how much time we have left before he explodes and really hurts her. I can feel it coming."

"I know, little diva." Trill tucked Nova into her side more tightly as she whispered back, "Just stay away from him for now and keep everything as calm as you can until Jaime is done with that earring, which she thinks will be tomorrow. I'm not saying you need to take any shit from that fucker, but keep away from him as much as possible so you don't trigger him. Right now, we need to keep Isadora as safe as we can."

Trill nuzzled Nova's ear as she continued to whisper softly to her. "When the earring is done and Isadora has it in her possession, we can spring our trap like we've planned then watch as his abuse is uncovered for the entire world to see. We will throw gasoline on those flames and burn everything he has and everything he is right down to the ground. Isadora will *finally* be freed from the hell she's lived for the past twelve years, when Lancaster is exposed as the brutal, violent bastard he truly is."

ை-ω-ை-ω-ை-ω-ை

With a vicious look on his face, Chad Lancaster stared at his laptop screen, tapping his fingers on the table beside him and thinking hard.

He'd first heard about Armstrong Protection Services—or APS, as everyone called them—when he and his wife had come to Indian Shores, Florida, last winter to visit his attorney, Andrew Matheson…wanting to discuss the proposed plans for his current production in person. During the course of their conversation, Andrew had casually mentioned the wife of a friend of his had disappeared—a friend to whom Andrew had originally intended to offer a contract to oversee the accounting piece of Chad's film.

There were rumors of domestic violence, Andrew had gossiped, although he had disavowed knowledge of any actual abuse that might have taken place. Then he'd told Chad there was a local organization who provided protection services for women, and his friend was positive they had something to do with her disappearance.

"It's called Armstrong Protection Services and it's run by all these dyke women. I don't know, it's really strange. Chicks protecting other chicks? I mean, who the fuck does that?" Andrew shrugged. "All I know is that they have this big fucking reputation in the Tampa Bay area as an organization who will cut off the dicks of anyone who so much as looks sideways at a woman with intent to harm. People are either in awe of them or fucking scared to death of them, depending on which side of the fence they fall on.

"Anyhow, if the wife went running to them for help, my friend might as well kiss his own ass goodbye…because she's gone with the wind. If you're going to be filming on the Gulf beaches, Chad, you might want to make sure your staff and crew watch it if they're into that sort of thing with their bitches. It sounds like those dykes don't play." Andrew had guffawed then turned the conversation back to the movie contracts discussion.

Chad had laughed with him but had failed to see how this APS would be relevant to his production in the overall scheme of things. How he chose to discipline his own wife in the privacy of his own home was *his* business. But then he had been startled to see an APS logo on the polo shirt of the reserved, observant female who had brought that raging bitch Nova MacLeod to their initial meeting.

Nova had said her car was at her mechanic's and her neighbor had been kind enough to bring her to their meeting, so Chad hadn't thought any more of it at the time. When Nova had stalked out abruptly after their clusterfuck of a meeting and had gotten into her neighbor's SUV though, Chad had come out to see the neighbor staring fixedly at him through the front windshield. It was not a friendly look, and Chad had been disconcertedly relieved when they had driven off.

Chad scrolled down through the website of the National Weather Service until he reached the information for Tropical Storm Audrey, the first named storm of the Atlantic hurricane season. He clicked on the details page so he could read about the forecasted track of the storm and its expected strength. His mind was racing.

He had *never* had trouble with a production like he was having with this one, and it was all because of that fucking MacLeod shrew.

She was a mouthy broad who didn't know her place and thought she could do what she wanted, when she wanted, because of the contract she kept throwing in his face.

Chad narrowed his eyes as he thought next about the person who was responsible for him having to deal with this thorn in his side…*Isadora.* His normally obedient wife had told him that she refused to do this movie unless Nova MacLeod was the food stylist who was hired to take charge of the food needed for the production, and who would serve as her coach for Isadora's role as a chef. Craig Acosta wasn't good enough, she had dared to tell him, which had earned her a couple of nasty punches to her kidneys.

Astonishingly enough, Isadora had continued to press for Nova MacLeod's involvement. She wanted another Oscar, she kept telling Chad, and Craig was not the food stylist who could get her there. But Nova *was*, and Isadora had been determined to have her way in this or else she would not do the film. Chad had admitted to himself that what Isadora had said made sense, but he still gave her a couple of physical corrections, lest she thought she could continue her unseemly behavior going forward.

Continuing to tap his fingers next to the keyboard, Chad looked at the forecast track of the storm. An idea was forming in his head on how to deal with the absolute shit storm he was positive was headed his way because of that fucking useless cunt MacLeod and her band of aggravating do-gooders.

It had been nothing but one war after another in dealing with her. She had refused to acknowledge Chad's supremacy on this production and had been doing her best to disrupt every single fucking thing she possibly could. She all but threw Chad and several of his staff out of her space and forbid them to come near her setup—citing proprietary information—and then had threatened to walk off the production if Craig Acosta was not removed immediately as her "supervisor." As the icing on this shit cake, she had informed him she was going to executive producer Tony Girardi to explain to him how she was going to cost him a fucking boatload of money if she pulled out of her contract, and why she was planning on doing it. In *explicit* detail.

Ignorant bitch cunt.

After their last altercation, Chad had stomped back to the production trailer in a fury and had just managed to calm himself down when a knock came at the door. One of the contract production assistants had stuck his head in after Chad had curtly called out to enter. Chad didn't know his name, but he knew the guy had been hired on contract through a local company Andrew had retained, because of his in-depth knowledge of the area.

"Mr. Lancaster, sir. I'm sorry to interrupt, but I have the information one of those food stylist people wanted." He waved a sheaf of papers at Chad. "I don't remember her first name, but she's the one who's married to one of the APS Seven. Something Malloy? I know we've been given instructions to avoid that part of the production lot, so I'd like to know what you'd like me to do."

"The APS Seven?" Chad had spoken slowly, feeling a *frisson* of disquiet run down his spine.

"Yeah, they're kind of a big deal around these parts. The Armstrong twins and the APS Seven are the management team that runs Armstrong Protection Services and they are some bad ass motherfuckers. Oops, sorry, Mr. Lancaster." The production assistant put his hand briefly over his mouth. "Anyhow, that one food stylist is married to one of the Seven and she's the one who's asked for this. What should I do if they don't want us near their setup?"

"Go ahead down with that and tell the chief food stylist that you are delivering some information Mrs. Malloy wanted. Ms. MacLeod is extremely prickly, but she shouldn't give you a problem since you are delivering something they asked for themselves. However, please don't linger because I'm not in the mood for any more fireworks from her today."

When the production assistant had left, Chad Lancaster had ignored the million things he had to do and did a web search on Armstrong Protection Services. What he found did not make him happy. APS did not maintain their own website, but Chad still saw hundreds of comments coming from *everywhere* about the organization and what they did for the protection of women in the greater Tampa Bay area. Someone had even cobbled together a simple website that gave a brief biography of each one of the nine owners, along with a basic blog that recounted more stories and comments about them.

Chad had felt the shock running clear down to his toes when a recent blog entry had hinted that Trillian Dacanay of the Seven was now dating a local food-styling legend—Nova MacLeod—and there was speculation the two of them would end up getting married…although the information couldn't be confirmed.

Everyone at APS, both the management team and the regular associates, played their cards close to the chest, and personal information about *any* of them was never released to the public. This website and this blog were like fan pages for individuals who were fascinated by the APS associates and their almost mythical capabilities, but they had no official affiliation with them.

Now that he thought about it, that roadie on MacLeod's crew had also had the look and feel of someone who could possibly be an APS associate as well. *Jesus Christ*. His eyes narrowed. It was like he was fucking surrounded by the assholes all of a sudden.

Coming back to himself in the present, Chad thought about what his conclusions had been after everything he'd read about APS that afternoon. It was a sure bet that Isadora had spilled her guts to that bitch MacLeod when she'd found out who Nova was dating. His wife was willful, despite her outward obedience, and probably thought this was a perfect opportunity to put an end to the corrections he gave her—ones that she sorely needed on an almost constant basis because of her propensity to make poor choices.

If it ever got out that he gave one of the most popular movie stars in the world physical corrections to keep her in line and to modify her conduct, however, *he* would be the one who suffered. Chad was a powerful man in Hollywood, but Isadora was adored by millions and his reputation might not survive the coming maelstrom. He had to figure out a way to keep his useless wife quiet before she destroyed them both.

Chad stared at the forecast track of Tropical Storm Audrey. The storm was expected to make landfall in three days just to the south of the Gulf beaches. The winds had already strengthened substantially and all production preparation had been suspended so that the crews could ensure the set and everything associated with it were secured.

Because the expected winds wouldn't exceed 40 mph—because Audrey was only a weak tropical storm—the manager of the four-star hotel where they were staying on St. Pete Beach had assured him they would be perfectly safe as long as they stayed indoors. *There would be no need to evacuate, not with a storm like this*, he had promised Chad.

Tap. Tap. Tap.

It would be tragic, Chad abruptly thought to himself, tapping his fingers more rapidly as a startling idea occurred to him, *if Isadora was lost in the storm by some chance.* His eyes widened as he considered the possibility. While it was true that her movies, appearances, endorsements, etc., had made him a fortune in the past—and continued to add to his already considerable coffers today—how much more lucrative would the Isadora Nightingale brand be *posthumously*? Chad stopped to explore the notion in detail, excitement curling through his belly.

Because she would have died so heartbreakingly young, her legacy would be idolized. She would reach an iconic status with the cult members who already worshipped her, much like Marilyn

Monroe had. Corporations would fight to represent her brand with licensing, marketing, and intellectual property. Add that to the fact that there was a multitude of dead celebrities out there who made more *after* their deaths—sometimes millions more—than they'd *ever* made while they were alive. Chad knew, just *knew*, that Isadora would be one of them.

And Chad himself would benefit greatly by Isadora's death as well. The world would come together to support the poor, grieving widower who had so tragically lost the love of his life. His reputation would remain intact, and he would undisputedly be at the top of the heap once the dust had settled and the initial mourning period had passed. Actors and actresses everywhere would say or do anything just have the privilege of working with him—*for* him—with absolutely no backtalk or resistance.

The best part? He wouldn't ever have to put up with Isadora's whining or defiance or incessant prattling about what *she* thought was best ever fucking again. The stupid, ignorant bitch didn't have the first damn clue about what was best anyway. He had built her brand from *nothing*, and it was only by his talent and efforts that she hadn't managed to demolish all his hard work.

Truth be known…he had never wanted to marry her anyway. There was nothing about her that had attracted him—had *ever* attracted him—and he would have never given her a second thought if she hadn't won an Oscar in her very first role. He'd seen her for the opportunity she was, nothing more, and had done what he needed to do to make sure he was *the* most powerful man in Hollywood—by using her and her baffling appeal to position the two of them as Hollywood's glamorous power couple.

In any case, it appeared that she was now outliving her usefulness to him. Although her appeal had continued to shoot into the stratosphere in recent years, Chad was tired of the constant need to monitor her behavior and issue as many corrections as he did, simply because the stupid bitch was incapable of following his direction.

It had been more understandable when she was younger and as yet unformed, but with the amount of training he'd given her over the years, it was clear she was totally incapable of doing what it was that he expected her to do. And now…she was jeopardizing his reputation, as well as everything he had worked for his whole entire life, because. *She. Didn't. Fucking. Listen.* It had become crystal clear that Isadora Nightingale had to go, before she brought about his complete ruin.

So…he would use these next couple of days to lay his plans, to make sure his schemes were absolutely foolproof, and do what it was he needed to do to make sure Isadora Nightingale was exactly where she needed to be at the time he needed her to be there.

And then he would kill her.

Chapter 16

"Were you able to hide the earring I gave you when you went back to your hotel room today, Isadora? Obviously, you were able to smuggle in your new cell phone and hide it from Chad just fine since you're calling me, but what about the earring? And where is that douche canoe anyway? I know there would have been no way for you to call me if he was still around."

"I hid the earring for now, in my tampon box like you told me to do with my cell phone. Chad went down to one of the hotel restaurants to meet a business acquaintance for dinner and told me to stay here and order room service. I really doubt that I'll see him before ten p.m. I suspect he's meeting with his attorney, Andrew Matheson, because Andrew and his wife live in Indian Shores. The weather is deteriorating fast, but Chad was apparently unconcerned with making him come out in it."

"Indian Shores? Isn't that swanky?" Nova rolled her eyes from her perch on Trill's lap then stifled a yawn.

It had been a long but productive day. Peyton had left the movie set with Nova's rig after everything had been disassembled and packed up, planning to park the rig securely inside the APS complex to protect it from the coming storm. Nova had also left and had headed for Pinellas Park in her own car to meet the woman from her latest extraction and take her to the airport.

By the grace of the Goddess, flights were still running, and Nova had been able to put her on a plane bound for Salt Lake City. The woman had flung her arms around Nova with tears streaming down her face and had promised to call her the minute she had landed safely and was with family again. When Nova had gotten home, she'd found Trill and a smirking Jaime Quintero there waiting for her. They'd assured her that everything had gone smoothly on their end, and that the woman's alcoholic abuser husband was going to get the shock of his life when his car was finally found.

After Jaime had left, Trill had thrown some fish under the broiler while Nova had fixed them a salad. After they'd eaten and done the dishes—Nova insisting on helping Trill this time—Nova had settled on Trill's lap to call Isadora before she collapsed for the night.

"Other than that, is everything okay?" Nova was still worried about the movie star. "I don't know what Lancaster's deal was, but he was fucking weird on the set this morning. The couple of times I saw him while we were packing up our rig to leave the set until the storm passes, he gave me this weird, really creepy half smile and walked in another direction. If I didn't know better, I'd think he had something up his sleeve."

Isadora spoke slowly. "He was—I don't know—almost *nice* to me today. I can't remember the last time he spoke to me as if I was anything other than a piece of gum stuck to the bottom of his shoe. Even Alyssa and Delaney remarked on it." Then amazingly, she giggled a bit. "Of course, you know your crew. Esmeralda said it was probably because his drawers weren't too tight and riding up his butt today."

Nova burst out laughing.

"That's Es for you." Then she rapidly sobered. "Seriously, though, are you sure you're okay? I really want you to put those earrings in tonight, Isadora. This uncharacteristic behavior from Lancaster has me a little bit on edge for some reason." Nova put her head down on Trill's shoulder. "If there's anything I've learned over the years, it's to listen to my gut feeling…and mine is telling me that motherfucker really *is* up to something."

"It looks like I'll be stuck in this hotel room until after the storm passes, which I guess is a good thing then. I doubt very much that Chad will touch me with so many people around because these walls aren't soundproof. He never does anything that will put him in a bad light, nor will he risk getting caught." Isadora sighed. Nova heard her digging around for a minute, then there was a brief moment of silence. "There. The earring's in, Nov. You said to squeeze the stud part of the earring to turn it on so it starts recording, right?"

"Right. Desi and Darcy—who are Jaime and Trill's number twos, or the associates who are the second-in-command of their crews—can access the feed directly, and Trill's going to show me how to use the app she installed on my phone so I can do the same. As long as you can keep that earring in your ear and turned on, Isadora, we can always see and hear what's going on in front of you.

"Jaime says you can keep squeezing the stud part of the earring to turn it on and off, like when you have to use the bathroom or want to take a shower and need some privacy. You'll hear one beep when it turns on, two beeps when it turns off, which will make it easy for you to know when it's recording or not. I really, really want you to keep your earrings in for now, okay? Jaime says the recording earring is waterproof and pretty indestructible, so you're good to go."

"Okay."

Trill mouthed the word "*Rosi*" to Nova, and she nodded. "Trill also wants me to remind you that when all this starts to go down after APS releases the video they capture of his abuse, an APS SUV will come and pick you up immediately at the hotel. I don't know who's going to be driving yet—although I suspect Peyton is going to insist—but whoever it is will lose any paparazzi following you and take you to Rosi Armstrong, the mother of the Armstrong twins. You are going to shelter with her, and she will take care of being your official spokesperson. Mama and Papa Armstrong are awesome, and you will be as safe with them as you would be with any of the APS associates."

"Okay," Isadora whispered again.

"It's almost over, honey." Nova felt her tears start. "You have to deal with one more physical abuse challenge from that mangy son of a bitch and then we can send him back to hell where he belongs. I want you to rest right now and remember we've got your back on this. I keep telling you…you aren't alone anymore."

When Nova hung up, Trill wiped her tears and kissed her gently then took her phone. "Here's the icon to access the feed from Isadora's earring right on your home page. Click it and you should be able to see what's going on in front of Isadora." Nova reached up and tapped the icon and a live feed filled the screen. Nova's mouth dropped open as she saw Isadora's hotel room as if she was standing in the movie star's place. Trill continued, "I'll also have my security associates monitoring this feed from the Recon Room 24/7, baby. Everything is being recorded continuously. Jaim is also going to check in with it frequently, so all we can do now is wait."

"I love you." Nova kissed Trill deeply before she pulled back and looked into her fiancé's eyes. "Isadora will be able to put an end to her nightmare with that prick because of you and APS. I would have never been able to do this on my own, Trill. Never."

"Don't underestimate yourself, little diva. Isadora found *you*, not APS. We've been able to help her as we have because *you* were the one who made it possible. Now, because you'll be here at home for the next few days, I want you to take this opportunity to rest and relax. My security specialists will have eyes on Isadora 24/7, so there won't be any need for you to monitor her constantly, and we don't expect anything to happen until the storm is over anyway.

Trill banded her arms tightly around the diminutive brunette. "The APS management team typically goes out during a storm to sweep the city and check on residents whenever possible, baby. Because Audrey will barely be a tropical storm, according to the forecast, the twins and the Seven will hit the road to see if we can help emergency personnel if there's a need, but we're not expecting anything major to happen. This apartment complex has a backup generator in case we lose power, so you can sit here and work on your food-styling plans in peace without that motherfucking dickhead up your ass."

Nova laughed then was inspired as an idea hit her.

"You know, Trill…Alyssa's apartment is in a low-lying area and she usually has to leave if there's any kind of a storm because flooding is so bad where she lives. If you're okay with it, I'd like to ask her to come here and stay with us, but I won't if that would make you uncomfortable. I was just thinking it would be a good opportunity for the two of us to finish going over Isadora's drawings together without being busted by any of Lancaster's minions…and since Del lives right down the hall, she can come and play, too."

"Baby. Give me a break." Trill kissed Nova's temple. "This is your home, too. You don't need my permission for shit like that. My couch pulls out into a very comfortable sleeper and Alyssa is more than welcome here any time. She's one of us, she's *always* been one of us, and you already know Jaime is determined to make that official…probably sooner rather than later."

Nova shook her head a bit skeptically, then she said, "I'm going to go ahead and call Lys. Audrey is hitting within the next forty-eight hours, so she needs to pack and head on over before the weather conditions get even worse."

"Tell her to call when she's on her way and I'll have one of my crew open the north complex parking door of APS for her. Someone will help her run across the street here to the apartments and we'll let her in. To this day, the twins and the Seven are still pissed as shit that we didn't think about putting in a covered skyway between the apartments and the APS complex. Maybe we'll add one someday if we can find the time to figure it out.

"In the meantime, little diva," Trill looked at her femme with heat in her eyes, "you make your phone call…then be prepared to be taken in every way I can take you." Nova whimpered as Trill gently bit the side of her throat and cupped one of Nova's breasts in her hand, thumbing the nipple through Nova's T-shirt. "If I'm not going to be able to have you for a couple of days, I need to make up for that…starting now."

ɞɷɞɷɞɷɞ

"Are we good? Everyone ready to take off?" Blake tossed an empty rucksack to Drew as the Armstrong twins and the Seven prepared to head out into the storm.

"We're good. The SUVs are loaded with supplies and are full of gas. Rowan and Kelly are with my mother, Brooke and our new friend Piper are bunking down in Hades, and Alyssa and Del are with Nova in her and Trill's apartment. They'll all be safe where they are, so no worries there," Riley informed them as she picked up a big duffel bag.

"Kelly squawked and wanted to come out with us—and I would have totally backed her on that—except Rowan specifically asked Kel to please stay with her. Kelly was disappointed, but you know how she feels about her big sister, so I told her there would probably be plenty for her to do after the storm blew through anyway."

"Jess and the rest of my team made sure Hades was ready for any friends or family that needed to shelter with us. Anyone we might have been expecting is already there." Casey slung another duffel bag over her shoulder. "Campbell said there's still plenty of room for anyone who might get caught in the storm whom we need to bring back. There's a lot of non-perishable food in the employee lounge, plus snacks for the kids, and a shitload of bottled water. Everything's good from my end."

Bryn was texting on her phone. "Noah's out on patrol too, and he says it doesn't look that bad at all…just the usual squally shit." Noah Armstrong, a Whimsy police officer, was Bryn and Riley's little brother. Bryn grabbed yet another duffel. "Thankfully, this should be an easy one. We'll still get some flooding because of the storm surge, but it should be minimal because this thing is barely a tropical storm at all." Storm surge was an abnormal rise in sea level caused by any type of tropical system.

Kenn caught the SUV keys Trill tossed to her. "Let's get out there and get on the road then. Casey's crew knows they can call my dad if they need him." Rich Weston, though retired, was a former Army Special Forces Weapons Sergeant and survival expert. Kenn looked at Trill. "You're with me, right?"

"Right. It's you, me, and Jaime in the first SUV. Bryn, Casey, and Blake will be in the second, then Riles, Drew, and Teag in the third. We're covering north Whimsy, Bryn's SUV is covering the east side up until you hit the estuary, and Riley and her team are taking the south along the Intracoastal. We don't need to worry about west Whimsy because it's a sure bet no one's going into that nature reserve to hike during a storm like this."

"I have my DarkMatter Katim phone in case we need it." Because Drew spent so much time on the dark web, she carried an expensive, very secure smartphone designed to withstand cyberattacks, hackers, and extreme field conditions. "I've only had this thing for a couple of years, and I haven't had the chance to fully test it out in hurricane or tropical storm conditions before. This could be interesting, although I doubt it will come to that."

"For a smartphone that cost almost two large with all its modifications, that fucker should be out there in this shit patrolling for us," Blake snarked. Drew rolled her eyes and shot Blake the finger.

"All right, assholes, let's get out of here." Bryn headed for the door. "We'll keep in touch via cell phone since we know our comms aren't all that great in inclement weather. You see anything unusual and you need backup, holler. Audrey will be making landfall in about six hours, but it doesn't look like it's going to be that dramatic of an event. Vince Masterson and the Whimsy police plus a bunch of our own associates are out as well, so we should be able to do two very thorough sweeps of Whimsy before landfall. Good luck, and we'll see everyone back here later this afternoon."

ఌωఌωఌωఌ

"I still cannot get over what this woman has been thorough." Nova sighed, her legs thrown over the arm of a recliner. She, along with Alyssa and Delaney, had been examining Alyssa's sketchbooks from her sessions with Isadora on the movie set for several hours. "How in the fuck did he manage to keep his abuse and his violence a secret for so long? You would think someone would have noticed something was off with them. It doesn't take a fucking rocket scientist to have figured out something was really wrong."

Alyssa was peering intently at one sketch in particular. "If I'm interpreting this right, those three queer bitches on her staff *do* know he beats her. His entire staff probably knows. But these fuckers in particular—hired by Mr. Douchebag himself as Isadora's personal staff—were probably paid a bunch of money to keep their bitchy mouths shut and weren't about to do the first goddamn thing to help Isadora…because their own careers and ambitions are more important to them. Assholes. We were pretty sure we'd already figured that shit out, but these drawings definitely confirm it."

She looked at Nova and Delaney, thunderclouds on her face. "Let me remind you that I've already called dibs on them. Those bitches are going to find out what it's like to have their prissy, pansy asses handed to them by a queer femme who doesn't suffer fools gladly…and who now has a fucking arsenal of very cool Krav Maga moves to shove up their asses."

"Lys. Holy crap, girlfriend. I swear, you are more bloodthirsty than the bad asses are." Delaney looked at Alyssa with her eyebrows raised.

Alyssa snorted. "You forget I know you, Del, and I know this is not cool with you on any level. Therefore, I'm willing to make book on the fact that you're patiently waiting for the show, popcorn in hand."

Delaney snickered then sheepishly shrugged in agreement.

The women were in Nova and Trill's apartment, riding out the tropical storm. According to the last weather update from The Weather Channel, they were about an hour from landfall, which was expected to take place just south of them in Sarasota County. Although the weather was squally and the rain bands coming through had produced some fairly gusty conditions at times, the three native Floridians knew this was a very minor tropical event and they were as safe as it was possible to be where they were.

Nova was still a bit worried about Isadora, but she consoled herself with the fact that Isadora was sheltered in a large, solidly built hotel that could withstand almost five times the amount of wind and rain this storm would produce. Unable to help herself, she kept peeking occasionally at the app on her phone to check on the movie star. Isadora was apparently reading in the living room of the large suite, ignoring Chad Lancaster, who was pacing back and forth. Nova frowned at his peculiar behavior but chalked it up to the fact that the Californian had never weathered a tropical storm before and was most likely just freaked out.

"I need this shit to be over with." Nova blew out a deep breath as she forced herself to minimize the app. "I'm about to break out in motherfucking hives from nerves. Now, this bitch," she gestured at Alyssa, "has me wanting popcorn. With butter and parmigiana cheese on it, so my ass can explode…because, why the fuck not?"

Alyssa and Delaney burst out laughing.

"Do you have the stuff to make it? If you do, I'm on it." Delaney rose from her seat on the couch as Nova got out of her armchair and went into the kitchen to help her.

About thirty minutes later, just as they had finished eating their snack, Nova's cell phone rang. She looked at the display and frowned. "Jesus. It's Isadora." She rapidly answered the phone. "Hey, what's up? Where's Chad?"

"Nova! Oh, my God, Nova!" Isadora whisper-screamed into the phone. "It's Chad, and I think he's lost his mind! I stood up from the couch and walked toward the bathroom, disconnecting my earring because I needed privacy to, you-know. As I got to the bathroom door, though, he grabbed me and threw me down onto the floor, saying that I'm a problem he should have gotten rid of years ago! He has a *gun*, Nova!" Alyssa and Delancy sat bolt upright from the look of horror on Nova's face. She quickly put her phone on speaker so the other two could hear the conversation.

"I managed to kick the gun out of his hand and escaped into the bathroom. I've locked the door, but he's…he's turned into some kind of lunatic, hammering on the door and screaming at me to open it. He's acting like he's pure evil! Now, he's yelling through the door and saying we're going to take a drive to the set, where he's going to make it look like I had a deadly 'accident' in the storm!" Isadora whimpered and choked in terror. "The door is splintering, Nova, and I don't know how much longer it's going to hold him back! Help me…dear God, help me!"

Nova felt a fear she had never felt before freeze her in place for a moment. "Isadora, listen to me. The twins and the Seven are out doing a safety sweep of Whimsy, but I'm going to send them to you right now!" She nodded frantically at Delaney. "Del just pulled out her phone and she's going to text Teagan so I can stay on the line with you. I promise you, we're not going to let that bastard son of a bitch hurt you! Hang on for me, honey! We—" Suddenly, Nova's phone went dead.

"Isadora! Isadora!" Nova screamed into her phone. She pressed the 'end' button then tried to call Isadora's phone back to no avail. "Jesus Christ, what the hell just happened?!"

"My phone's dead too. I have no idea if my text to Teagan went through or not." Worry and fear were evident in Delaney's voice as she tried to call her spouse. "Damn it, it goes straight to voicemail. The only thing I can think of, based on what Teag has taught me, is that the cell phone tower took a hit of some type. They're usually pretty invulnerable in a little storm like this one, but it could have gotten hit by debris or big tree branches or something like that. All it would take is the exact right strike at the exact right time to disrupt the communications."

"I have to go after her! She said he's going to take her to the set and make it look like she had some kind of fatal accident." Nova flew into her bedroom, stripped off her shorts, and pulled on a pair of jeans. She threw a warm hoodie over her T-shirt, yanked on her sneakers, and went back out into the living room to find Alyssa doing the same.

"Shut the fuck up, homeslice." Alyssa poked her forefinger in Nova's direction at the look on Nova's face then glowered as she pulled on her own sneakers. "The fuck I'm letting you go out alone in this, especially if we need to deal with that motherfucking maniac. Del can stay here and watch for the bad asses.

"Actually, it would probably be better if Del went back to her own apartment because she's in a corner unit and her apartment looks right out onto Dunbridge. Yours doesn't. That way, she can keep a lookout for either anyone who goes into the APS complex across the street or comes back here.

"Almost all the APS bad asses are out patrolling, but they have to come back sometime. Right now, it's not like any of us can call the skeleton crew that's on the inside over there in the complex or anyone sheltering with them to tell them what the fuck is going on either, because hello? *No. Fucking. Phones.*" Alyssa was pissed through her worry.

"Okay. Okay. My car isn't huge and will probably slide on the roads some because it's pretty lightweight and it's windy as fuck out there…but we should still be all right." Nova went charging into the office then returned and stuffed a large wooden board into her backpack. She arched an eyebrow at Alyssa who was looking at her as if she had lost her mind.

"What? It's a photography background board we use for food-styling photo shoots. Tell me I won't slam that motherfucker right across the head with it if I get a chance, Lys. Isadora said he had a gun, but something tells me that jackass has no idea which end of it to actually use." Nova was trying to cover her fear with snark.

"We're out of here." She grabbed Delaney in a tight hug then stepped back as Alyssa did the same. "Trill is probably going to kill me, but I can't leave Isadora out there all alone. If we could have reached them, *any one of them*, we would have kept our happy asses here and waited for them to do what it is they do. But they're not here, we can't reach them, and I refuse to let that evil son of a bitch take anything more from that sweet woman.

"I *promised* her she was no longer alone." Her voice wobbled a bit. "I could never live with myself if something happened to her and there had been even a slim chance I could have prevented it but didn't." Nova swallowed down the tears that were starting to drip down her face.

Delaney was openly crying. "I get it. Just please…*please* be careful. Lancaster is unhinged as hell and if he has every intention of killing Isadora, he won't have any qualms about taking you out, too. He *hates* you, Nov, and you know it. I'll keep trying to get ahold of someone while I watch for them." She ran out of Trill and Nova's apartment and navigated down the hallway with the other two then opened the door to her own apartment as Nova and Alyssa headed out the front door.

"We're taking my SUV, homeslice. It's heavier than your car and won't slide as easily. Desi gave me a remote when I got here yesterday, told me Jaime said to keep it in my vehicle for now, so I'm parked in the APS parking garage across the street." They ran across Biscayne Street South to the APS complex, hunched against the wind and rain, and Alyssa let them into the garage through the north entrance. When they got into Alyssa's SUV, Nova pulled the seat belt across her chest, buckled it, then gave Alyssa a grim look, her honey-brown eyes dark. "You ready to do this thing, Lys?"

The corner of Alyssa's mouth lifted with no humor as her own light blue eyes darkened as well. To Nova's total shock, she pulled a gun in a shoulder holster out from under her driver's seat and handed it to Nova. "I was born ready, sister." With resolute, determined intention, Alyssa put her vehicle in gear and the two femmes sped off into the storm—determined to save a broken, battered woman from the man who was equally determined to take her life and permanently snuff out the hopes and dreams he had shattered long ago.

Chapter 17

"I can't believe communications are down," Trill grumped as she, Jaime, and Kenn made their way back to the APS complex. The SUVs carrying the other two teams had met up with them in downtown Whimsy and they were all headed back to the APS complex together. Tropical Storm Audrey had made landfall about thirty minutes before on Longboat Key, a barrier island south of Anna Maria Island between Sarasota Bay and the Gulf of Mexico, and reports of flooding and damage to the Whimsy area were minimal. Although there was currently no way to reach them, the management team assumed their crews would be coming back shortly as well.

"We did dodge a bullet, though…despite losing our phones and comms, which has sucked," Kenn remarked, crossing over Biscayne Street as she headed east on Dunbridge to the north entrance of the APS complex. "Who would have thought a measly little pissant storm like Audrey could take down a fucking cell tower? I'm sure Teag will tell us the details as soon as she finds out what happened for sure."

As she turned into the complex parking garage, however, she suddenly slammed on her brakes. "What the fuck? Is that *Delaney*? What in the motherfucking *hell* does she think she's doing?" The three APS butches peered through the driving rain at a small figure dashing down the street toward them. They saw Teagan jump out of the SUV behind them and run to meet her, scooping her up and heading into the garage out of the weather.

When they were parked and back inside the complex, the APS management team found Teagan and Delaney in the back hallway that led to the north parking lot, Delaney crying and clutching Teagan's biceps as Teag banded her arms tightly around her wife's waist. She was clearly shaken by Del's uncharacteristic panic. "Slow down, angel. *Slow down* because I can't understand a goddamn word you're saying. Why the fuck were you out in this shit? And where's Nova and Alyssa?"

Delaney took a deep, shuddering breath and forced herself to calm her panicked words as the management team surrounded them. "Isa-…Isadora called Nova earlier," she hiccupped. "She was locked in her bathroom at her hotel, completely hysterical because Chad Lancaster had pulled a gun on her! She said he was raving and screaming at her that she was a problem he should have gotten rid of years ago!

"I don't know how, but she managed to kick the gun out of his hand, got into the bathroom away from him, and locked the door. She pulled out that little prepaid phone Nova had gotten for her—the one she'd told Isadora to keep hidden in her tampon box in the bathroom—and she called Nova. Chad kept yelling at her through the door that he was going to force her to go to the movie set with him, then he was going to kill her! He's going to make it look like she had an accident in the storm."

An angry silence swept through the group.

Delaney wiped her streaming eyes with one hand. "Isadora said he was trying to smash his way into the bathroom and that the door was starting to splinter. We knew he was determined to make her go with him to Madeira Beach where the set is, but we had no idea what his plans were past that or how he was going to make it look like she'd had an accident. Nova promised her we were going to find you all immediately and send you to her, but then the phones went out! Nova lost touch with Isadora and we couldn't contact anyone else, no matter how hard we tried. Our communications were completely gone."

Delaney turned in Teagan's arms and looked at Trill, still shaking. "Trill, Nova headed out in the storm to go to the production set to find Isadora herself. Alyssa went with her because she said there was no way in hell she was letting Nova go up against a maniac like Lancaster alone. And Nova said…Nova said," she drew in another deep, choking breath, "she said that she could never live with herself if something happened to Isadora because she ignored even a tiny chance that she could stop whatever it is that Lancaster was planning to do."

"Baby, when did they leave?" Teagan's voice was calm in the midst of the rage that surrounded them.

"About an hour ago. Audrey was about thirty minutes from making landfall when Nova heard from Isadora. She and Alyssa took off for Madeira Beach in Alyssa's SUV, and my job was to wait for you all and grab you the minute I saw you. Grab *anyone* I saw from APS, whether it was someone coming out of the complex or coming into the apartments, and tell them where those two had gone and why." Delaney started to cry again.

"I am so scared for both of them, and for Isadora. Lancaster is fucking psychotic and I told Nova he would kill her just as easily as he would Isadora, because he hates her with a *passion.* And he has a *gun.* He can't make this look like a simple accident if he shoots them, but I honestly think he might be too far gone to care. He is determined to get rid of Isadora, and he'll kill Nova with no qualms whatsoever if she gets in his way."

"If that motherfucker touches even *one* hair on my woman's head"—none of them had *ever* heard the kind of deadly rage that was emanating from the normally cool, calm, collected Trillian Dacanay before—"I will burn Madeira Beach to the ground. Chad Lancaster is a *dead* man." She started to walk rapidly toward the Recon Room. "I need to grab one of my sniper rifles and then I am fucking *out of here*." Her fury shimmered in the air around her as she strode angrily down the hallway, seething hate in every line of her body.

In the next moment, however, Trill found herself slammed face first against the wall and pinned by Drew, Casey, and Riley. "You three need to get the fuck off me before I do something I might regret." In a flash, Trill's voice went from red hot rage to one coated in ice. "I have never in over thirty years raised my hand to any one of you motherfuckers in anger, but today just might be the goddamn exception to the rule. What part of the woman I love is in danger and might lose her life if I don't get to her *now* do you fucking bastards not understand?!" Trill was screaming by the end, struggling violently.

"You think I don't understand, when my wife was kidnapped by one of the vilest pieces of shit we've ever gone up against? One who was planning on *raping* her and forcing her to become pregnant? You think I don't get it?" Riley spoke calmly into Trill's ear, holding firm against Trill's savage attempts to get free. "*Broki*, I get it. Bryn gets it. Teag gets it. I hope to *Christ* none of these other assholes ever has to learn what it's like…but if God forbid they ever do, we'll be there for them, the same as we're here for you."

"Don't make us drag you to lockdown, cuz, please." Drew's voice was equally calm. "It would kill me to do it if I had to…but I'll do it if it means keeping you safe from yourself. You know I will. You need to focus and get your shit together because Nova needs you right now, and we can't take you to go get her if you don't get your fucking head back in the game. You *know* that."

Casey spoke up last. "You have one of the smartest women I've ever seen in my life, Trill. The APS femmes are absolutely amazing. You *saw* what she and Alyssa accomplished in Hades, and you know that motherfucker is going to be eating his own dick by the time the two of them are done with him. You need to calm down, realize you have your posse at your back, and remember that none of us are going to let the first fucking thing happen to those two.

"But Drew's right, cuz. You need to get your goddamn head back in the game." Casey squeezed Trill's arm in support as they all finally felt Trill's body start to relax. "We need to get there *now*, but we have to do it as the cohesive team we've always been. There's no room for error or bad judgment on this, Trill. *None*."

Trill slumped against the wall and leaned her forehead against the wall after a long moment, blowing out a deep breath. "Okay. Okay." She felt the red haze of rage that had fallen over her dissipate as she became more clearheaded and stood up. "Fuck. I'm sorry. I don't know what the hell came over me."

"I do." Delaney, who had still been standing with Teagan, went over and hugged Trill fiercely. After a moment, the APS team lead hugged her back just as hard. "You love her, Trill. You love her, and you want her to be safe, and it makes you crazy to know that she's *not* safe at the moment. That's why you lost it for a minute there.

"I've known every single one of you since I was in kindergarten, and it's amazing to me how much you've always had each other's backs. None of us is perfect and we've all done things we aren't especially proud of…but that's just one of the reasons you all have each other. At the end of the day, you keep each other sane when this kind of insanity happens in your lives." Delaney stepped back and squeezed Trill's hands warmly even through her worry.

"You said you're sorry, I can already tell they know it was just a blip on the radar screen, and now *all* of you are going to find Nova and Alyssa. And may the Goddess have mercy on Lancaster's soul, because none of you sure as hell will."

ত৩ত৩ত৩ত

"There's his rental car." Alyssa switched off her lights in the murky, rainy gloom and stared at the Mercedes-Benz S-Class sedan parked in the middle of the deserted lot. "Does he have her in her own personal trailer or are they in his production trailer? *Fuck*, I can't tell. There are lights on in both of them."

The two femmes sat there for a minute, letting their eyes sweep over the rest of the parking lot. "It's a sure bet that pansy-ass motherfucker won't be coming outside himself for long. He's too much of a pussy to be out in this kind of weather," Nova snarked despite her anxiety.

"We need to figure out what kind of an accident he wants her to have," she mused next, almost to herself. "Except for the key set construction, just about everything else has been removed and put into storage. There isn't anything laying around that she could fall on…and then there's the question of what excuse he's going to give people to explain why Isadora was on a deserted movie set in the middle of a tropical storm."

"Right? She's from California. Californians never deal with tropical systems like this, and it wouldn't be something most Californians would be eager to test out, especially a movie star like Isadora." Alyssa was also thinking, drumming her fingers on her steering wheel. "Let's talk this through, Nov. He has a gun, but his intention is to make her death look like it was an accident…so he can't shoot her if that's what he wants people to think. Therefore, we're going to assume he has the gun to force her to go where he wants her to go, rather than to actually inflict bodily harm."

"Okay. I can buy that." Nova was still staring at the set. "We've already said the set has been stripped, so there's really not anything that's been left here that could be used as another type of weapon. She also can't have an accident *inside* one of the trailers if he wants to make this look believable either. That's protected shelter from the storm, so it wouldn't be smart to stage any kind of fatal accident in there. That might cause eyebrows to raise and could actually trigger an investigation, which he'd want to avoid at all costs."

Alyssa narrowed her eyes. "I'm betting he'll leave his rental here in the lot to make it look like Isadora drove to the set all by herself and had her accident without him around. He'll probably go down to one of the hotel restaurants or lounges alone and pretend he's never left the Don CeSar. He'll make it seem like Isadora stayed up in their suite and then be just as shocked as everyone else when she turns up missing. His act as the bereaved widower will start when they find her body in Madeira Beach."

"How does he plan to get back to the Don from the production set after he kills her then? Is one of his fucking little minions in on this with him?" Nova was still staring at the production set. "And what will he possibly say about why Isadora would leave him and come to the movie set in the middle of a tropical storm? Unless," she pondered, "he makes up some kind of bullshit story, like she lost a very sentimental piece of jewelry on the set right before the production crew shut everything down because of the storm.

"I know she owns a child's locket that she *always* has on her person somewhere, and has for over fifteen years. Isadora told me her mom died when she was five years old, so that locket is something deeply personal to her because her mom gave it to her. It's the only thing of hers that Is has. That scumbag would probably play the grieving husband card and fabricate a loss like that to explain why she would sneak out and come to the movie set alone when it wasn't safe."

"I'm really starting to hate this fucker even more than I already do." Alyssa's expression was full of disgust. "You know, I bet he wouldn't take the risk of calling one of his minions because he'd be afraid they'd try to blackmail him or something. He'll probably get that sleazy lawyer he does business with here in Florida to come and get him, then he'll cut him in on all the money he'll make from Isadora's brand posthumously. A big shot entertainment lawyer stands to lose a fuck of a lot more than three gay boy flunkies if something like this goes south."

All of a sudden, Nova gave a huge gasp and her eyes grew wide in the dim light before her head whipped around and she turned to stare at Alyssa. "Oh, my God! Lys! I think I know how Lancaster is planning on killing Isadora!"

ᘐωᘐωᘐωᘐ

Smack! Isadora Nightingale sobbed as the vicious blow to her face snapped her head back. "You have no idea how fucking relieved I'll be to get rid of your whiny ass, you bitch! You are nothing but a disgrace, and you have *no* idea how unbearable you've made my life over the past twelve years." *Smack! Smack!*

"Why couldn't you just fucking *listen* to me, Isadora! I told you back when I gave you your very first correction that you would have a good life if you would just. *Listen. To. Me*!" Chad Lancaster kicked her ankle hard enough that she heard something snap and an almost unbearable pain shot up her leg.

"Now, I have no choice but to get rid of you for my *own* peace of mind. I have reached the end of my rope with you! Once you're gone, I'll *finally* have some much-deserved peace and quiet. And, as a bonus, I'll make more from your brand when you're dead than I *ever* made while you were alive! I'll consider that money my compensation for. *Every. Single. Thing* I've had to put up with from you through the years.

"It feels *so* good to finally give you the beating you so richly deserve, and not have to worry about avoiding your face because people would question the bruises. You're going to die in this tropical storm, you stupid bitch, and the authorities will just chalk up any battering to your face and your body to you getting caught out in it." He punched her in the eye savagely.

Isadora realized with a sorrowful heart that she was going to die tonight, tears flooding down her face from both the knowledge of her looming death and the pain of the cruel hammering she was taking at the hands of her husband.

But…in the midst of the savage beating, she suddenly felt the spirit of Nova MacLeod swiftly fill her with the essence of everything she had *ever* wanted to be her whole entire life. Sweet, funny, protective Nova, who'd answered her cry for help and had done everything in her power to get Isadora away from the cruel tyrant she was married to.

Out of the blue—for the very first time since she was nineteen years old—Isadora suddenly felt fierce and unstoppable. She was astonished as it occurred to her that meeting Nova, Alyssa, and Delaney had at long last given her the courage to live life on *her* own terms. Not anyone else's…let alone those of Chad Lancaster.

Right then and there, she vowed to herself that her death would have a meaning her life had never had—that she was more than just a bankable Hollywood movie star, Chad Lancaster's sycophant wife, and an abused woman who had never dared reach out for help…believing she had deserved everything she'd been given in some deep, buried part of herself. As these thoughts flashed through her head in the blink of an eye, and the beautiful movie star remembered who she *really* was, her eyes narrowed in hate and determination. If her bastard husband wanted her dead, that evil son of a bitch was going to have to *work* for it.

And then—Isadora Nightingale finally, *finally*, struck back at the man who had made the last twelve years of her life a living hell *with a vengeance.*

After pulling herself to her feet and putting all of her weight on her good ankle, she made a fist and struck Chad right in the nose as hard as she could—her rage and her craving for revenge filling every ounce of her body. She exalted when she heard a loud *crunch!* And Chad's hands flew to his face.

"Go ahead and shoot me, asshole," she taunted as Chad let out a sound of pain, pulling back in shocked disbelief, as blood started pouring from his nose. "Explain that one to the fucking cops." She backhanded the gun out of Chad's hand and was relieved when it went skittering off into an unlighted corner of the production trailer. "You want me dead? You'll have to fucking *earn* it, you piece of shit.

"I should have punched you back the first time you *dared* to raise a finger to me. You're nothing but an insecure little bully who's ridden the coattails of *my* talent and success for years, Chad. You would have never been anything but a second-rate director without me. I think the world deserves to know who the *real* Chad Lancaster is." She punched an immobile, still frozen Chad Lancaster in the face again.

But then Chad shook off his stupor and roared with rage, punching the slight woman back until she fell to the ground and stomped on her bad ankle. Isadora screamed from the pain and rolled to the right, but she wasn't fast enough to avoid a nasty kick to her ribs. Chad reached down and grabbed her by her long, blonde hair, wrapping it around his fist, then started to drag her to the trailer door.

"You are fucking *dead*, you little cunt," He seethed as he reached the door and pulled Isadora's prone body through it and down the trailer stairs. Isadora's head bounced off the metal stairs and she struggled to stay conscious from the repeated thumps. "I am taking you up to the catwalk," he raised his hand and pointed up into the sky to where an overhead steel walkway ran the length of the set, "and I'm going to throw you over the railing so you fall to your death. It doesn't matter how much damage they see on you when they find your body then…they'll just assume your injuries were made by the fall.

"I'd already planned to tell everyone you'd been distraught over something you'd gotten from your dead mother that you were sure you'd lost on the set, but we'll let the mystery of why you were up on the catwalk remain a mystery. I'll be too busy playing the bereaved, grieving husband to worry about why you would have done anything so foolish in the middle of a tropical storm." Chad laughed, an evil, malignant sound, as he continued to pull her body along. "Goodbye, you ignorant piece of trash. Because *I. Win.*"

I tried, Nova. I really tried. But I failed, Isadora thought through a flood of bitter tears. She felt unconsciousness eating at the edge of her pain and sadness as Chad dragged her over to the stairs that led up to the top of the catwalk. *Please don't ever forget me, my beautiful friend. I already know that wherever my spirit goes, I will never,* ever *forget you.*

Chapter 18

"ETA to Madeira Beach, ten minutes." Riley checked her watch. "It's still nasty out here, but the storm feels like it's losing strength pretty fast now that it's made landfall. We can only hope Lancaster is enough of a pussy that he decided to hunker down until the winds calmed some." She glanced over her shoulder at Trill, who was riding in the back seat of Drew's SUV, staring out of the window.

"We're almost there, *broki*. Kenn threw a couple of your sniper rifles in the back of her SUV, but only you can decide if you're up to shooting them in this weather if needed." A shadow of surprise crossed Trill's face and she turned back facing forward to look questioningly at Riley, who snorted.

"Dude, give me a goddamn break. Every single one of us has lost our shit at times and it just so happened to be your turn…even though you're not typically the one who gets a wild hair. *We. Fucking. Get. It.* You think my twin and I have put up with your ass since we were three years old for you to bail at the first opportunity? I don't fucking think so, so cut the shit."

The corner of Trill's mouth lifted almost imperceptibly despite her worry. "Noted. I only wish I would have known what I was in for when I fell in love with Nova MacLeod and found out she loved me just the same. I swear to Christ, I'm going to be gray in a year." She blew out a deep breath and rubbed her hand over her face.

Even in the midst of their strain, Riley burst out laughing. "When Kelly and I got engaged, Bryn asked me if I ever thought two confirmed bachelors like the two of us would have ever gotten caught by a couple of Virginia girls like we did. I told her she would have been lucky if I hadn't punched her in the fucking face if she'd ever said that to me in the beginning."

Drew snickered.

"Oh, you go ahead and laugh, fucker," Riley informed her. "You know what Mrs. Santoras told Teag, and the hell I'm messing with any of that shit. I come from an extended Puerto Rican family that believes in *espiritismo*…and if the spirit world can intervene in the human world as she and Mama are convinced it can, the spirits have every one of us by the short and curlies.

"You're eventually going down just like the rest of us, *broki*, so don't think you're fucking exempt." Drew snorted in disbelief. Riley paused for a moment as she peered at the cross streets they were passing. "We're just about there, *mi corillo*."

Trill's heart hammered in her chest as they approached the beach access parking lot on Madeira Beach where the production set for Isadora's film was located. The skies were rapidly darkening with the coming twilight and a strong wind mixed with rain still blew, although it appeared Riley's assessment was correct—Audrey was losing strength. As they turned into the front parking lot for Madeira Beach access, the other two APS SUVs pulled in right behind them.

Riley turned around to glance at Trill one more time. The look on her face was ice cold. "No matter what, you know we've got your back, Trillian Dacanay. For over thirty years, we always have…and we always will. We've got Nova and Alyssa, too." She unbuckled her seat belt and prepared to step out of the SUV into the storm. "That motherfucker had better hope and pray he hasn't harmed them in any way, because we will fucking *destroy* him if he has."

ઝ-ωઝ-ωઝ-ωઝ-

"Lys! The trailer door is opening!" Nova sat bolt upright in the passenger seat of Alyssa's SUV. "What in the fuck is that miserable piece of shit doing? Is that *Isadora* he's dragging like she's a goddamn sack of laundry?! By the fucking hair?"

Alyssa gasped then growled with anger. "I swear to you, I am going to *kill* that fucking bastard!"

Nova was livid.

She had just finished telling Alyssa that she thought Lancaster's plan was to force Isadora at gunpoint up onto the catwalk, where he could then push her over the railing so she would die in a fatal fall. It was a steep drop; the survival rate for anyone falling over the rail wouldn't be assured, although it did appear there was a fair possibility Isadora *could* survive.

Because the fatality rate wouldn't be one hundred percent, however, Nova was positive Lancaster planned to murder Isadora before he tossed her over the guardrail to make sure she was dead. When the trailer door opened and Lancaster appeared, pulling Isadora by the roots of her hair down the metal stairs of the trailer—letting her head bounce hard off the steps—Nova unbuckled her seat belt in an absolute fury.

"For some reason, it doesn't look like he's armed, unless he has the gun shoved down his pants next to his tiny little dick." The diminutive brunette was breathing fire. "Here's what we're going to do, Lys. There's no place for us to hide out here, but daylight has waned quite a bit and we're wearing dark clothes.

"He might not see us right away if we crouch low while we're running over to them, and he's still occupied with Isadora." Nova rapidly pulled the photography board out of her backpack and tucked it under her arm. "I'm going to slug that motherfucker right across his balding head and pray to the Goddess that I knock him out.

"At the very least, I want to give us enough time to get a head start so that we can get up onto the catwalk with Isadora. I don't think heading back to the SUV across this open parking lot would be very smart. The lot is wide open and deserted, so we'll have nowhere to hide or take cover, and I have no idea if she's able to walk at all. At least that way, I can pull her up the stairs backward while she's on her butt and you can cover us since you're armed.

"She's not completely unconscious because I see her arms and legs moving, even though her movements are feeble. She's hurt bad,

Lys." Nova stifled the sob that rose into her throat. "There looks like there's about thirty feet between the stairs and the endpost of the catwalk and it's about a fifteen-to-twenty-foot drop to the ground. You *can* survive a fall from that distance, but I'll bet you any money he's planning on breaking her neck first so it looks like the fall killed her and he can make sure she's really dead."

"When we get her up there, we need to make it down to that endpost." Alyssa was grim as she swiftly reached up onto her overhead console to turn off her inside and door lights, then she strapped on her shoulder holster. "It's a more defensible position because Lancaster won't be able to sneak up on us from behind. Come on, homeslice, we gotta bounce. Stay low, move fast, and whale the shit out of that motherfucker's head when we get there. Then we grab our girl and *move*."

With one last fierce look at each other, Nova and Alyssa opened the doors of the SUV and slid out into the storm.

"Fucking cunt. What the hell have you been eating?" Chad Lancaster paused at the bottom of the steel steps that led to the top of the catwalk and wiped his brow, which was sweaty despite the rain and wind. "I can't believe I have to drag your goddamn ass the whole way to the top of these stairs." He looked up the metal stairs and groaned.

"So much for me making you walk up the stairs at gunpoint like I had originally planned. But *no*…you had to make me break your ankle, and then you smacked my gun out of my hand! I don't know what you thought this last little act of defiance would buy you, Isadora, except make me angrier than I already am." He took a fresh grip on Isadora's hair. "Let's get this over with so I can get back to the Don and have a *very* well-deserved brandy for all my trouble."

"Brandy *this*, motherfucker," a new voice said from behind him. Startled, Chad started to straighten up when a tremendous blow to his head came out of nowhere. Chad let go of Isadora's hair and collapsed to the ground, unconscious.

"He's out! Come on, Lys, we gotta move!" Nova bent over Isadora and gently took her friend's face between her hands. "Isadora, honey? Can you hear me?" Isadora's eyes fluttered open and she stared at Nova, uncomprehending, as they could see her mind start to clear. "Come on, my sister, we have to go. I knocked Chad out and he's unconscious, but I don't know how long he's going to stay that way, so time is of the essence. Alyssa is here to help, but this will be much easier if you can actually stand on your own two feet with our assistance."

The two APS femmes could see Isadora gritting her teeth as she shook off the last of her grogginess and forced herself into a sitting position. "I think my ankle's broken, girls. I can probably hop up the stairs, but I'm going to be slow and I'll definitely need some help."

Her voice caught for a moment. “I can’t believe you’re here. I really can’t. I thought for sure…” They heard a noisy swallow as Isadora plainly fought to keep her emotions under control.

“We’ll tell you the story when all this bullshit is over with.” Alyssa gently took Isadora’s other arm as she and Nova helped her to stand. “Isadora, where is his gun? I have mine,” she patted the shoulder holster she’d put on before she and Nova had left the SUV, “but I sure as fuck don’t want to get into a gunfight with that douche on Madeira Beach in the middle of a tropical storm.”

“It’s in the production trailer. I smacked it out of his hand while we were fighting and it flew into a corner somewhere. He never bothered to go and find it because he was able to get me down on the ground after that and I was unable to fight him anymore.” Now that Isadora was standing, Nova and Alyssa could see the additional damage she’d taken besides the broken ankle—her eyes had been blackened, her lip was swollen, and there were deep purple bruises starting to form up and down her arms. As Isadora tried to hop, she let go of Nova and Alysa to clutch her side.

“Jesus, you’re fucking amazing, Is.” Despite her rage at Isadora’s physical condition, Nova breathed out a sigh of relief. “That’s one less thing we have to worry about right now then. I want you to sit on the stairs and pull yourself up backward up the steps while you’re sitting on your butt. Can you do that? I have a feeling that’ll be a lot faster if you think you can manage, although I know it’s going to be painful as hell. I think it will be easier in the long run, though.”

"I'm friends with some bad ass bitches who've taught me all about grit and determination." Isadora lowered herself to the stairs, careful to avoid banging her broken foot. The look on her face made it clear that even the smallest movement was excruciating, and she was steeling herself for the ordeal.

"I'm going, and I promise I'll pull myself up as fast as I can possibly go. If you need me to do anything different, just tell me." She started to scoot herself backward up the stairs, Nova and Alyssa keeping pace with her. Nova was on the same stair as Isadora to make sure she didn't fall and Alyssa was on the step right below her, keeping her eye on Chad Lancaster.

When Isadora was almost at the top of the catwalk, Lancaster groaned and rolled over, then started to struggle to his feet. His eyes widened and then filled with fury when he saw Nova and Alyssa flanking Isadora at the top of the staircase. "You two fucking bitches are *dead*," he hissed as he started to storm up the stairs toward them. "I am going to end all three of you goddamn cunts if it's the last thing I ever do!"

"Don't fucking think so, dickweed. Duck, Lys!" When Alyssa crouched down on the stair she was standing on, Nova hurled the photography board she was still clutching at Chad Lancaster's head. It struck him right in the forehead and he tumbled back down the stairs, landing flat on his back in the parking lot. He was clearly dazed, and they used the opportunity to get onto the catwalk to make their way down to the endpost.

"It's really windy, Is, so hold on as tightly as you can to the guardrail while you hop." Nova's voice was calm despite her fear. "Lys, when you get to the end, I want you to cover Isadora as much as you can from directly in front of her. Keep her behind you and as close as you can get, and both of you crouch down as low as possible. Don't shoot unless you absolutely, positively have to…it's too fucking windy up here and your aim is going to be off. I'm going to stay about halfway down the catwalk and defend us that way. Let's hope those Krav Maga moves Casey and Jess are so fucking proud of don't fail us now."

As the three women finally got to where they needed to be, they heard Chad Lancaster stomping angrily up the steel staircase again. He appeared at the top, absolutely *enraged*, then a vicious grin spread across his face when he saw Nova in the middle of the catwalk.

"Say bye bye, bitch," he spit out, that maniacal grin growing broader. "You're a fucking dead woman, Nova MacLeod, and I'm the one who gets the privilege of getting rid of you forever! The last thing you're ever going to see in this lifetime is my ecstatic face right before I snap your neck!"

"Look! Up there!" Blake yelled, pointing up at the top of the catwalk at the edge of the production set. The APS management team saw Chad Lancaster at the top of the steel staircase leading to the catwalk, balancing himself against the wind. About halfway to the end, another small figure stood, crouched down with one arm wrapped tightly around the guardrail in front of her. Trill felt her heart freeze as she realized it was Nova, facing off against Lancaster. Trill couldn't hear what they were saying, but it was evident that Nova was seriously enraging him.

"Cuz, none of us are willing to try and shoot that son of a bitch because if we miss, we'll hit little diva." Kenn's voice came calmly from beside her. "There's still wind circulation in the atmosphere even though the barometric pressure is rising. Any bullet's trajectory will be uncertain as hell.

"I can't even pull up any information on current conditions because the fucking phones are still out. There's no way for any of us to determine an accurate wind correction, Trill. We'd be running blind if we tried to get him in our sights like this. Unless you have some kind of night optics with you that would be effective in a wind storm, that's not a path it would be smart for us to take right now."

Trill shook her head no as her mind raced, searching frantically for a solution.

"We could try to get to him from the staircase, but then we run the risk of him rushing Nova and potentially causing her to fall. The guardrail looks like it's pretty high, but she's tiny and I wouldn't put it past that motherfucker to pick her up and throw her over when he saw us coming." Jaime's voice was angry and worried.

"He has Alyssa and Isadora trapped up there as well. That staircase is the only way up onto the catwalk…which is good in the sense that the soon-to-be-dead motherfucker can't sneak up behind them. As far as possible rescue routes go, however, it sucks giant green monkey dicks."

Suddenly, Trill saw Nova let go of the guardrail and step into the center of the catwalk. "What in the goddamn motherfucking *hell* does she think she's doing?" she yelled, staring incredulously up at the tiny brunette, her heart thundering in her chest. "She weighs maybe a hundred pounds soaking wet! All it will take is one stiff breeze to blow her right the fuck over the rail!"

Her eyes widened as Nova started to advance toward Chad Lancaster, who had been determinedly making his way to her. "Is she fucking crazy?! I…She…" Trill's breath stuttered to a halt in her chest as Nova crouched down and stabilized herself, then lifted her leg and kicked Chad Lancaster right between the legs when he reached her.

ᘐωᘐωᘐωᘐ

"I like you better when you're not fucking talking and wasting the planet's oxygen, loser," Nova taunted the director, clinging to the guardrail. "Working with you in the future is at the top of my '*never-fucking-ever*' list. I should have realized at our very first meeting that Isadora is the one with the talent. You're nothing but a fucking hack who's built his career on the backs of everyone else around him. You scum parasite. You aren't worth shit."

"You goddamn *cunt*. What the fuck would someone like *you* know about talent?" Lancaster screamed, his face turning purple with rage. "My bitch of a wife owes *everything* she is to me! I made her and I can break her just as easily. She would have been *nothing* without me and my connections…just another starlet willing to spread her legs to get ahead!"

Nova ignored his hateful words. "Yeah…pretty sure they don't give Oscars to just anybody in their debut role, or call their performance '*transcendent*,' if they're nothing. She was also offered that role without your 'help.' You had absolutely nothing to do with either her discovery *or* her launch, Lancaster. It was all *her*.

"I'm also pretty sure that industry giants like Peter Jackson or Ron Howard would have been frothing at the mouth to direct her without what you laughingly call your 'influence.'" Nova took a firmer grip on the guardrail as she continued to taunt him, trying to force him into making a mistake.

"What do you think Hollywood is going to do when they find out the omnipotent Chad Lancaster is nothing but a bully and a domestic abuser? That he's controlled and beaten one of the brightest stars in the Hollywood sky just so he could stay relevant? Because without her, *he* was nothing, just a fucking second-rate loser.

"I'll tell you exactly what Hollywood's going to do, fucker. You're going to become *persona non grata* in that place. There is a fuck of a lot of sexual abuse and corruption and domestic abuse that goes on in Tinsel Town…but rule number one? *Don't. Get. Caught.* And you not only got caught, you stupid jackass, you lit it up for the whole fucking world to see. Everyone will be running away from you as fast as they can because they won't want to get tarred with *your* brush."

"I fucking *hate* you like I've never hated anyone else in my life before, you goddamn bitch." Even through the sound of the wind and rain, Chad sounded as though he was eating ground glass.

"Shocker." Nova shrugged as though she was unconcerned. "For some reason, I don't think I'll be losing any sleep over it, though. You see, I may just be a *food stylist* to you, Chad, but I have people lining up from *everywhere* to work with me. Print. Television. Film. Commercials. When word about *you* gets out, as well as the fact that you tried to *murder* your wife, the only thing people are going to be lining up to hire you to direct is a prison Christmas production." Nova let go of the guardrail and stepped into the center of the catwalk.

"*Bitch!*" Lancaster screeched at the top of his lungs and lunged with murderous intent toward Nova, forgetting where he was for a moment. With one decisive move, Nova crouched down, centered her body, and nailed the director with a hard kick right between the legs with her foot.

ᘐωᘐωᘐωᘐ

Lancaster screamed in pain and bent over, grabbing his balls with his hands. Nova kneed him in the face then nailed him with a series of open palm strikes to his head, just as she'd been taught. Chad staggered backward and Nova began to pummel him with savage punches, driving him backward to the steel staircase. When they had reached the beginning of the catwalk right where the stairs began, Nova punched him square in the face one final time with everything she had.

She watched coldly as Chad Lancaster cartwheeled, screaming, then lost his balance and fell down the staircase, a look of horror on his face as he tumbled hard down the metal stairs. He finally landed on the ground at the bottom on his back, his head cocked at an odd angle, and didn't move.

The APS management team came barreling through the parking lot from where they had parked their vehicles. Trill pounded up the stairs to where Nova was standing, frozen, a look of shock starting to creep over her face. Trill grabbed Nova and pulled her to her chest, wrapping her arms firmly around her shaking fiancée. "Baby? Talk to me, little diva. Are you hurt anywhere?" She kissed Nova on the top of her head as Nova burrowed into her.

"I'm fine. But Trill, Isadora is in bad shape." As usual, Nova was more concerned with a domestic abuse survivor than she was about herself. "She has a broken ankle, two black eyes, a split lip, and a million cuts and bruises all over her. She also has some pretty bad pain in her side, but I'm not sure what that could be unless it's her ribs. We need to get her to the hospital just as fast as we can."

"Drew and Blake already have her, baby. They'll be taking her to the emergency room at Bayfront right away." Nova looked up to see Isadora hopping toward her while leaning on the two tall, strong APS team leaders. As they reached the end of the catwalk, they stopped for a moment so that a greatly shaken Isadora could wrap her arms around Nova, tears flooding down her face.

"Nova. My God, Nova." Despite her obvious pain, Isadora leaned back and gently held Nova's face. "You could have been *killed*, Nov! What in the *hell* were you thinking? I…I…I don't even know what to say! You and your friends," she released Nova's face to grasp Drew and Blake's hands, "you put yourselves on the line every single day for women like me. We owe our lives to you. But I would rather have had Chad kill *me* than to lose someone like *you* to his evil."

Nova very gingerly hugged Isadora back, mindful of her injuries. "But, honey…we don't think of it like that. My older sister was once a victim of domestic violence and I almost lost her because of it. When I got her out of that situation, I vowed I would do whatever it took to help other women who were at risk as well. I've known the APS management team since we were all in fifth grade and, for as long as I can remember, all *they've* ever wanted to do was protect women from the violence of the world.

"This," Nova pulled a smiling Trill forward, "is my fiancé, Trillian Dacanay…one of the infamous APS Seven." Trill softly shook Isadora's hand and squeezed it, also conscious of her extensive damage. "You need to get to the hospital, Is, but you'll get to meet all of them when you're better. We'll tell you a lot more about what we do then. I promise." With a kiss to Isadora's cheek, Nova stepped back.

Drew very gently swept the severely battered star up into her arms and they started to slowly navigate down the staircase, Blake leading the way to give Isadora an extra layer of protection. "Hide your face against Drew's shoulder and don't look down at Lancaster, Isadora," Nova heard Blake instruct the injured woman firmly as they neared the bottom where Chad Lancaster's body lay. "We'll take care of everything. Your job when you get to the hospital is to get better, and *that's it*. We've got you, my friend, and there's absolutely *nothing* for you to worry about. Not anymore."

Nova then saw Jaime with her arm wrapped firmly around a flustered Alyssa, bringing up the rear. When they reached Nova, Alyssa pulled away from the APS team lead to wrap her arms around her friend just as Isadora had done and kissed her cheek. "You did good, homeslice. Make sure you get some rest because that was some intense shit that went down.

"My mom and dad are still at their cabin in North Carolina for the summer, but I'm going to their house to clean up and crash, since I'm sure my place is flooded. It will probably take forever for the hot water tank to heat up, but I'll deal…even though a hot shower sounds like fucking heaven right now. I'll come by and get my stuff from your apartment tomorrow." She held up her hand as Nova opened her mouth to object.

"You and Trill need to be alone tonight, Nov, and frankly…so do I. I'll call you in a few days." She kissed Nova on the cheek again then continued to walk down the stairs next to Jaime.

When they were finally alone at the top of the staircase, Nova gave a deep, gusty sigh. "I killed him, Trill." Her voice was quiet as she rested her forehead against her fiancé's. "I knew without a doubt that I was going to do it, too…it was just a question of figuring out how while staying within the boundaries of the law. When I saw what that piece of shit had done to Isadora, I decided right then and there that he was too evil to let live.

"Alyssa and I saw him drag Isadora out of the production trailer by her *hair* while she was lying prone on her back, and he yanked her down those metal stairs so that her head kept ricocheting off them. That's when I thought…oh, *fuck* no. It's time for this motherfucker to *go*." Her eyes then filled with tears.

"I was so damn scared when we lost the phones. Isadora had called me from her bathroom when Lancaster first started becoming psychotic to tell me what was going on. I was worried, but I knew I could send you all to her in a flash. As a matter of fact, Delaney was in the middle of texting Teagan to let her know what was going on when we lost all communications. That's when I started to freak.

"I couldn't abandon her, Trill." Nova's voice was whisper-soft, then she started to cry in earnest. "She's been alone and abandoned since she was five years old, and I just couldn't do it. Not as long as there was even the slightest chance I could get to her before he killed her. And if the worst would have happened, Goddess forbid, at least she would have known at the very end there was someone out there who cared about her and tried to save her for the *right* reasons."

"I know, little diva. I know. I was scared too, and I *completely* lost my shit at one point, but I'm not angry with you. I understand why you did it." Nova looked at Trill in puzzlement as she tried to bring her tears under control. The corners of Trill's mouth tipped up. "It was the first time in our over ten-year existence that those fuckers threatened to drag me to lockdown if I didn't get my shit together and make sure my head was in the game."

Nova's eyes grew huge as she gasped.

"We can talk more at home, baby. I think we need to get you out of this wind and rain, go home and take hot showers, then eat. Nothing's open and I'm sure the fuck not cooking, but scrambling eggs isn't hard." Trill held Nova for one more long minute before she kissed her forehead and took her by the hand.

"Bryn already signaled to me to get the hell out of here and get you home, so we're going to take Drew's SUV since she's with Blake and Isadora. I know you're worried about Isadora, baby, but there won't be much you can do at the hospital tonight. Thankfully, none of her injuries are life-threatening—although they're painful as fuck—and it's going to take several good months for her to heal completely, especially with that broken ankle."

"Okay." Suddenly, Nova felt as though every ounce of remaining energy she had was draining completely out of her body and she slumped against Trill. "I'm so glad this whole nightmare is over for her, honey. I wish I could feel sorry for Chad Lancaster for dying the way he did, but I can't. Not after everything he put Isadora through all these years.

"She needs to focus on healing and then decide what *she* wants to do with her life. I don't know that there's much I can do to help her at this point, but I'll be there for her if she needs me."

Trill took her by the hand and they started to walk down the staircase. "We already have other APS reinforcements arriving. Riles and Bryn have taken off, presumably to go to their parents' house to bring them up to speed on everything that's been going on. I saw them leave. I suspect Mama Armstrong is going to insist that either the twins or Papa Armstrong bring her to the hospital so she can immediately establish herself as Isadora's official spokesperson.

"There's going to be a motherfucking shit storm when word gets out that Chad Lancaster is dead and Isadora was severely injured when Audrey made landfall." Nova looked dispassionately at the sheet-covered body lying in front of them when they reached the bottom of the stairs before shaking her head and moving toward the parking lot.

"Mama A will slit the throat of any media fuckwits who try to disturb Isadora right now, and she'll use the initial medical evaluation period to figure out what all needs to be done as far as Chad's estate and their production company goes." Trill led Nova by the hand to a group of black SUVs in the middle of the lot. "The folks at Bayfront *don't* play, so they'll make damn sure Isadora is protected while Mama A figures out the business and personal piece of it."

"You okay, little diva?" Kenn, who had clearly been waiting for them, hugged Nova and kissed her on the cheek before giving Trill a high five. "A bunch of our crews showed up about ten minutes ago, cuz. You probably saw them from the staircase. Casey and Teag went to the Madeira Beach police station to report Lancaster's death, Jaim took Alyssa home, and I have the keys to Drew's SUV for you.

"I don't know that there's anything our crews can do at this point, but the police are going to want to interview Isadora just as soon as possible. Casey is going to have the Madeira Beach police chief contact Vince Masterson on our behalf, and Papa A will serve as her attorney of record. As far as we're concerned, this was a horrible, tragic accident…but because Isadora is such a big star, Papa A will simply tell the two police chiefs that everyone wanted to make sure she was protected during this tragic time. Because Vince is the Whimsy police chief, we'll fill him in on the real story as soon as the dust has settled."

Nova snorted, then her eyes widened.

"Trill! What do we do if Lancaster's douchebag attorney shows up? You know, the one who lives in Indian Shores, who we were fairly certain also stood to benefit from Isadora's brand posthumously?" She put her hands on her hips and arched a belligerent brow.

Trill and Kenn looked at each other for a long moment before their mouths curled up in identical, malicious smiles. “Let him show up, little diva.” Trill banded her arms around Nova’s waist and nuzzled her behind her ear. “I’m pretty sure he knows who we are, and I’m also pretty sure he knows he doesn’t want to land on the wrong side of us.

“Trust me, I don’t look for any trouble out of him…I’m betting he’s going to distance himself from Lancaster immediately. Now, I think it’s time to get you home, and out of this rain and wind.” Nova kissed Kenn on the cheek and climbed in the passenger seat of Drew’s SUV. Trill caught the keys Kenn tossed to her.

“Everyone was so incredibly proud of you and Alyssa tonight, baby, and what you both accomplished. Because Isadora was able to find you and figured out a way to establish contact with you, she now has the chance to live the life she always should have been living. She has a long road ahead of her—with a shitload of physical and emotional healing to do—but I think with the help of her new friends in the APS posse, she’s eventually going be just fine. Domestic violence survivors are some of the damned *strongest* women on the planet, and Isadora Nightingale is going to be kicking ass and taking names before we know it.

“Although…I have a feeling Ms. Riker is going to end up over Jaime’s knee shortly—because our femmes can’t seem to manage to stay out of trouble for very long. We’ll let those two fight it out, though.”

Nova rolled her eyes as Trill shared a brief, amused glance with Kenn before she swung into the driver's seat.

"Let's go home, baby." Trill reached out briefly and stroked the side of Nova's face before she put the key in the ignition and started the SUV. "I need to take care of you, and I need to feel my woman safe in my arms again. You are everything to me, Nova MacLeod…my world, the love of my life, and the woman I'm going to marry. Until death do us part, forever and always we'll belong to each other, my precious little diva.

"And don't think I was kidding when I said I would have burned the world down if something would have taken you from me. Like I've said before, no one would *ever* be prepared for the hell I'd unleash to avenge you if it was necessary."

Chapter 19

Nova's brows scrunched together in confusion when she read the text she'd just received from Trill. She had been getting a head start on dinner before Trill got home from work when the handsome butch had sent her a cryptic message, saying she should be ready to leave in ten minutes because Trill was coming to get her. To Nova's recollection, she and Trill hadn't made any plans to go anywhere that night.

Life had finally been getting back to normal for everyone after a chaos-filled six weeks in the aftermath of Chad Lancaster's death and all the events surrounding it. As Nova ran to change her shirt, she couldn't help but reflect on the past couple of months as she thought about all the changes that had taken place in that time.

Because Isadora had been so gravely injured the night Chad Lancaster had been killed, the movie star stayed in the hospital for two full weeks while the worst of her injuries started to mend. Thankfully, her ribs had just been bruised and not broken, and her doctors had assured her during her final examination the day before she was discharged that they would most likely be fully healed in another week or so.

Her broken ankle was by far more serious, however, and her doctors had been reasonably certain the break would need a full ten weeks before her cast could be removed. There would only be faintly lingering evidence of her black eyes and her split lip when she left the hospital, however—though the bruises on her arms and torso had still been discolored and would require a little more time to heal because they were so deep.

"Really, it's no big deal," she told a pissed-off Nova wryly during one of Nova's many trips to visit her. "I'm probably going to go into shock when there are no bruises left at all, Nov. Chad always made it a point to make sure I was marked in some way, so eventually being bruise-free will be like an early Christmas present."

Isadora gratefully—and in total trust—signed a power of attorney giving Rosi and Oliver Armstrong carte blanche to handle her medical, property, and financial affairs. The senior Armstrongs spent a lot of time with Isadora while she was recovering in the hospital, getting a feel for how her business was structured—although the blonde actress admitted she didn't know much.

"Chad always said it was none of my business and I wasn't intelligent enough to understand any of it. That I needed to leave it to the men and let them handle it," Isadora confessed with an embarrassed look at Rosi and Oliver during one of their discussions.

"*Querida.*" Rosi leaned over the hospital bed and grabbed one of Isadora's hands, squeezing it tightly. "First of all, you are *anything* but unintelligent. Second, I have full faith that the three of us will figure all of this out eventually. I plan on firing everyone who's ever been even the slightest bit involved in your affairs and starting from scratch anyway—since all of them were *his* pick—so we'll have a fresh, clean start with a lot less work for us in trying to make sense of it all.

"When we establish your new company, you'll be in on the ground floor right from the beginning, so you will understand *everything* that goes on in your business from day one. And third," her brows lowered, "my only regret is that I can't kill that *mamabicho* myself, but I suppose you can't have everything."

Oliver winced.

"Do I want to know what that means?" Isadora whispered as she looked at the twins' tall, blond father.

"No, love, you don't." Rosi's attorney husband raised his eyebrows, then a twinkle came into his blue eyes. "Suffice it to say it is a very crude term used to describe someone who visits oral gratification on a member of the male sex."

Isadora's cheeks flamed and her mouth dropped open in shock before she actually giggled and hugged Rosi.

Rosi also handled the press with shocking ease as media outlets from everywhere had clamored for an update on Isadora's medical condition, as well as pressed for details surrounding the night Chad had died. The Hollywood vultures, as Rosi had disdainfully started to call them, descended in droves, digging up questionable information from a myriad of sources and causing a maddened frenzy—until Rosi sternly made it quite clear that any official recounting would come from her and her alone, unless it was from Isadora herself.

"Anything you would like to know in an official capacity about the occurrences of the night in question as far as the death of Mr. Chad Lancaster goes will have to come from Chief Tobias Winthrop of the Madeira Beach Police Department. Beyond that, the only authorized source of information with respect to Ms. Nightingale will be *me*, or Mr. Oliver Armstrong in his legal capacity as her attorney. Once Ms. Nightingale is back home in California, I will be holding some *closed* press conferences—with her in attendance—to answer questions and to give the press more details about this very tragic situation.

"You can be sure, however, that whoever continues this disgraceful speculation and printing of half-truths and lies will be banned from my briefings…and I will make certain the names of those who have been excluded are publicly released, so that interested individuals will know any information these hacks attempt to peddle is worthless."

Trill threw her head back and howled when Nova and Isadora, with wide eyes, told her about Rosi's edicts during one of their visits to check on Isadora.

"You should prepare yourself for the fact that Mama A is just getting started, little diva. She hasn't been married to a former

Florida state attorney for over forty years for nothing." Then, she smiled at Isadora, dimples flashing and amusement clearly evident in her eyes.

"You should also know that Rosario Reyes Armstrong is the only woman in the entire world whom every single associate in the APS organization is scared shitless of…*including* her twins, Bryn and Riley." Isadora's eyes grew even wider. Trill shook her head and laughed some more. "Welcome to the APS family, Ms. Nightingale. You're one of Rosi's now, so just strap yourself in and enjoy the ride."

In the wee hours of the morning on the day before Isadora's official release from the hospital, a black unmarked SUV pulled quietly into one of the restricted loading bays at Bayfront Health. Rowan Holland—in a wheelchair with a fake cast on her foot, her head wrapped snugly in a large black shawl with a pair of dark sunglasses covering half her face—slipped into the back seat of the SUV with Bryn Armstrong's assistance. Bryn shut the back door and then climbed into the driver's seat, an impassive Blake Seibert riding shotgun. Bryn backed out of the loading dock slowly then pulled out into the street and headed for I-275.

Anticipating that Isadora Nightingale would be leaving early in an attempt to avoid the media, there were sounds of slamming car doors as reporters dashed to their vehicles. Before long, there was a convoy of cars following the black SUV. Bryn and Blake led them on a merry chase as if they were trying to lose them, taking them first to the small Albert Whitted airport—which had no commercial flights—then to the joint civilian-military St. Petersburg-Clearwater airport, and finally, to Tampa International.

While the two APS associates and Rowan were diverting the media, another black SUV backed soundlessly into another loading dock at Bayfront Health. Rosi and Oliver Armstrong wheeled the real Isadora out in another wheelchair while Teagan Malloy and Drew Hollister stood by the SUV, ready to help her into the vehicle. Rosi and Oliver climbed in beside her, their luggage—including some essentials for Isadora—already loaded into the SUV.

The group headed for Albert Whitted airport, where the plane APS often chartered in the course of their business dealings was waiting for them. Nova hadn't gone to see Isadora off, everyone wanting to keep her departure as discreet and secret as possible, but she called Isadora right before the plane was ready to leave for Los Angeles.

"I will see you in about a month, my sister, when you come back for your next checkup," Nova said to a tearful Isadora, tears flooding down her own face. "I love you and you've got this. Mama and Papa Armstrong will tear anyone who doesn't act right a new asshole…and just know you can call me whenever you want, even if it's just to chat or scream and start getting some of that bullshit out.

"You *will* get through this, Is. You have family at your back now—although I'm not saying any of this is going to be easy—but at least you *never* have to be alone again."

Rowan gleefully told Nova what had happened when she, Bryn, and Blake had finally stopped—at an all-night diner they'd gone to after Bryn had circled a couple of times around Tampa International airport and then had headed back south down I-275 across Tampa Bay—and Rowan climbed out of the SUV.

She'd used the time they were on the road to remove her fake cast, unwrap her blonde curls from the heavy black shawl, and remove her dark sunglasses. When a stream of cars followed them into the parking lot of the diner and eager reporters jumped out of the vehicles after haphazardly parking every which way, they froze in their tracks to see a small blonde—who was very obviously *not* Isadora Nightingale—standing next to two tall, slightly menacing APS bad asses who had their muscled arms folded over their chests.

"It was *epic*," Rowan reported animatedly, laughing after she called Nova. "Those fools had absolutely *no* idea what to do, and they were clearly *not* going to ask Bryn and Blake where Isadora was. Because who in their right mind would ask an obviously unfriendly APS butch *anything*…especially when it was quite evident the reporters were the ones who had screwed up. I was so excited, I made Bryn take me into the diner and buy me pancakes. This subterfuge stuff can really give you an appetite!"

Because Rosi, Oliver, and Isadora arrived in Los Angeles by private plane, they were able to inconspicuously land at the private Van Nuys Airport instead of Los Angeles International. Isadora also absolutely refused to stay in Chad's house on Malibu Colony Beach—which was filled with nothing but bad memories for her—so she and the senior Armstrongs booked two premium private cottages at the Calamigos Guest Ranch and Beach Club in Malibu.

"It's not a real working ranch as far as visitors go," Isadora said with a secret smile as they made the reservations, "but the vineyards are beautiful, and it will be a nice place to rest and relax. Plus, it's only about twenty minutes away from Chad's house on Malibu Colony Beach, so you can do whatever it is you need to do there but come here to get away from it all."

Trill took Nova out to dinner to update her on Rosi's progress the night after Isadora and the senior Armstrongs had reached California. "Mama A is wasting no time," she informed Nova with a smirk as she cut into her favorite medium-rare rib eye at the Pier House Grill. "She no sooner had Isadora checked in and comfortable at the Calamigos Guest Ranch, she left Oliver to stay with her and then took the private car they'd hired to Chad's house…along with a very professional and highly recommended security team she's hired.

"Because California is an at-will employment state—just like Florida is—and employers don't need to give any reasons or justifications for letting someone go, Mama A walked into that house, fired the entire house staff on the spot, and gave them one hour to pack their shit and get out."

Nova put her fork down and stared at Trill in amazement as Trill chuckled.

"Better yet," Trill's smile then broadened, "she called Isadora's personal stylist—that Harrison Blackridge bitch who had ignored the bruises all over Isadora for years because his own ambitions were more important to him than her health and welfare—and fired *his* sorry ass over the phone. She told him she was going to ruin him in Hollywood and make sure he wasn't so much as hired to pick up the trash for anyone in Orange County…then she did the same thing with the other two assistants. She's loaded for bear, little diva."

"And I'm missing the show," Nova bemoaned, picking her fork up again and stabbing a fat shrimp. "Isadora deserves every ounce of revenge that Mama A can exact on her behalf. I hope every single one of those bitches is ruined. It's like I told Lancaster that night: *Don't get caught*. The last thing a potential employer wants to hear is that you're nothing but a snake in the grass who can't be trusted. Mama A will *definitely* make sure everyone in Hollywood knows that too. Boo hoo, bitches."

The hardest part for Isadora had been the memorial service held for Chad Lancaster about two weeks after they had arrived in Los Angeles. Rosi had released a short, simple statement to the media that said, *"The outpouring of support in the wake of the loss of Chad Lancaster has been very much appreciated. Due to the tragic nature of his death, a private memorial service will be held, and his wife asks that her privacy be respected during this difficult time."*

At dinner one night before the memorial, Rosi fretted because Isadora was still expected to attend Chad's service, no matter what kind of severe trauma she had suffered in the tropical storm. She would have to weather the memorial service while dealing with quite a few Hollywood celebrities and acquaintances, because there would have been no way to keep the memorial service completely private without raising questions and causing a bigger frenzy. Isadora gave her a slightly cynical smile and leaned over to hug her.

"There's a reason I've won three Oscars and three Golden Globe awards, Mama A.," Isadora smiled reassuringly at Rosi. "Yes, this is going to be harder than anything I've ever done before in my life because all I want to do is scream to the world and finally tell everyone what an evil piece of crap he was…*but*, I'll put on the performance of my life so I can walk away with no worries and no additional public speculation when it's all over.

"Because—and you might want to prepare yourself for this, you two—when Chad's memorial service is over, we're going to announce to the world that I'm retiring from acting."

Rosi stared at her, shocked, as Isadora continued, taking a sip of her wine.

"Everyone will automatically assume it's because of my grief over Chad's death because we were married and had worked together for so long…but as far as I'm concerned, they can think what they want. In reality, I used to love acting, but my late husband killed that joy for me. I also have *no* love for Hollywood. I know there are more than a few people there who always suspected Chad's abuse over the years as well, but they never did the first thing about it. So screw them.

"I'm going to retire, we're going to sell the Malibu Colony Beach house, we're going to sell and get rid of everything else that's even remotely connected to Chad, and then," a joyful smile illuminated Isadora's face, "I'm going to buy a nice working ranch up in Big Sky, Montana, and go back to doing community theater like I did when I was a teenager, to see if I can't recapture the magic."

Oliver threw his head back and burst out laughing as his wife's mouth dropped open in sheer disbelief. "That, love, is probably the best thing I've heard in months. Positively *brilliant.* But…Montana? Why Montana?" Oliver inquired since Rosi's vocal cords were still failing her.

Isadora actually giggled as she twirled some pasta on her fork. "Not many people know this, Papa A, because Chad didn't want anybody to realize I came from such humble beginnings, but I actually grew up in an orphanage in Bozeman. That's where my mother was from. I was five when she died and had no other living relatives, so I became a ward of the state.

"I was one of the lucky ones, though—I was never adopted, but the foster families I stayed with always treated me pretty well. I got into acting in high school, moved to Hollywood after I was released from the system when I turned eighteen, and was chosen to play the lead in my very first role when I was nineteen. But I did community theater for years up in Montana before I moved away.

"Ironically, the director in Bozeman when I was doing community theater in high school is in Big Sky now. Caleb Poindexter." Isadora's face colored unexpectedly. "He'd been hired not long before I left Bozeman and he's a *wonderful* actor. I think he was only about ee-four when they hired him as the director because he's so good. I've actually…I've been texting with him this week."

Her blush deepened. "He's so excited I'm moving back to Montana and that I want to do community theater again."

"Isadora." Rosi finally recovered her voice, her dinner forgotten. "How long have you been thinking about this, *querida*? Don't get me wrong, I think this is an excellent plan for you—getting away from Hollywood and all these *lambónes*, these bootlickers here. Doing community theater also sounds wonderful and very healing as well. But owning a working ranch? Really? Do you even know how to ride a horse?"

To Rosi and Oliver's surprise, Isadora threw back her head and screamed with laughter. "You are *clearly* a Florida girl, Mama A," she teased, leaning over to hug Rosi again and kissed her on the cheek. "I grew up skiing, biking, and hiking a lot with the foster families I lived with. One of them kept horses, so I learned to ride when I was about eight or nine."

Rosi's mouth dropped open again.

"A lot of people refer to Bozeman as 'nature's playground' because there's just so much to do outdoors there. Big Sky is only about forty-five miles away and you'd be surprised how many high-profile people live there. The skiing is tremendous, and I always loved to ski before I moved to California. I begged Chad to take me to Lake Tahoe or Mammoth Lakes at least because I missed skiing so much, but he never would."

Rosi rolled her eyes in disgust.

"I think I've actually found a ranch that I'm quite interested in. It's small, only about 300 acres, but I don't know that I'd want anything bigger than that, to tell you the truth." Isadora gave a little squeal of excitement and bounced up and down in her chair, as animated as they'd ever seen her. "Caleb has driven out to see it and says it looks perfect for me.

"It has great grasslands, a beautiful live stream *without* any public access—which is really important with all the fly fishermen around—and some impressive mountain views, he said. The ranch hands have been there for a long time and handle all the grazing and running livestock. He also says I can lease the hunting rights to my property if I want to as well, although I don't know if I'm that crazy about letting people that close. Anyhow, he would like Papa A to call him so they can start discussing it with me."

Oliver patted her arm kindly. "I don't know the first damn thing about ranching, love, but we will figure this out. I'm sure your friend will be a tremendous help, although I should warn you: He better hope he passes muster with my twins and the Seven of APS. You belong to them now, you know, and they are very protective when it comes to their little sisters."

He arched a blond eyebrow pointedly as Isadora colored some more and then smiled. "However, it sounds as though you finally have the opportunity to reshape your life in any way *you* want, Isadora. I could not be more pleased."

Rosi was beaming and grasped Isadora's hand tightly. "You plainly have been working and thinking things through just as hard as we have, *querida*, and you have come up with an absolutely *amazing* plan for yourself. It looks like we just need to get you through this memorial service, and then you can spread your wings and fly."

"Nova has already been doing a ton of research to help me. We talk every night, and I've already told her about my ranch and community theater ideas. I think she's ready to fly out to Montana tomorrow to make it happen." Isadora laughed softly. "I need to go back to St. Petersburg and see my doctors about two weeks after the memorial service, so we can talk more then. I need to get through that first…and then I *know* I'll feel like things are really, *finally* over."

Chapter 20

In the present, Nova sat down on the couch in the great room and waited for her fiancé. The apartment looked much different than it had when Nova had first moved in. Caprice and Alice had tackled her practically the first thing after Isadora had gone back to California and the initial excitement had settled down.

They'd firmly told her they were redecorating before Trill had a chance to change her mind and that Nova could tell them what colors she wanted…but beyond that, this was a Mom thing and they were taking control. Nova had rolled her eyes, knowing her mother's taste was extremely similar to her own so she wasn't too worried, and left the two of them to scheme on their own while she went to the Dream Creamery to start planning her fall menus.

When Caprice and Alice were done, Nova had to admit the apartment was beautiful. The plain, sterile gray walls were now a silver gray with a barely discernible lavender undertone. One wall had been painted a deeper lavender color, which had warmed the room significantly and coordinated perfectly with the gray-marbled porcelain tile floor. The original black accents were now mixed with some deep purple touches and the stark black furniture had been softened by the muted lavender tones. All in all, the makeover had satisfied Nova's need for color while respecting Trill's more conservative taste, and the pair had been extremely happy with the result.

Nova heard the click of the front door lock and Trill came into the apartment. She swept Nova up into her arms and kissed her deeply. "Are you ready, little diva?" she asked when she released Nova's mouth. "I just want you to know that while this was our idea—the entire APS management team—we needed some assistance to pull off the execution of it. None of us have the first clue about decorating and shit like that. It's a good thing we have moms who do."

Mystified, Nova pulled back from Trill's arms and raised her eyebrow at her fiancé after blowing her bangs out of her eyes. "Do I even want to know what the fuck you are babbling about, Trill? Decorating what? Your mom and my mom took care of our apartment. And why the hell would it take all nine of you to try and figure out *decorating* shit? Are your inner femmes coming out?" she snarked with a smirk. Her eyebrow elevated even higher.

Trill tightened her arms around her woman's waist. "That's a spanking offense, little diva. As in, I'll tie you face-down in our bed, naked and spread-eagled, spank this gorgeous ass while I tease you with my fingers, and deny you release until you're *screaming* for my mercy."

Nova felt a gush of liquid escape her body to soak her panties.

A sinful laugh reached Nova's ears as Trill bent her head to nuzzle her woman's neck. "My baby loves the thought of being spanked by me, it seems. But that's quite all right. I love the thought of spanking and teasing her just as much. Now," Trill pulled back with a wicked grin, "I suggest you go and change your panties before we get out of here, little diva. Wearing damp underwear isn't always the most comfortable."

Nova huffed at her fiancé and headed for the bedroom.

When they left, Nova looked at Trill, surprised, when Trill took her down to the hallway that led to the four apartments on the north side of the building instead of out the front door. The way the APS apartment complex was configured, there were four apartments running directly down the right side of the hallway on the south side of the building once you'd entered the front door of the complex: Teagan and Delaney's, Casey's, Trill and Nova's, and Kenn's. A small hallway led to the right between Casey's apartment door, and Trill and Nova's to the other side where there were four more apartments: Drew's and Blake's to the right and Jaime's to the left, along with an empty eighth apartment at the furthermost northwest side of the building next to Jaime's apartment. Trill had once told Nova it was extra storage for the Seven.

To Nova's astonishment, there were quite a few people milling around in the hallway outside the entrance to the empty storage apartment. Nova saw Rowan and Bryn, Kelly and Riley, Teagan and Delaney—who were due to leave for Ireland in a few days for a delayed three-week honeymoon trip—Brooke, Alyssa, Jaime, and Blake. Nova's eyes widened when she saw that a few of the APS moms were there as well: Marsha Sedgwick, Kathleen Malloy, Alice Dacanay, and Caprice McLeod.

"What," Nova wanted to know, "in the royal red hell is going on down here?" The femmes looked bewildered, the APS bad asses looked smug, and the moms looked like they were about to jump out of their skin.

Caprice cleared her throat and stepped forward until she was standing at the head of the group by the front door of the empty apartment. "Rosi can't be with us because she's in California with Isadora, but you should know she was involved in this as well." She smiled warmly at Rowan and Kelly.

"Anyhow, this all started when Trill mentioned that Alyssa had stayed with Nova and Trill during Tropical Storm Audrey, because the streets and property around Alyssa's apartment *always* flood during a storm. Staying with Nova during a storm was something Lys always did when Nova still had her apartment with Gillian, but now Nova lives in this complex with Trill.

"You coming here now was *definitely* not a big deal as far as Trill was concerned," Caprice assured Alyssa, "but Trill also said you were worried about being in the way and you were afraid you might make her feel like someone was invading her private space." Alyssa nodded slowly. "Also not true, honey, because you're *always* welcome in any of their apartments any time because of who you are, but…here we are."

"On top of that, it then occurred to the bad asses—as you call them—that the femmes in their posse really don't have somewhere safe they can go in a group to do what they call 'girl things' together anyway." Alice was up next. "Watch a movie, listen to music, cook together, anything like that. The twins and the Seven discussed it in one of their morning management meetings. They came to the moms—to us—and asked if there was anything we could do with this empty apartment if they cleaned it out, to make a get-together space for the APS femmes."

Six jaws dropped open in disbelief. Nova stared at Trill with huge eyes that had started to well.

Kathleen and Marsha beamed. "The moms all got together," said Kathleen, "and not only figured out what you would need in such a place, but also decided what it should look like. It took us a month, but this is now a fully equipped apartment where all of you can get together with each other—a safe place where you can hang out and have fun, but you'll be somewhere your bad asses won't have to worry about you. Marsha?"

Marsha smiled at Delaney, who already had tears running down her face. "Since you are our classic literature buff, my beautiful daughter, can you tell everyone what happens after Wendy Darling gets hurt in Peter Pan?"

Delaney started to cry as Teagan wrapped her arms tightly around her wife. "When Wendy was injured in the story, Peter Pan and the Lost Boys built a small house around her right where she had fallen, to keep her safe and warm. And to this day, small playhouses for children in places in the UK and South Africa are known as 'Wendy Houses'."

"That's right." With tears running down her own face, Caprice gestured to Blake, who swiped a key card and entered a code in the keypad to unlock the door to the apartment. “Welcome to your Wendy House, my lovelies. Every single one of us expects to be invited to the housewarming when you have it.”

When Nova walked into the apartment with everyone else, she thought her heart was going to explode from her emotion. The ceiling was painted a soft blue, as if mimicking the sky, and the walls were covered with a floral gardens mural scattered with butterflies. The furniture was soft blue and comfortable, a large flat-screen TV was mounted on the wall, and one peek into the kitchen showed that it was extremely well-equipped.

The floor was the same gray porcelain tile that was in Trill and Nova’s apartment, adorned with pretty throw rugs; the coffee table, end tables, and other storage cabinets were a vintage white; and a glass dining table with six pale green fabric-covered chairs sat in front of the window that looked out toward the back end of Seashells.

“The bedroom is completed as well, so you can give guests a place to stay if you want without having to give up any of your own living space. Like Isadora, when she comes to visit you,” Trill murmured into a crying Nova’s ear. “We wanted to do this for all of you, little diva.

“I don’t think you girls have any idea what your love and support means to us. You still give us some motherfucking heart attacks half the time with the shit you get yourselves into, but at least this way, we have a bigger chance of keeping you the fuck out of trouble.

Hopefully," she snorted even as she cuddled a sobbing Nova gently to her.

The APS femmes were undeniably overwhelmed and touched by the effort the bad asses and the moms had gone through on their behalf. There were tearful hugs and kisses all around—even Brooke was resting her forehead against Blake's and thanking her profusely with tears streaming down her face as Blake wrapped her strong arms around Brooke's waist.

Nova couldn't help but notice, however, that Alyssa was avoiding Jaime and staying on the complete opposite end of the living room from her. She didn't look angry, only incredibly sad even as she hugged and kissed the moms, and she was clearly struggling to keep from breaking down.

"This was *so* thoughtful," Alyssa managed to say as a small tear escaped and ran down her cheek. "Really, I never expected anything like this when Jaime left me the voicemail about meeting everyone here because the moms had something to show us." Obviously, Alyssa was avoiding Jaime's calls as well, and Nova gave Trill a slight frown.

"This will be a great place for us to hang out. Thank you." Kelly wiped her eyes then gave Riley another kiss. "And we will definitely have some kind of a housewarming for the Wendy House when Teag and Delaney get back from Ireland. That would be a great opportunity for them to tell us all about their trip, too. I think Teagan can probably burn all the photos to a CD and we can put them up on the big screen in here in a slideshow so everyone can see them. I can't cook for shit, but I'm pretty sure Rowan, Nova, and the moms will have that covered."

A babble of excitement arose as everyone talked all at once with suggestions and ideas. Nova raised up on her tiptoes, pulled Trill's dark blonde head down to her, and kissed her passionately.

"I love you, Trillian Dacanay," Nova whispered in Trill's ear when she had ended their kiss. "My bad ass dominant who is also my closet romantic. The most intelligent butch in seven counties, who has also made it so much easier for me to do domestic violence rescue and supports me all the way.

"All the different shades of color in our life together just astounds me, honey. You're everything I've ever wanted, as far back as fifth grade. When I first looked into the intelligent gaze of a serious, handsome, ten-year-old baby butch, I never in a million years dreamed this is where I would be lucky enough to be twenty-five years later."

"Being able to call you Mrs. Nova Dacanay can't come soon enough, little diva." Trill held Nova tightly. "We'll both keep doing what we're doing, making the world safer for women everywhere. My crew is jonesing to see you, by the way…and Val especially made me promise to remind you that you owe them a night out at Seashells to explain more about food styling."

Nova laughed. "I'll text her and we'll figure out a day and time that's good for everyone. Just so you know, I'll probably have to increase my ice cream production a bit while Del is in Ireland, because we won't have any baked goods to go with it until after she gets back." Nova stroked Trill's face.

"We're all going to be really busy in the next few months, but I hope we get a bit of a breather right now until Del's bakery is ready to open. Isadora will be coming back right after the Malloy's return from their trip to *finally* get that fucking ankle cast removed…and she says she owes everyone a night out at Seashells too, now that Lancaster is no longer here to prevent her."

But Nova frowned as she glanced around the crowded apartment, people still talking and laughing about the Wendy House surprise and the upcoming housewarming. "Honey, where's Alyssa? She was over by the dining room table a few minutes ago, but I don't see her now. Maybe she ran to the bathroom?"

"I doubt it, little diva, because Jaime looks like she's about ready to fucking explode." The dark-haired, dark-eyed butch was quietly talking to Bryn and Riley in Spanish next to the hallway that led to the bedrooms and the hall bathroom, thunder on her face and her arms crossed aggressively across her chest.

"I'm thinking Ms. Riker found a way to sneak out of here without saying goodbye to anyone, which is pretty much a guarantee she's going to find herself across Quintero's knee in short order." Trill's light brown eyes looked steadily into Nova's honey-brown ones. "You know as well as I do that the one thing a femme does not do, *ever*, is run from an APS butch when there's a discussion to be had."

Nova blushed, remembering her efforts to avoid Trill in the beginning.

"But you spanked me because I was doing domestic violence rescue in a way that you didn't consider to be safe, not just because I was avoiding you," Nova pointed out, feeling obligated to defend her friend. "Lys may be avoiding Jaime, but I hardly think that warrants a spanking, even if it does piss Jaime off."

"Lys barreled straight into danger with you during Tropical Storm Audrey when she jumped into her SUV and went after a scum motherfucker with one of her posse…but strapped on a shoulder holster that contained a loaded weapon, *without having any idea* how to shoot a gun in high wind conditions *or* at a considerable distance. Things like bullet drop and wind speed start to play a factor in that environment, and she didn't have the *first fucking clue* what to expect.

"I've been shooting my whole life, little diva, and even *I* wouldn't take the risk to shoot that night. Jaime wouldn't for one minute blame her for going with you and helping you to save Isadora from that goddamn maniac…but introducing a loaded weapon into the mix under uncertain circumstances? Baby, Alyssa is going to be lucky if she's able to walk after *that* punishment spanking takes place."

Nova's eyes were huge.

Trill kissed her fiancée's temple. "Like I said before, though, we'll let the two of them work it out. Jaim is fascinated by Alyssa, little diva, much the same way as I was fascinated with you. Under that cool, impassive APS facade is an intense, passionate Puerto Rican who is bound and determined to tame a fiery, stubborn little redhead…and I have a feeling we're all in for one hell of an entertaining show when the fireworks begin."

ھ-ω-ھ-ω-ھ-ω-ھ

Seashells was filled to the brim with Whimsy residents, plus many more, as word rapidly spread that the legendary Isadora Nightingale was there hanging out with the APS femmes and numerous APS associates. Isadora was bubbly and gracious—signing a ton of autographs, shaking hands, and laughing animatedly—her casted foot propped up on one of the chairs, as she exalted in the fact that her ankle cast was finally going to be removed the next day, after a full ten weeks of healing. Sitting next to her, talking with Bryn, Riley, and Kenn as if he had known them all his life, was her new boyfriend, Caleb Poindexter.

Recently, Isadora and Caleb had very secretly started dating, not wanting to give the gossip mill any excuse to start churning because it had only been a few months since Chad Lancaster had died. Isadora shared many details about what her life with Chad had been like in several private conversations with him, and an extremely *angry* Caleb Poindexter had vowed to Isadora that she would never be unsafe, unprotected, or abused in her life *ever* again.

"We like him a lot, little diva," Trill had informed Nova after one of the APS morning management meetings. "He is squeaky clean, has an amazing reputation in Big Sky and Bozeman, and our sources couldn't find the first person who had anything bad to say about the man. He is clearly crazy about Isadora and has been doing everything he can to help her process through her trauma—driving her to therapy appointments, taking her anywhere she needs to go since she can't drive yet, making sure she eats right. She's got a good one there, baby, who will take care of her like she deserves.

"Of course," Trill's light brown eyes had twinkled as her deep dimples peeped, "I don't think it hurt that a 5'1" little diva with honey-brown eyes and a fairly threatening manner alluded to whacking something off if he stepped out of line."

Nova had shrugged, unrepentant.

Isadora left Hollywood not long after Chad's memorial service and, with Caleb's assistance, had moved to Big Sky, Montana, after purchasing the pretty little ranch she had liked so much. Rosi and Oliver had hired a highly recommended financial services firm and were in the process of liquidating and selling all of Isadora's Hollywood assets, such as the mansion on Malibu Colony Beach, and setting up a completely new portfolio for her. After hiring a firm to refurbish the inside of the main ranch house in Big Sky, Isadora had met with the ranch hands about the ranch operations—calling Nova that evening and giggling.

"They were all super polite and very formal at first, referring to me as Ms. Nightingale and barely cracking a smile. You can tell they don't think much of Hollywood actresses even though they were quite mannerly! But then, when I mentioned that I had been born and raised in Bozeman and started talking about ranch operations like I'd run a ranch all my life, they did this complete one-eighty. By the end of our meeting, Gus—an old, grizzled ranch hand if ever I've seen one—was calling me Izzy." Nova had burst out laughing with her.

Now, Nova was relaxing with everyone else at Isadora's informal Seashells meet-and-greet. "Do you need something to drink, Nov? Is this fucker slacking?" Kendall, Darcy, Val, Melanie, and Peyton stopped by Nova's table where she was sitting next to Trill and Isadora. Trill shot her crew the finger as they all smirked.

"I'm good, guys, thank you." Nova waved a still half-full bottle of beer at them.

"I have to tell you, little diva, hanging out with you the other night and hearing all that shit about the food-styling industry still has me crazy," Val enthused. "We have to do that again soon because that was *amazing*. Some of those fuckers on the other crews were bugging me like a bunch of little bitches because they wanted to join in the next time, and I told them to get off my dick—little diva was *ours*." The rest of the crew gave each other a high-five while Nova shook her head and laughed.

"Now that Teagan and Delaney are home from their Ireland trip, we need to sit down and decide when we want to have the housewarming for the Wendy House. The femmes are all getting together tomorrow night at the Wendy House to talk about it. Alyssa, as usual, tried to wiggle out of it, but I told her I would kick her fucking ass if she dared."

Nova snorted.

"I don't know what the hell has crawled up her ass in the last couple of months…since that night, actually," she looked apologetically at Isadora, who looked at her with unperturbed eyes, "but I'm fucking done with her bullshit. If something's wrong, she needs to spit it the fuck out to her posse. And don't think I won't be jumping on her ass tomorrow night about it, either."

Casey and Blake had volunteered to drive Isadora and Caleb to the doctors' the next afternoon to get Isadora's cast removed. Since the pair was staying at the Wendy House, Caleb said he'd meet some of the bad asses at the Pier House Grill for dinner so that the girls could have the Wendy House to themselves to plan the housewarming.

"Alyssa Riker had better understand that I'm not playing with her anymore," Nova informed Trill as they lay in bed that night. "I don't know what's wrong, but something is worrying her to death because this isn't fucking like her. She needs to tell us what's wrong so we can fix it. She still has Brooke covering her art therapy sessions—which Brooke said was fine, she's got it—but she's worried too. We all are. Lys is avoiding *everybody* right now and I fucking want to know why."

"All I know is that I think Jaime has reached the end of her rope, little diva. There *is* something going on with Lys and I'm sure Jaim knows exactly what it is, even though she hasn't said dick to any of us. But we respect that too…because if it's something that's not hers to tell, then that's how it should be." Trill nuzzled the shell of Nova's ear. "We won't keep secrets from each other, we never have, but we'll never betray the secrets of someone else. I think that whatever this is that's going on has something to do with the two of them, however…and Jaime Quintero has finally fucking had *enough*."

ခωခωခωခ

That night in the new Wendy House, the APS femmes—Rowan Holland, Kelly Armstrong, Delaney Malloy, Nova MacLeod, Brooke Marino, and Alyssa Riker—plus Isadora Nightingale, were sprawled out on the couches and armchairs, making plans for its official "christening." Because the space wouldn't be big enough to accommodate all the APS bad asses, femmes, and parents they wanted to invite at the same time, Rowan suggested they make it a Sunday afternoon open house, so people could come and go at will, much like she did for the opening of the WAC and the Dream Creamery. Everyone agreed that would be the most sensible plan.

"Also, because it will be in the middle of the afternoon, having little nibble dishes set out on the dining room table will be more than enough for refreshments," Nova mused. "No one will be expecting a full meal or anything like that. And you, Ms. World Traveler," she threw a piece of popcorn at Delaney's head, "Teag is still going to burn a CD with all your amazing honeymoon pictures, isn't she?

"We can put them up on the big screen on a rotating loop." Delaney hadn't been able to stop talking about her amazing three-week trip to Ireland with her spouse, how wonderfully warm and welcoming Teagan's extended family was, or how incredibly lush and beautiful she'd found Ireland. Delaney nodded happily.

"And now that *that* part is over with…" Nova folded her arms across her chest and raised her eyebrows at Alyssa, who was sitting on one of the armchairs with a quiet, pale face. "You, my bitch, need to know that your posse has been worried sick about you and we want to know what the fuck is going on. You haven't been yourself since the night all that bullshit went down with Lancaster. It's been two-and-a-half months, Lys, and you're still acting like a fucking hermit and avoiding everyone. Jesus Christ…Brooke is *still* taking care of your art therapy sessions for you! I mean, what the hell, sis? You need to tell us what's going on with you."

"You know I couldn't give two shits about stepping up for you either," Brooke rushed to assure Alyssa, her gray eyes anxious. "I'll take care of those sessions for you for as long as you need me to do it. You *know* that. But," Brooke then pinched the bridge of her nose, "I don't like feeling there's something really wrong, but you haven't felt like you could come to any one of us for help. Not because you think you can't trust us, but because something is throwing you for a goddamn loop and you have no idea what the hell to do about it."

"Should I leave?" Isadora questioned, looking back and forth between all the concerned faces. "Lys, it's perfectly okay if you want me to go because you don't feel like talking about whatever it is in front of me. You won't hurt my feelings, I promise. I mean, I love you all madly already, but we haven't really known each other for very long. I totally understand if you want to keep it between the six of you."

Alyssa was staring at her lap, not saying anything. She had been quiet all afternoon, contributing little to the conversation about the Wendy House housewarming and giving every indication she was only there because Nova had not given her a choice. At her continued silence, the femmes and Isadora looked at each other uneasily.

"Lys." Kelly tried next, leaning forward with her elbows propped on her thighs. "Do I have to kick someone's ass? This isn't like you, and you are freaking me the fuck out. What the hell *happened*? What do we need to do to fix this?" Everyone was alarmed by the sudden slow tears that started to roll down Alyssa's face.

"Honey?" Nova jumped up and went over to perch on the arm of Alyssa's armchair. She wrapped her arm gently around her friend's shoulders. "You know us, and you know we won't pry into your business if you want us to back off. All you need to do is tell us that. But I think it's something you want to talk about, you just don't know how to start. Whatever it is, it's something that has you worried to death."

Alyssa's tears rolled faster.

"Lys, the night of Lancaster's death, when everything was finally over—you were a little bit flustered and shaken up when Jaime helped you down off that catwalk, but you were still *you*. Then you both left and Trill told me Jaime was going to take you home…but the woman I've seen after that night has been this uncommunicative, closed-off, zombie of a person whom I don't have the first fucking clue how to reach."

"Did Jaime do or say anything to cause this?" Kelly's brows lowered as a thought suddenly occurred to her. "Because if she did, I will kick her ass from here to eternity. You two are like oil and water sometimes, although I know you can give as good as you get because I've seen you in action. But if she did anything fucked up right after you'd been through a trauma like you'd been, I'll…I'll…"

Delaney the peacemaker jumped in. "Jaime is one of the *kindest*, most protective souls I know under that mean, bad ass exterior. I can't see her doing anything like that—*ever*—but things were pretty crazy everywhere that night. I honestly don't know if *anyone* was thinking that clearly, especially with the phones out like they were. Did she say something to you that has you upset, Lys?"

Alyssa dropped her head into her hands and mumbled something that none of them could hear.

"Honey, none of us got that," Rowan urged softly, still looking at Alyssa with worried eyes along with everyone else. "Can you repeat that for us? Let us help you, Lys. *Please*." There was a long moment of silence.

"I said," Alyssa lifted her head from her hands and took a deep, quavering breath before bursting into tears, "I said I slept with Jaime Quintero that night."

ə-ωə-ωə-ωə-

Everyone froze in shock as a stunned silence fell over the group. Nova wrapped her other arm around her friend as Alyssa leaned her head on Nova's shoulder and cried harder.

"Wh-when Jaime and I left that night, it was still r-raining pretty hard and the wind was still bl-blowing in gusts," Alyssa finally stammered through her sobs. "I told Jaime she would have to t-take me to my parents' house because more than likely, the r-r-roads to my place were still impassable. Sh-she said she assumed since my parents' house was shut up for the summer because they're at their c-cabin in North Carolina until October, the hot water probably wasn't on…and I-I said that was true, but that was okay. I'd be fine." She started to calm.

"She told me there was no way in hell she was going to let me take a cold shower after everything I'd been through that night. I needed a hot shower and warm food, so…she brought me here to her apartment instead."

"She. Did. *What*?!?" Rowan, Kelly, Delaney, and Nova screeched in a chorus. Brooke and Isadora looked at each other questioningly and Brooke shrugged her shoulders, baffled. Alyssa stopped sobbing for just a moment and frowned at the four of them.

"Why is that such a big deal? There were probably a lot of people that night who borrowed a friend's or a relative's shower because their apartment or house was inaccessible or their plumbing wasn't functioning properly."

"Lys." Delaney hesitated for just a moment before she plunged on. "When I first moved in with Teagan, she told me neither the twins nor the Seven ever invited a woman to her apartment. *Ever*. That, as sexual as they all are, their apartments are sacred spaces to them and are not a place they take casual hookups.

"But when Bryn met Rowan and Riley met Kelly, Teagan reconnected with me, and Trill finally claimed Nova…the very first thing they did was bring us to their homes. Because to them, that's exactly where we belonged." Alyssa's face grew paper-white. "I think there's a deeper meaning there that you need to be aware of, honey," Delaney concluded quietly.

"What happened next, Lys?" Rowan's soothing voice spread across the group.

Alyssa did her best to refocus on her story after the bombshell Delaney had just dropped. "When we got here to Jaime's apartment, I told her I didn't have anything with me. I had some stuff at Nova's because I had stayed there for a couple of days before that whole clusterfuck started, but I had no way to get it until Trill and Nova got home. Jaime told me not to worry about it, she had a big T-shirt I could borrow, and she had plenty of soap and shampoo. I took a shower while she made me something she called '*revoltillo*'…which was basically scrambled eggs with a lot of veggies in it."

"Mama A makes it for the twins if they have to go over there early in the morning for whatever reason," Kelly murmured as Rowan nodded in agreement.

"I think everything hit me then. The crisis was over, I was clean, I was warm, I had some food in my belly, and I just…I just lost it. I started to bawl, like I *never* do in front of people, let alone one of the APS bad asses. She didn't say a word, but she plucked me up out of that chair like I weighed nothing, swept me up into her arms, and brought me into the bedroom. She laid me down, lay down next to me and pulled me to her, then put my head on her shoulder and wrapped her arms around me while I cried. Hard, like I haven't cried in *years*."

"Oh, honey." Isadora's face was full of sympathy.

"She kept stroking the back of my head and murmuring to me really low in Spanish…trying to comfort me, I guess. I've never heard her be that gentle, since we're usually too busy snarking at each other. When I finally calmed some, she uncapped a bottle of water on her nightstand, made me sit up and drink some, then handed me a handkerchief so I could blow my nose and clean up my face. I know I looked like a beast, with my eyes all swollen and the front of her T-shirt soaked in tears. I was really embarrassed."

Delaney's voice was soft as she smiled with perfect understanding at Alyssa. "Bet she didn't care one bit though, did she?"

"She didn't." Alyssa sighed. "When I was done, she laid me back down again, wrapped herself back around me, and just held me. No pressure, no words. It's like she knew I needed to know someone was there, that I need to feel safe. I f-felt…felt like there was nothing in this world that could get to me as long as I was in her arms. But then…" Alyssa's voice faltered for a moment.

"Then, I looked up at her and I saw a look on her face I'd never seen before. She was looking at me almost in awe, like she couldn't believe I was there with her. That I was something…*precious* to her. I couldn't help it. I reached up and I…I kissed her."

The room was dead quiet.

"She kissed me back for a minute, very tenderly, and then she raised her head up and stroked my cheek. She told me she's wanted me forever, but she wasn't going to take advantage of my state of mind. That it would be *more* than okay if we just slept in each other's arms that night…because simply holding me and then waking up to me was a dream come true for her." Alyssa closed her eyes for a moment, tears sliding down her face once again. "But she said I also needed to know that if I decided I still wanted this, wanted *her*, it meant that *I was hers* and she was *never* going to let me go."

Nova blew her bangs out of her eyes then took in a deep breath. "And you still slept with her, even after she said that?"

"I did. And without giving any details…it was the most magical night of my life. Even with all our snarking and arguing, I know I will belong to Jaime Quintero for *infinity*. I fell completely and irrevocably in love with her that night, when I saw *everything* she was deep down inside under the surface." Her tears ran faster.

"The world sees a kind, funny APS butch, one of the fabled Seven, who can also be a mean-as-fuck hardass when the situation calls for it. But just like the rest of the management team, when all's said and done…it's protecting women that's her *life*. It's the reason why she breathes, why *any* of them breathe.

"There are also complications I never saw coming." The pain in Alyssa's voice struck them all like a fist. "And if I would have known any of it before I slept with Jaime that night, I would have walked away from her without a backward glance."

Chapter 21

"Why, Alyssa? *Why*?" Nova demanded, taking Alyssa by the shoulders. "You're *finally* admitting you're in love with Jaime. Without a doubt, she is also in love with you. You're *perfect* for each other, despite all your snarking and bickering. The two of you are going to give new meaning to the word 'combustible'…but what the fuck can we expect when a fiery Puerto Rican butch claims a stubborn redheaded femme? The gang has been calling you two *Kelly and Riley 2.0* for months."

Kelly shot Nova the finger.

"I have to keep her safe," Alyssa whispered, her eyes still welling. "I know what she is, Nov, and I know what she's capable of doing. She's APS's physical security risk assessment expert. You once told me Trill called her a 'magician' when it came to breaching physical locations, so I know there's no one more capable of keeping me safe. But I refuse to put her at risk because of *my* shit…and I would if I continue to let things with her go any further. You have to *swear* to me you won't ever tell a soul anything I'm about to tell you."

"Whoa, whoa, *whoa*, sister. What in the actual fuck are you talking about?" A suddenly irate Kelly Armstrong jumped to her feet. "What the hell changed between the time you and Jaime connected that night, to you doing this fucked-up about-face a day later? I haven't known you for very long, Lys, but the one thing I *have* figured out about you is that you're a straight shooter. You're not a tease nor are you one of these bitches who's all over the place. You would have never in a million years accepted Jaime Quintero's claim on you one minute, then turned around and changed your mind the next. That's not how you fucking roll."

Brooke snorted. "No, it's not. Del and I have known this bitch since kindergarten…she's one of the most real and most honest people we know." With her arms folded across her chest, Delaney nodded silently, staring fixedly at Alyssa. "I'm thinking someone better start fucking talking and explain what the hell is going on because I'm about to lose my shit."

Alyssa leaned forward and propped her elbows up on her thighs, leaning her head in her hands for a brief moment before she raised up to look at them all. "You know what I do, that I'm an art therapist, but I'm going to explain it a bit more in detail for a minute…for Isadora's sake, if nothing else, because that's kind of central to the discussion." She turned to look at Isadora.

"I have a dual degree: a Bachelor of Fine Arts, and a Bachelor of Arts in psychology with a focus on narrative therapy, Is. In a nutshell, that means I use art to help people who have been severely limited in their lives because of things like horrible self-perception, feelings of inadequacy that can be downright crippling, nonexistent self-worth, or skewed notions of who and what they really are. Challenges like that.

"I teach them how to write a new story or 'narrative' about themselves, one that's more positive and affirming. That's what I do. I run group art sessions for people who have been sent to me by the state and other private institutions, to help them get a handle on any self-destructive tendencies they have…and to get them to a place where they can start to create a narrative about themselves that's more constructive and productive."

Isadora's eyes were wide. "Now I know exactly why you were so amazing when we were on the movie set. You are one impressive woman, Alyssa Riker."

"You don't even know the half of it," Brooke murmured.

"Anyhow…I don't take clients who are parolees or have a history of violence of any kind or anything like that. That's a whole different skill set and something I'm not adequately trained to handle. My clients have never been in trouble with the law, are nonviolent, and are more on the spectrum of having tough challenges managing their lives because of the things we've talked about. My clients are not anyone I would ever have to worry about in that capacity…or so I thought anyway." The eyebrows on six pairs of eyes lowered.

"There's this one client I had, who came to my weekly sessions for about three or four months, who had started getting…clingy. A big part of his issues came from the fact that he had been in love with this girl who hadn't returned his feelings, which only exacerbated his self-perception and feelings of inadequacy.

"As a result, it's a common occurrence in the therapy world for a client or a patient to project the feelings they have about an important figure in their life onto one of their therapists. It's a phenomenon we call 'transference,' and it happens all the time.

"Normally, there are things we can do to make the client understand their feelings aren't 'real,' and we can work through it…but I finally had to tell this guy about two weeks before Audrey hit that I didn't think we could work together anymore.

"He had absolutely refused to manage the situation with me, and I couldn't see where anything I had been doing was making a difference. No forward progress at all. I ended up calling his regular therapist to explain what was going on and I told the therapist I was ending our sessions, because his patient had gotten far too aggressive and obstinate. I thought that was the end of it."

"Yeah, you left me notes about that dude and all the petty bullshit he was pulling," Brooke rolled her eyes. "What a little tool."

Alyssa continued, twisting her fingers in her lap. "The day after Jaime and I were…together…I told her I was going to go get my stuff from Nova and Trill's, then go home for some clean clothes. Everything was fine, we were fine, and I fully expected to meet her at her apartment after she got off work. But…" Alyssa heaved a huge breath and started to cry again.

"When I got home, my apartment had been *destroyed*." The femmes and Isadora gasped. "Someone had broken in and totally gutted the place. Ceramics were broken, all my artwork and supplies had been slashed to ribbons and thrown all over the place, everything in my kitchen cabinets had been pulled out and dumped on the floor. It was an absolute mess. There wasn't one thing left intact or was salvageable.

"I called the Whimsy police and Noah Armstrong, of all fucking people, was the responding officer. He told me lootings and break-ins were not uncommon in the aftermath of a storm, but the extent of the destruction in my apartment seemed to be a little extreme for someone who was simply looting. I told him I had no idea who would do something like that, but…" She stopped before she wiped her eyes and continued.

"There had been a note left in the center of my living room floor. It wasn't signed, but I *knew* it was from Ivan Olsen. It said that I was *his*, and if I didn't dump the piece of shit I had hooked up with the night before, that 'woman thief' was going to find herself with a bullet in her head before she knew what had hit her. Then it said I was to tell no one, or the people around me would start dropping like flies. That's the real reason I've been avoiding you all, not just because I slept with Jaime. I figured the farther away I stayed from you, the safer you'd be.

"You c-c-can't tell her and you *have* to pretend like you don't kn-know any of this," Alyssa stammered through her sobs. "I told Noah I didn't want *anyone* from APS to know either because they would have lost their shit…not to mention, the twins and the Seven would have interrogated the hell out of me until I finally told them my suspicions. Then they would have tried to do something about it, gone after Ivan themselves, and one of them would have ended up getting *killed*.

"*NO*, Kelly," Alyssa screamed defiantly when she saw the angry look on her friend's face. "*NO*! You will *not* tell them! *Ever*! *Especially* Jaime. I'd rather she thought I was the biggest two-timing bitch in the galaxy rather than her end up dead because of me!"

"Ssshhh. It's okay, Lys. We understand." Nova wrapped her arms around her uncharacteristically hysterical friend and glanced at Kelly, whose face was filled with fury. "Calm down, honey. There has to be a way out of this eventually without putting anyone at risk. I respect your need to keep to yourself right now, considering what you've told us, but I want you to promise me one thing if you can. Okay?"

Alyssa raised her swollen, tear-stained face and nodded.

"I want you to promise me you'll at least text us. That motherfucker can't read your texts, so everyone will still be safe if you keep connected to us like that. You won't feel so isolated, and we won't worry about you so much. Can you do that?" Alyssa nodded again, considerably calmer. "As far as the bad asses are concerned, we met this afternoon to talk about the Wendy House housewarming and that's it. Now, I'm going to assume the reason you haven't gone back to work yet is because that dickhead plans to force his way back into your sessions?"

"Yes. As a matter of fact, he's really mad because I haven't gone back to work yet, but I didn't want to face him. I also didn't want to put any of my other clients at risk if he started to perceive someone was getting more attention than he thought they should or anything like that."

"Not to worry, sister, I got you." Brooke's voice was pissed. "Little Dick can fuck all the way the hell off for now. I'll make sure all the available seats are taken and there's no room in any of the sessions for his skanky ass. I have a big project coming up—a new craft brewery is opening up in St. Petersburg—but there's no reason for me to think I can't manage both for now."

"Kelly." Alyssa hiccupped. "I need you to promise me you're not going to say anything to the bad asses. *Promise* me, Kel. We need to keep them safe and Ivan is unhinged as hell. I have no idea what he's actually *capable* of doing, but his threats were enough to convince me that we *can't* let them know."

"I promise you from the bottom of my heart, Lys, that I am not about to do the *first* thing that will put any one of us in danger." Kelly crossed her heart. "The priority is to keep *everyone* safe and I'm all over that." Alyssa nodded, an obvious look of relief crossing her face, as she took the Kleenex Nova handed her and blew her nose.

Nova kept her expression impassive, but it didn't escape her notice that Kelly hadn't actually promised not to say anything to anyone—she'd only promised that she wouldn't do anything that would put anyone in danger. Nova caught the subtle warning look that Kelly tossed at her and she nodded at Kelly discreetly, letting her know her message had been received and understood.

"I need to get back to my parents' place. I told Mom and Dad there had been some damage to my place because of Audrey and I was staying at their house for a while. They were cool with that. I'm pretty sure Ivan knows where I am, but my dad has the security system from hell installed, and there's no way that douchebag can get in there without setting off a million alarms. Dad is former Navy, and the man doesn't ever play when it comes to security."

With a bit of her spirit recovered, Alyssa rose from her seat. She looked around at her assembled friends and tears filled her eyes once more. "I haven't been back to my own apartment in over two months. I hired someone to cart away anything that looked perishable or had the potential to rot or mildew, but beyond that, it's still in the same condition it was when I found it. I just can't face looking at it right now." She hugged them all, one by one.

"Thank you," Alyssa hiccupped again after she had embraced each one of them. "Truly. I hope you all realize that I have *hated* keeping anything from you, but I couldn't take the chance that he would hurt one of you. I couldn't live with myself if he ever did."

Rowan hugged her again. "But now you know you can text us and not feel so alone, right? There may not be a lot we can do personally, but at least we can be there for you whenever you need to talk. We'll see you at the housewarming, okay? We love you, Lys. We'll figure this out."

The minute Alyssa had left, Kelly whipped her phone out of the back pocket of her jeans. "This is some motherfucking *bullshit*," she fumed as her fingers flew through a text. "I'm letting the twins and the Seven know we need to have an emergency meeting right fucking *now.* I need to tell them what the hell's been going on with Alyssa over the last several months because every single one of them has been confused. It *hasn't* been like her, her behavior since the storm, and they don't know to make of it."

Kelly laughed slightly. "This is ironic as hell, considering I ran myself when I first got to Whimsy because I thought my presence would put them in danger, but I sure as fuck know better now. Jaim is going to *freak* when she finds out what's been up and why Lys has been avoiding them."

"Trill told me just last night that Jaime was at the end of her rope anyway, so this isn't going to be pretty." Nova shuddered. "Having been the recipient of an APS punishment spanking, I don't envy Lys one bit…because there is no way in *hell* Jaime is going to let this slide." She caught Isadora's curious eyes. "Don't even ask, sister," Nova advised the blonde actress. Rowan, Kelly, and Delaney all shuddered in turn as Brooke rolled her eyes.

"Roll your eyes all you want, my bitch," Nova told her as the rest of them headed to the door. "For your sake, I hope Blake doesn't ever catch you doing something you're not supposed to be doing, Brooke. As the head of Utopia, Blake is built for speed—with the reaction time from hell—and there would be no chance of ever escaping *that.*"

Brooke snorted and rolled her eyes again.

"Okay, bitches. I'll report when there's anything to report. I'm heading over to the APS complex now." Kelly opened the front door. “I’m going to tell the twins and the Seven every single thing Lys told us today. I hope to *hell* Ms. Alyssa Riker is ready for the fiery Puerto Rican hurricane that’s about to hit her shores when Jaime Quintero finds out what the fuck has been going on.”

Epilogue

Jaime Quintero swiped the key card and punched the access code to her apartment when she got back to the APS apartment complex after her meeting with Kelly Armstrong, the twins, and the rest of the Seven. She calmly walked inside, took off her leather jacket, unstrapped her concealed carry holster, and went into her bedroom and master bathroom.

After a hot shower, letting the steaming water pound into the back of her neck and her shoulders in an effort to relieve some of her tension, she toweled off, put on a clean pair of jeans and a T-shirt, then went back into the main room, her boots in her hand. Sitting on the edge of her sofa to put them on, she paused and settled back on the sofa to think for a couple of minutes, trying to calm her still-churning brain.

Alyssa Riker. The femme Jaime had been in love with practically her whole life.

When Jaime and her mother had moved to the Whimsy area from Puerto Rico after Jaime's father had died when she was six years old, Jaime had been withdrawn and apprehensive: grieving, not knowing a word of English, and unsure of what her place in this new world should be. Two new classmates, Bryn and Riley Armstrong—whose mother was Puerto Rican—had befriended her immediately…along with their close friends, who had also accepted her right away. Despite Jaime's determination to learn English as quickly as possible, it had been a huge relief to have friends who spoke Puerto Rican Spanish as if they were *boricua*, or Puerto Rican-born.

Not long after school had started, a small kindergarten girl with copper-red hair and light blue eyes, whom Jaime had noticed from the very first day, had paused by Jaime's lunch table one afternoon. Jaime, a first grader, had been tongue-tied when the little girl had beamed and given her a big, juicy red apple. "I know you don't speak English yet," she had said, still with that gorgeous smile, as she turned her head and looked at Bryn. "Please tell her I said, 'Welcome to Whimsy,' okay, Bryn?" With a knowing grin, Bryn had given Jaime Alyssa's message in Spanish—along with her name—as the pretty little girl with the copper-red curls had skipped off.

Jaime Quintero had fallen in love with Alyssa Riker that day.

Alyssa had eventually grown up into a firecracker of a woman—still beautiful, with her copper-red curls and big light blue eyes—but also playful and mischievous, with a snarky sense of humor that covered the biggest heart of anyone Jaime had ever known. After graduating from high school, Alyssa had headed off for the University of Florida at Gainesville, the year after Jaime had joined the Marines, to earn a dual degree in fine arts and psychology. When Alyssa had graduated from college, she'd then headed back to Whimsy to start her new career as an art therapist.

The year before Alyssa's graduation from college, Jaime had also started at USF when her active tour of duty was complete. Like Alyssa, she'd also pursued a dual college degree—her majors being in criminal justice and security management, since she had decided her strengths could best be used as the physical security risk assessment expert for the new protection company venture she was starting with her best friends. Only the most imperceptible trace of a Spanish accent was now evident in her perfect English, and her passionate Puerto Rican nature was typically hidden under layers of cool, detached appraisal. Like the other bad asses of APS—as they had been nicknamed—she could turn mean and threatening when the situation warranted, but the APS associates were generally known as a kind, helpful, community-minded group amongst the residents of Whimsy.

As they had grown up, Jaime and Alyssa had settled into a snarky, bickering relationship with each other—the fiery Puerto Rican butch and the stubborn redheaded femme often going head-to-head in arguments that ignored their intense attraction to each other. More than once, Jaime had caught Alyssa staring at her thick, black-cropped hair, her dark brown eyes, and her substantially hard-muscled frame when Alyssa thought Jaime wasn't looking—and the handsome butch had basked in the knowledge that Alyssa was just as attracted to her as Jaime was to the beautiful femme.

Someday, Jaime had long vowed to herself, she was going to claim Alyssa Riker for her very own, leaving Alyssa no choice but to realize she belonged to Jaime in every single way it was possible for a femme to belong to a butch.

On the night Jaime had brought Alyssa back to her apartment in the aftermath of Tropical Storm Audrey, she had been determined to get the weary, bedraggled art therapist clean, dry, and fed immediately. While Alyssa took a hot shower, Jaime had made her a simple Puerto Rican breakfast dish that was warm and filling. When Alyssa had finally eaten something and a good deal of her tension had melted away because she was safe and warm, Jaime had been astonished when the usually tough-as-nails femme had started to cry unexpectedly.

Recognizing an imminent breakdown teetering on the edge of shock, Jaime had swept Alyssa up into her arms and brought her into her bedroom. Laying her down and wrapping herself around the shaking redhead, Jaime had tightly held a crying Alyssa, crooning to her softly in Spanish, until she felt Alyssa's tears start to slow and she had started to calm.

When Alyssa had kissed Jaime, and then given herself to the APS butch unreservedly—wordlessly accepting Jaime's claim on her at long last—Jaime had taken Alyssa with a passion that had startled them both. When Jaime had put her mouth on her femme for the very first time, bringing Alyssa to a screaming release that had her crying out her love for Jaime without reservation, the Puerto Rican butch had felt the culmination of every dream she'd had in the almost thirty years that had passed since she first laid eyes on Alyssa Riker. When morning came after that enchanted night, Alyssa had kissed Jaime goodbye lovingly, saying she was going get her overnight bag from Nova's then pick up some clean clothes at her apartment before meeting Jaime back at her own apartment after work.

That was the last time Jaime had seen or heard from her.

Jaime laced her hands behind her head as she furiously contemplated what she and the rest of the APS management team had learned from Kelly that afternoon. First of all, Jaime Quintero had already known that—if she knew Alyssa Riker at all—Lys was anything but a player. Alyssa had left her the morning after the night they'd spent together with a warm, passionate kiss goodbye and unmistakable affection in her eyes.

Something drastic and serious had happened after Alyssa left Jaime's apartment that had caused the petite redhead to cut off all communications with her, and Jaime had been going crazy trying to figure out what the fuck it was. She hadn't had the first clue—until the emergency management meeting Kelly had called today, where Kel had spilled every single detail about the conversation she and the rest of the APS femmes had had with Alyssa in the Wendy House that day.

And Jaime. Was. *LIVID*.

The APS butch stretched out her long legs in front of her. Alyssa already had a reckoning due for bringing a loaded weapon with her when she and Nova had raced off to rescue Isadora Nightingale in the midst of Tropical Storm Audrey. While there was no way Jaime would have ever been upset with Alyssa for trying to save a life the way she did when she clearly didn't have any other options—and it had been more than evident Isadora would not have survived had Alyssa and Nova not done what they did—on what fucking level did her woman *ever* think wielding a gun in high wind conditions was a good goddamn idea…*especially* when she was a novice at shooting? Oh, *fuck* no. Lys was going to find herself over Jaime's knee at the first opportunity for that one.

But when Jaime had found out Alyssa had also been hiding from her and from everyone else—even her posse—because some skanky piece of shit motherfucker was trying to stake a claim that wasn't his to stake, and had *threatened* Jaime's woman? That Alyssa had cut off all communications with everyone because she was terrified and thought this was the only way to keep *them* safe? The Armstrong twins and the Seven had jumped to their feet when Jaime had started to curse violently in Spanish, all of them ready to drag the enraged butch to lockdown if she didn't get her wrath under control. Jaime had managed to hold on to the impending explosion by the skin of her teeth.

"*Broki*. I get it," Kelly had said quietly and had looked deeply into Jaime's eyes, willing her to calm down. "I was in Lys's position once too, remember? I know what she's thinking. When people you care about are under threat, the only thing you can focus on is doing whatever it takes to keep them safe. This Ivan Douche Canoe told her he was going to *kill* the people she loves if she didn't do what he said…and there's no way she was going to risk that *or* us."

Casey had crossed her arms, a malicious glower on her face. "I'm thinking Lys needs to get her fucking ass back on the mats to start practicing Krav Maga with Jess again, cuz. I suspect Kenn also wants to get her hands on her so our little sister can focus on her shooting lessons…while learning there are silly little things like wind correction and trajectory in this world." An equally pissed Kenn nodded, her own arms folded across her chest. "That is, of course, after my cuz here informs little Ms. Riker that running from APS never ends well for *anybody*."

Jaime had been oddly relieved after finding out what the real issues with Alyssa had been—it didn't have a thing to do with the two of them and their budding relationship—although she was still extremely unhappy Lys had chosen to hide rather than come to them when everything had first gone down with this fucking dickhead.

"*Mia fogata* is going to understand that hiding her worries and her fears from us—let alone hiding from us period—is not acceptable. *Ever*," Jaime had informed them grimly. "You know I haven't laid eyes on her or talked to her since the day after Lancaster was killed, except for once, because she's been hiding from every single one of us. But she is going to understand right fucking now that. *She. Is Mine*. She gave herself to me the night of the storm, which means she is *officially* my femme and I am her butch. When shit like this happens, it means she *comes to me*…she doesn't hide and try to take care of this bullshit by herself."

Bryn and Riley had looked at each other with huge smirks on their faces as Blake had said, "All right, fucker, what does that mean? *Mia fogata*? Why are the twins laughing? And do I need to make book on whether or not this is going to piss Lys off or not?"

Jaime had given them all a predatory smile. "*Fuego* is the Spanish word for 'fire,' *broki*. *Fogata* means 'bonfire,' and *mia fogata* is 'my bonfire.' I figured that was a little more appropriate than *fuego* since my woman and her attitude are bigger and more intense than a regular fire.

"And a little harder to bring under control…but I think I'm up to the challenge." Her humorless smile had broadened as she'd looked around the table at the rest of the management team, her momentary ire forgotten. "I'm not sure Alyssa knows exactly what she got herself into the minute she let me know she was mine, but she's sure as fuck going to find out, now isn't she?"

In the present, Jaime leaned over to put on her boots then stood up to strap on her concealed carry holster and slid her arms into her leather jacket. Alyssa had been staying at her parents' house this entire time and Jaime had respected her obvious decision to cut all contact with everyone for a time, as hard as it had been to stay away from her. Now that she knew the full story, however, Jaime was *done* letting her femme live in fear—believing that she had to keep away from everyone because she might put them in danger if she dared to establish any kind of communications with them.

She missed her beautiful femme. She wanted to wake up every morning and see Alyssa's gorgeous pale blue eyes looking back at her with love in them. She wanted to create a *home* with her, a place where they both could live and love in security and peace. Jaime had gotten a tiny taste of what a life with Alyssa would be like the night she had claimed Alyssa as her own, and she was already addicted.

Mr. Ivan Olsen was going to understand *today* that he was nothing more than a pissant little piece of shit whom the APS organization would stomp like a fucking cockroach under their boots. Her Alyssa had a fucking army at her back, almost fifty associates strong, and Jaime's own crew would tear Olsen's throat out if he dared to so much as raise one finger against them or frighten her woman anymore.

He *definitely* didn't want to land on the bad side of the associates on the APS Physical Security team, who were about to find out they had a new little sister of their very own. Angel had grown up in Whimsy, so she already knew Alyssa pretty well, but the rest of her crew only had a passing acquaintance with her from functions they had all attended together, like Kelly and Riley's wedding.

It didn't matter. Whereas Lys had been an only child up until this point, she was going to understand she now had a handful of bossy, assertive siblings who would drive her out of her fucking mind with their security going forward…as well as an insanely protective butch lover, who was going to make sure the world understood that Alyssa Riker belonged to Jaime Quintero—body, mind, and soul.

A slow smile spread across Jaime's face at the thought as she strode to her front door. "I am coming for you, *mia fogata*, my fire," the black-haired, dark-eyed Puerto Rican butch said softly before she pulled open the door and went out of her apartment, a predatory look in her deep brown eyes.

She stalked out of the entrance of the APS apartment complex and headed determinedly toward an unsuspecting copper-haired femme drawing with isolated sadness at her parents' house…a lonely, melancholy woman oblivious to the fact she was now in the crosshairs of a dangerous, formidable butch who was intent on bringing her home—forever.

ABOUT THE AUTHOR

Tiffany E. Taylor writes sensual Sapphic romance fiction within the passionate butch/femme dynamic in a variety of genres: action-adventure, contemporary, and paranormal. She lives with her spouse and their daughter in an idyllic queer-friendly little town on Florida's west-central coast. You can find out more about Tiffany at www.tiffanyetaylor.com, or you can follow her at:

Facebook: www.facebook.com/tiffany.taylor0627
Instagram: www.instagram.com/tiffanyetaylor_sapphicauthor
Twitter: www.twitter.com/TiffanyE_Author

And before you go… REVIEWS are like rocket fuel for authors. You keep us going when you take some of your precious time and tell us what you think. I know you're busy, but I'm asking you to take just a few minutes to post a review on Amazon. It doesn't have to be long—just a few sentences would be lovely—but I will be immensely grateful.

Next in the Whimsical Dreams Series:

Whimsical Fire

(Book 5, Jaime and Alyssa's story)

Jaime Quintero of the APS Seven moved to Whimsy, Florida from Puerto Rico after her father's death when she was just six years old: grieving, not knowing a word of English, and wondering where she fit into this new world. Meeting the Armstrong twins, whose mother was Puerto Rican, and their friends helped an enormous amount—but when a small kindergarten girl with copper-red curls and big blue eyes skipped up to Jaime to welcome her, wearing a gorgeous grin and holding a big red apple gift in her hand, it was game over.

Jaime fell head over heels in love with Alyssa Riker that day.

Now, almost thirty years later—just as Jaime *finally* claims Alyssa for her own—the feisty femme art therapist finds herself the target of a dangerous hate obsession. Stung by Alyssa's rejection of him, Ivan Olsen wants nothing more than to eliminate the APS butch whom he calls 'the woman stealer,' promising Alyssa he will shoot and kill not only Jaime, but anyone else who gets close to her. Frightened, Alyssa tries to stay away from everyone she loves to keep them safe, but Jaime—the Physical Security Risk Assessment team lead for APS—refuses to let her, vowing she will hunt down

Ivan Olsen and make him pay for every ounce of fear her woman has suffered because of him.

When Alyssa falls into an insidious trap set by Ivan, Jaime and the rest of APS race to find her against the clock when they see the truth of Ivan's plans for her. But an unlikely rescuer gets to Alyssa first and deliberately puts herself in harm's way to rescue the tenacious art therapist, little dreaming the two of them were about to uncover a larger plot—one that strikes at the very heart of Whimsy itself.

Whimsical Haven

(Book 1, The Whimsical Dreams series)

When Rowan Holland of Woodbridge, Virginia lands squarely in the crosshairs of a psychotic stalker, fleeing to Whimsy, Florida might be her only chance of escape.

There, she'll meet the head of lesbian-owned Armstrong Protection Services. Possessive. Protective. Deadly.

Bryn Armstrong, one of the owners of APS, is immediately captivated by an equally-mesmerized Rowan, and vows she will do everything in her power to protect Rowan from this psychopath.

When the stalker follows Rowan to Whimsy, staying hidden in the shadows, it's up to Bryn—along with her twin, Riley, and "the Seven," the butch management team of APS—to cut him down and put an end to Rowan's nightmare.

But, as the stalker draws closer to Rowan and the increased danger to Bryn's woman becomes more real, Bryn and her team know they must find and stop the psychopath, who just may be a killer in disguise.

TW: This work of fiction contains a scene of disciplinary spanking and other instances of light BDSM that some readers may find triggering.

Whimsical Princess

(Book 2, The Whimsical Dreams series)

Kelly Holland is everything her sweet older sister, Rowan, is not: Kelly is bold, bad ass, and the best covert and clandestine operations analyst the CIA has ever had in their agency.

Kelly also has a secret. A very big, very explosive secret.

Riley Armstrong, Bryn Armstrong's twin, is intrigued by the flame-haired femme, but wonders why a simple information analyst like Kelly has attracted the attention of the head of Percutio—a malignant crime organization headquartered in Florida. Grigor Reizan is pulling out all the stops to get to Kelly, and Riley wants to know why.

Because Kelly Holland belongs to her.

When Riley, Bryn, and the Seven of Armstrong Protection Services learn Kelly's secret—and find out why Grigor Reizan has been so unyielding in his efforts to capture her—they are stunned. After Kelly loses her CIA agency status and protection because of a mole planted by Reizan, they vow they will do whatever it takes to keep Kelly safe.

But Reizan is just as determined to take Kelly for himself. He knows he can use her and her rare "superpower" to become the most powerful man in Florida—if not the world—and he's not about to let anyone stop him.

No matter who he has to kill to succeed.

Whimsical Angel

(Book 3, The Whimsical Dreams series)

Teagan Malloy of the APS Seven has long been known as "Casanova" in the tiny community of Whimsy — a magnet for the hordes of women who've fallen for her brilliant green eyes, hard muscled body, and killer smile. But Teagan has always played the field in an effort to forget the shy, beautiful femme she loved and lost over fifteen years ago. She's always resisted attempts by women to become "the one" in her life…because if Teag can't have Delaney Sedgwick, she isn't interested in having anybody.

Then the day arrives when Delaney finally comes home to her after many years away, and makes Teagan believe in miracles again. The happy couple soon finds out, however, that Delaney hasn't come home alone.

A viciously jealous ex bent on revenge is determined to destroy Teagan and Delaney, and wants nothing more than to watch them explode in a shower of hellfire and pain. Tina Schaffner will do anything to make that happen, and she won't rest until she's wiped them from the face of the earth. It's the man whom Tina has hired to help her who's the real threat, however — someone who will not only crush Teagan and Delaney at Tina's behest for a hefty fee, but who will also stop at nothing to take over the very lucrative security and protection business run by APS in Tampa Bay.

Planning to defraud clients and put them at risk in his quest to come out on top, Frank Bellwood proves he will do anything to be crowned the undisputed king of protection as well as the big money winner in this game. Even if it means he must engineer the total destruction of APS itself in the process...

One More Chance

(Book 1, The Dance series)

Seven years after her wife's tragic death, a still-mourning Aimée "Jake" Charron finds herself unexpectedly intrigued by a personal ad sent to her by one of her best friends. It was a femme sucker punch right to the gut, and Jake finds her inner alpha butch responding with an almost predatory desire.

After two failed relationships, Geneva Raineri doesn't believe in fairy tales and happily-ever-afters anymore. Her neighbor posts a personal ad Gen wrote as a joke on a butch/femme romance site—and when a self-professed alpha butch named Jake responds, Gen finds herself swept up into a sensual game of cat-and-mouse that soon has a captivated Gen feeling like Jake's prey.

Jake knows she's already had one chance at a forever love, but lost it when her wife died. She wants Gen with a desire she'd thought was long dead—but Jake believes expecting to find another great love after you've already had one and lost it is a fool's game.

Gen, however, is determined to prove to Jake that anyone lucky enough to be given another shot at happiness needs to grab it with both hands and never let it go.

As Jake and Gen navigate personal journeys that include heartbreak, self-discovery, passion, and courage, they both discover that risking everything to take one more chance on love might ultimately be their salvation.

Painted Hearts Publishing

Painted Hearts Publishing has an exclusive group of talented writers. We publish stories that range from historical to fantasy, sci-fi to contemporary, erotic to sweet. Our authors present high quality stories full of romance, desire, and sometimes graphic moments that are both entertaining and sensual. At the heart of all our stories is romance, and we are firm believers in a world where happily ever afters do exist.

We invite you to visit us at www.paintedheartspublishing.com.

Printed in Great Britain
by Amazon

60312256R00198